"When I read this book, I lived the life of Dr. Hamilton's family right along with them. In today's economic world we are increasingly seeing the separation of the classes—the 'haves' and the 'have-nots'—and it doesn't take too much imagining to place yourself in one of those categories. While credit cards are so readily available—even to our children—it's easy to get trapped with the materialistic quagmire of 'want vs. need,' and soon finances are spinning out of control. In the year 2027, if your finances keep going like they currently are, which will you be? A 'have' or a 'have-not'?"

Angie Rice
Educator
Author's Wife

"Debt—the elephant in the room that no one wants to acknowledge. I found this to be very entertaining, easy to read, and a wake-up call for all of us. Not only did this book hold my attention, but it left me pondering if there is something we can do now, or is it already too late for us?"

Mary Kathryn (Kitty) Sims
Administrative Assistant

"David Rice's debut novel is a skillfully-written, smart combination of adventure, history, philosophy, religion, and the behind-the-scenes world of American politics. Set twenty years in the future, the unique and intriguing storyline gives us a startling insight into the world that could lay ahead if we continue down the road of mounting debt and apathy toward the state of our society."

Lynda Huenefeld
Editor

"Through his poignant writing, David Rice uses the history of our own nation as a predictor for the future state of our society, thus giving us a glimpse of a world lived to self. Though fiction, this novel forces us to look into the depths of our own souls and examine our values and motives, and then question 'what will we do with this?'"

Marilyn Jones
Educator

THE YEAR *of* JUBILEE

THE YEAR *of* JUBILEE

Can a presidential hopeful win the hearts of the hopeless with an ancient plan of grace?

a novel by:

DAVID RICE

Tate Publishing *& Enterprises*

The Year of Jubilee

This title is also available as a Tate Out Loud product. Visit www.tatepublishing.com for more information.

This novel is a work of fiction. Names, descriptions, entities and incidents included in the story are products of the author's imagination. Any resemblance to actual persons, events and entities is entirely coincidental.

This novel is a work of fiction. However, several names, descriptions, entities and incidents included in the story are based on the lives of real people.

This book is designed to provide accurate and authoritative information with regard to the subject matter covered. This information is given with the understanding that neither the author nor Tate Publishing, LLC is engaged in rendering legal, professional advice. Since the details of your situation are fact dependent, you should additionally seek the services of a competent professional.

The opinions expressed by the author are not necessarily those of Tate Publishing, LLC.

Published by Tate Publishing & Enterprises, LLC
127 E. Trade Center Terrace | Mustang, Oklahoma 73064 USA
1.888.361.9473 | www.tatepublishing.com

Tate Publishing is committed to excellence in the publishing industry. The company reflects the philosophy established by the founders, based on Psalm 68:11,
"The Lord gave the word and great was the company of those who published it."

Cover design by Elizabeth A. Mason
Interior design by Stephanie Woloszyn

Published in the United States of America

ISBN: 978-1-60462-731-2
1. Christian Fiction: General/Contemporary Social Issues
2. Fiction: Religious/Political
08.03.06

In a world that has gone blind there walks a madman, for he still believes that he can see.

To Mom and Dad…
…You taught me to believe.

Hear, O heavens! Listen, O Earth! For the LORD has spoken: "I reared children and brought them up, but they have rebelled against me…Ah, sinful nation, a people loaded with guilt, a brood of evildoers, children given to corruption! They have forsaken the LORD; they have spurned the Holy One…and turned their backs on him.

Isaiah 1:2–4 (TNIV)

They sell the righteous for silver, and the needy for a pair of sandals. They trample on the heads of the poor as upon the dust of the ground and deny justice to the oppressed.

Amos 2:6–7 (TNIV)

Your country is desolate, your fields are being stripped by foreigners right before you, laid waste as overthrown by strangers…Unless the LORD Almighty had left us some survivors, we would have become like Sodom, we would have been like Gomorrah. Hear the word of the Lord you rulers of Sodom; listen to the law of our God, you people of Gomorrah! "The multitude of your sacrifices—what are they to me?" says the LORD…"They have become a burden to me; I am weary of bearing them. When you spread out your hands in prayer, I will not listen. Your hands are full of blood; wash and make yourselves clean. Take your evil deeds out of my sight! Stop doing wrong, learn to do right! Seek justice, encourage the oppressed. Defend the cause of the fatherless; plead the case of the widow. Come now let us reason together," says the LORD. Though your sins are like scarlet, they shall be white as snow; though they are red as crimson, they shall be like wool. If you are willing and obedient, you will eat the best from the land; but if you resist and rebel, you will be devoured by the sword. For the mouth of the Lord has spoken.

Isaiah 1:7–20 (TNIV)

A Pillar of Salt

It was 4:58 on an August afternoon as Michael Hamilton stood in the pastor's office of Calvary Church, an office he had occupied for the past six years. As the late afternoon sun shone through the window, he noticed the rays as they made their way through the dust that had been stirred that day. He was surrounded by boxes packed full of his life at the church. There were boxes full of books he had studied preparing countless sermons and study groups; boxes that held his lifelong trophies—softball championship; best series in bowling; a plaque from the Adult II Sunday school class; and yes, a simple but elegant plaque from the Hamilton kids for "Best Dad Ever." While some may choose to decorate their office with art and monuments to self, Michael's walls had been filled with pictures of family and friends; pictures of special moments and memories; pictures of moose and buffalo captured on film while on vacation in Wyoming last year by Ian, his nine-year-old budding photographer.

He stared numbly at the empty box on his desk—a box waiting impatiently for the last few photographs and diplomas that hung behind his desk.

Summa cum laude, Southwest Seminary, he recalled his days in graduate school as he placed the diploma in the box. How proud his parents had been at graduation. He recalled the sacrifices of his wife, Allie, placing her own graduate studies on hold to make his doctoral work possible. Somehow, just looking at the diploma brought back the taste of peanut butter. He almost laughed remembering how they lived during those days at seminary, but this day was far too sad.

"Almost finished?" His secretary, Sandy, stepped through the doorway, wiping the tears away. "Does it really have to be this way?"

Like so many churches in the past few years, Calvary would close its doors for the last time tomorrow. Times were tough all over. Hundreds of churches across the nation had closed.

Michael looked up at Sandy. She was the first to greet him when he moved his things into the office six years ago. Their hopes for the church had been so high, but the economics of a nation falling apart had finally caught up with Calvary.

"They're just not tithing, Sandy. Some have lost their jobs. Some have jobs but no benefits, and so many others are staggering under incredible debt. We just can't pay the bills..." his voice trailed off. "Maybe it's my fault, maybe it's no one's fault. I don't know anymore."

He placed the last few items in the box and began the laborious task of loading them into the van. When he finished loading, he stepped back into the empty office. One more look...One more deep breath...One last memory...The dust whirled in the sunlight as he left.

Dinner was already in progress when Michael arrived home. The house was completely empty except for a few suitcases and a bucket of cleaning supplies.

"Looks like you've been working hard," he said, trying to break the tension as he walked into the kitchen.

"I ordered pizza," Allie said and looked up at him. "Everything's packed."

"Have we blessed this feast?" Receiving only blank stares, he assumed the answer was no. "Lana, would you say the blessing for us?"

His precious seven-year-old daughter nodded, bowed her head, and began to pray. "Dear Jesus, thank you for this day and thank you for our food, ame—and thank you for Mom and Dad and Ian and Mark. And Jesus, why do we have to move?"

"Amen." Michael gently put his hand on Lana's.

Mark, as only a two-year-old can, broke the moment by spilling his cup of soda all over the floor. Even the mess was a welcomed distraction.

"Phil and Don came by to help us clean." Allie winked at Mark as she wiped up the spill. "I think everything is ready."

As a going-away gift, the church was paying for all of the moving expenses. Most of the furniture and large boxes had been loaded on a huge moving van the day before and were already in route to their new home in Iowa.

The rest of the evening was uneventful. The Hamilton family slept on the floor in sleeping bags. They rose early on Sunday morning and dressed for church, ate their last breakfast at the parsonage, took their last look around the house, and headed to the church.

Michael had thought about this day for a long time. He had written and rewritten his sermon, but when the time came to deliver it, he just folded it up and spoke from his heart. Looking over a sanctuary that once held more than five hundred bright, shining faces, he would now speak to less than thirty. They were all in their regular seats: Ms. Jones on the front pew, offering her usual supportive smile; Allie off to his left with the kids; Sandy and her family halfway back on the right; and old Ed Farmer dead-center with his usual scowl. Ed blamed Michael for the demise of the church—a church whose foundation had been laid by his grandfather.

His heart went out to them all, but he had no great words of wisdom or comfort. He spoke for less than ten minutes. It was not an inspired oration. When he finished, they sang a song and were dismissed. The Hamilton family stood at the back door to bid the congregation farewell and then watched as the last car pulled out of the parking lot. Michael locked the door and ushered his family to the van. Driving away, he fought the urge to take one more look at the church. He remembered Lot's wife leaving Sodom, and he thought to himself, *I don't want to be a pillar of salt.* With that, he drove away and thought about the future.

Seven years later...2027

This Side of Heaven

"Good morning, Hill City, Iowa! Rise and shine. It's five thirty on this beautiful Monday morning! Get up, you sleepy heads. It's a school day, the first day of the 2027 school year. Rise and shine! This is Sunny Jack for WROE, Roe College Radio for a new generation of rockers," the DJ on the radio blared as the alarm clock went off in the Hamilton home.

"Dad, can I have the keys? I have to get going." Ian fell on top of Michael in the bed.

Not yet coherent, Michael could only stare at his eager sixteen-year-old grinning from ear to ear, thinking about his first chance to drive to school after getting his license a few weeks earlier.

"Why are you up so early, and what do you mean, 'Can I have the keys'?" Allie asked before Michael could open his mouth.

"They're on the dresser, son." Michael grabbed Ian and flipped him over on the bed. "Remember what we talked about last night. Straight to school and straight home."

"Thanks, Dad!" Ian bolted off the bed, grabbed the keys, and ran down the steps.

"Straight home," Michael reminded him.

Allie, still shocked, found her voice again. "Where is he going so early, and why did you let him take the car?"

"Football practice before school. I had a long talk with him last night about driving. He's a good kid. I trust him." Michael thought about his oldest and how proud he was of him. Straight A's, starting tailback at Hill City High School, well...maybe second string, but a father's pride will sometimes embellish.

The first day of school was always big, especially since it was Lana's first day of high school. Obviously, her brother left without her, but she was probably still sound asleep anyway. Lana loved few things more than her mutt, Sebastian, and sleep.

Along with new beginnings, it was also a day of endings. Seven years ago, Michael had gone to work for Roe College as a professor of religion and history. Leaving the pastorate was hard, and he was unsure of himself in the college scene. Dr. Henry Johnson, Social Science and Religion Department Chair at Roe, was a godsend. Dr. Johnson not only took Michael under his wing, teaching him the "ins" and "outs" of faculty life, but was also a source of wisdom and comfort as Michael dealt with his career change. Dr. Johnson was retiring today.

As Michael stepped out his front door, he looked across Fairmont Street at the perfect campus. Roe College, founded in 1859, was a beautiful campus full of classic buildings surrounded by mature trees, well-manicured grounds, and a grand church that sat just at its edge. The history building was halfway across the eighty-acre plot, but he enjoyed the early-morning walk.

This morning, just as he had done for the last seven years, he met Dr. Johnson at the church. Each day they would meet and sit in one of the back pews. They seldom talked much, but it was a great way to get their heads together before a hectic day of academics. The light shining through the nineteenth century stained glass was beautiful as it fell on the wooden pews and stone floors.

The air smelled of rich wood and sweet incense. Michael wondered if they would ever share moments like these again.

After twenty minutes of silence, Dr. Johnson turned to Michael. "Well, son, it's your turn now. I met with the Board of Trustees last night, and we agreed that you should be the next Department Chair."

Michael was in shock, but he fought the urge to respond with anything other than complete calmness.

"I am…honored, but are you sure they want me?" he finally uttered, not hiding his surprise nearly as well as he would have liked. "Dr. Mestrovic has been here so much longer, and Dr. Terry is—"

"They want you."

"But—"

"No buts. They want you. They want your ideas; your fresh view—"

"They think I'm crazy," Michael interrupted.

"You are!" Dr. Johnson let his head fall back with a laugh that came from the depths of his old soul. "You *are* crazy, Michael, crazy enough to think differently, to look for new ideas, new solutions. History, especially religious history, can be so boring. You give it such life. The students love you," he paused. "I love you, Michael. You've been like a son to me. I would be so honored if you would take this torch from me. Take it and light the way for a new generation."

"I…I…" Michael fumbled with his words.

"Ask not what your college can do for you," Dr. Johnson said in his best New Englander. They both had a good laugh and traded several more political quotes in their best statesmen voices.

As the time to head to class arrived, Michael stood, but Dr. Johnson remained seated.

"Are you ready, Henry?"

"I'm going to stay a little while longer. It's time for you to go on without me."

As Michael left the church, he let his mind wander back over the past few years. Dr. Henry Johnson was a man among men: scholar, teacher, awesome speaker. Although in his late seventies, he had a commanding presence. When Henry Johnson raised his deep baritone voice, he could stir the heart and calm the spirit at the same time. He was a man of vision who taught Michael many things about life. "People don't care how much you know until they know how much you care"—a well-worn phrase that only had meaning because of Henry's sincere heart for people, especially for Michael. Michael arrived at Roe College a little lost, somewhat disillusioned, and definitely uninspired. Dr. Johnson took a failed preacher and groomed him into a model teacher, and now he would pass the mantle of leadership on to him.

"Hi, Dr. Hamilton," a bright, cheery voice snapped Michael out of his stroll down memory lane. It was Shelly Tate, a senior history major who had taken just about every class Michael taught. She was definitely one of "his" kids.

"Hi, Shelly." They walked together across the campus, exchanging stories about the summer and admiring the well-groomed campus that welcomed them back for the new year. Not surprisingly, Shelly was in Michael's eight o'clock class—20th century American history.

Michael stopped by his office in the history building before going to the classroom. There was a note on his desk from Dr. McPherson, the college president:

Michael:

Welcome back. Hope you had a great summer.
Please stop by my office when you get a chance.

Peter

After completing the normal morning routine—checking e-mail, phone messages, and a few letters—he headed out the door for class. As he closed his door, some activity in the office next door, Dr. Johnson's old office, caught his attention. He did not have time to check it out, but he pondered the activity.

He scrambled up two flights of stairs to room 312, a room he knew well. The walls were lined with maps, historical charts, and all manner of "Indiana Jones" memorabilia. He paused just outside the door and listened to the voices floating into the hall. He made a mental list of "*his*" students:

Shelly Tate, loyal, bright, unbridled energy; Larry Finner, brilliant, kind of nerdy, *brilliant;* Ginny Long, save the planet, save the whale, save the date, the demonstrator, the passionate rebel. Robert Washington III, trouble, money, trustee's son, a little lost in his journey, good heart; Lenny Pete, California cool, the class clown when he spoke, potential; Danielle Winters, nine-year college veteran, majored in everything, something special waiting to emerge; Sarah Johnson, Dr. Johnson's granddaughter, she can't be a junior, beautiful young lady, beautiful spirit.

And one more voice that, surprisingly, seemed absent from the mix this morning—a voice of leadership, sometimes a rebel without a cause, a brilliant mind in search of a brilliant idea, a young man's man with destiny written all over him—Ben Wallace, preacher's kid, best friend's kid, awesome young man.

There were countless other voices in the mix. In the last few weeks leading up to the new school year, Michael's "enthusiasm" about returning from the lazy summer had wavered, but the sound of the young voices rekindled his passion for teaching.

"Good morning. Welcome back." He finally entered the room and sat down on the edge of his desk. Seventeen students looked back at him. Michael was a very humble and unassuming man.

Despite this nature, however, he had quite a following among the students. Shelly Tate was not his only fan. The student admiration stemmed from his genuine concern for them, as he truly had taken Henry's advice of caring to heart. His faithful followers had definitely been recruiting for this class. Although it contained mostly seniors, who, by nature, tended to be more serious, Michael chuckled as he looked over a group of wide-eyed students ready to hang on his every word.

Not one to beat around the bush, Michael threw out his first question: "What can you tell me about twentieth century American history?"

Instantly, the class was buzzing with answers. He began to write on the whiteboard as fast as he could:

Automobiles-Henry Ford-the assembly line-the middle class

The Wright brothers-flight

Space-John Kennedy-" We shall go to the moon, not because it is easy, but because it is hard..."

World Wars- Germany- Hitler- Japan- Pearl Harbor- D-Day

Vietnam-we lost

Korea-we lost

Middle East-we don't know what we did, but the oil guys loved it

Communism-we won-Ronald Reagan-

" Mr. Gorbechov, tear down that Wall."

60s-The Beatles-rock and roll-peace, love, hippies

80s-Wall Street, greed

90s-Debt, Clinton-" I did not have sex with that woman!"

20s-Prohibition-gangsters-flappers-Babe Ruth

30s-The Great Depression-draught/dust bowl-Hoovervilles-

Roosevelt and the New Deal

"Where did we go right?" he primed their thoughts.

Civil Rights movement

Higher Education Act

Medicine-cures for diseases

Computers-technology

"Where did we go wrong?"

Computers-could have had a fifteen-hour workweek-we chose fifty-plus

Health insurance-cures for the rich-not the poor

Social Security-no lasting plan for the future

No anything plan for the future-everything shortsighted

Greed!

Debt! Debt! Debt!

Class time was up, but not one student moved. The room was still ablaze with ideas. Michael handed out the syllabus and dismissed the class.

*What a start to the year. Department Chair...great class...*Then he remembered Ian driving to school for the first time and that jarred him back to reality. He checked his cell phone—no calls. *Well, at least Ian must have made it to school.*

Another dose of reality awaited him in the hall—Dr. Harry Terry. Somehow, Michael always had a hard time taking Harry seriously with that name, a problem that Harry—that is, Dr. Terry, as he reminded anyone who failed to use his full title—did not share. He was a stern little wart of a man with a cartoonish head and an "unfulfilled" moustache stacked on top of a squatty five foot two, two hundred fifty-pound frame of pure arrogance. His tired suit matched his personality—crisp, with a special "sp" starched to the hilt.

"Good morning, Dr. Hamilton, have you—"

"Call me Michael, Harry."

"It's Dr. Terry, Dr. Hamilton. We must maintain discipline for the students."

"Okay, Harry. Have I what?"

"Doc...The department chair, have you heard?" Dr. Terry wrinkled his nose at the informality.

"Henry just retired today," Michael retorted with his own wrinkled nose and best sarcasm, all along smiling to himself at the news he was withholding.

Harry could hardly contain himself. "I know there was a special meeting in the president's office last night, so something is up. I spoke to Dr. McPherson this morning, and he sounded like he was hiding something."

"What does that sound like, Harry?" Michael teased. "Let it go. When there is news to know, I'm sure we'll know."

Once again, in his usual condescending tone, Harry pressed, "You don't think they will give it to Mestrovic, do you? Sure, he's been here forever, but he has not been published like I have, and he's never matched my class load. I...I...I want it. I deserve it. I—"

"I-I-I see." Michael seethed at the words he was hearing. Dr. Nikola Alexioff Mestrovic had been at the college for over twenty years. In the early 1990s, Dr. Nick, as the students called him, endured the hardships imposed in Yugoslavia by the "Butcher of the Balkans," Slobodan Milosevic. Nikola often recounted the story of the Vukuvar Massacre that claimed the lives of his parents and brother. After several days of fighting during late November 1991, in his northeastern Croatian town, the Serb forces prevailed. Several hundred refugees, including Dr. Mestrovic's family, gathered at the city hospital. With the promise of safe evacuation, they were taken to a farm in nearby Ovcara, but the promises of safety soon turned into beatings and shootings. Nikola, his uncle, and several other young men slipped away in the mass hysteria, but they did not escape the sights and sounds of the massacre. The refugees were killed and then buried by bulldozer in a mass grave. As they ran from the scene, they saw buses unloading other refugees into a makeshift prison camp housed in old brick storage buildings. They watched as the prisoners ran between rows of Serbian troops who beat them with their guns and clubs.

At the end of the conflict, Nikola and a few of his zealous friends took a vow to assassinate the leaders of the camps. Although a youthful pact, it was a very sincere vow. One day, while Nikola was walking the streets of Vukuvar, he passed a storefront church and wandered inside. In his words, "I found Jesus in that little church." He abandoned his assassination vow. A year later he came to the United States. He worked his way through college, got married, and began to pastor a small church. He later earned his doctorate in letters and came to Roe College to teach. He was one of the finest religion professors Michael had ever met. Countless numbers of students had Dr. Nick to thank for passing Greek. He was a meek man who loved to teach.

"Nikola Mestrovic doesn't have my credentials, and neither do...well...you," Harry blurted out with his usual sense of tact.

"Go to class, Harry."

"Doctor...Michael, you let me know if you hear anything."

Michael replied with a simple look of disgust. The grasping for power revolted him. Why did it always seem to be those uninspired, uninformed, un-everything types that deemed themselves fit for *everything?*

Just as Michael turned to walk to his next class, the dreaded cell phone rang. "Hello," he snapped, still disgusted with Harry.

"Well, hello to you too," came Allie's voice. "It's only the first day. That bad already?"

"Sorry. It's actually been a very interesting day. I'll tell you about it at lunch."

"That's why I called. I need to get some things done before lessons this afternoon, so I'm going to have to miss lunch." Living right across the street from campus had its advantages. Michael and Allie usually found time to eat lunch together at home. It was a great midday pick-me-up.

"Sounds good. How many students do you have?"

"Two piano and one voice student today. I think I'll have about ten altogether. So what is your news?"

"Sorry, Al, I gotta run to class. I'll tell you tonight. Any word from Ian?"

"No. Are you worried?"

"N-n-no."

"You're not very convincing," she teased.

"Thanks. Gotta run. Love you. Have a good day." No lunch plans might actually be good. That would give him a chance to run by Dr. McPherson's office.

Religion classes were on the fifth floor—the top floor. *Closer to God,* Michael always mused. Although his plan was to work out more, he viewed the climb up and down the stairs each day as healthy, and it kept him from complaining about the hike.

Room 502: Religion, Jewish history. This would be an elective class for most students and was only offered every few years. The room was filled with the usual suspects, including the eight from his morning history class. This morning, however, it was not so much those who were present that caught his attention, but one who was not—John Stanley. John would be a senior this year, but there were rumors of family financial difficulties and the possibility that he would not be back. His absence seemed to confirm those concerns.

Michael assumed his usual position on the edge of the desk and took a moment to survey the faces in the class; twenty-two bright, shining faces. So many of the professors complained about "the students of today...They just don't care." Michael always found them to be hungry for knowledge. Was he just lucky to have great students? He often wondered at the difference. He and Allie talked about the students, and she always reminded him of Dr. Johnson's words of wisdom about caring for the students. Michael thought there must be more to it, but whatever the reason, he was grateful for awesome students to teach.

"What up, Doc? You zonin' on us up there?" Robert Washington III eyed his teacher from the front row.

"Hey there, Number III. Just taking you all in." In his usual jump-right-in fashion, Michael opened with a question. "In the beginning, God created...Do you buy that statement? Is the Bible truth?"

The answers began to fly, everything from "God said it, so I believe it" to "I don't know," with all the usual college answers—answers from wannabe sages and scholars trapped in their not-quite-yet-adult minds, a characteristic of college students Michael loved most. So often they possessed great knowledge, but the real beauty was their sincere belief that anything was possible—their "not yet tainted by the real world" view of life. Perhaps that is why one remark drew his utmost attention.

"No, I don't buy it." The stern comment bellowed from the most unlikely of sources—senior class president, Ben Wallace. Usually the ring leader, it was not unusual to hear him speak forcefully, but this answer was out of character for Ben, a Pastoral Ministries major. Though Ben was an old soul, usually too serious for his own good, he was not the "angry young man" type. His comment caught most of the class, as well as Michael, off guard.

The debate flourished for the rest of the hour, but Michael had a hard time concentrating. He slipped into shepherd mode, leaving the ninety-nine "sheep"—at least mentally—to search for the one who was missing...a very special *one.* Michael had known Ben for seven years. He was a preacher's kid. He had been a leader in high school and at church. Ben just had that "something"—something Michael couldn't put his finger on...call it charisma, a special gift. He was a well-rounded young man who participated in everything high school had to offer, everything from sports to choir to honor society and student council. As a southpaw with a wicked slider, he led the Hill City Indians to two straight undefeated state championship seasons his junior and senior years. He set school records for victories, strikeouts, and ERA. He was an Iowa baseball legend, his name splashed across newspapers all over the Midwest. The scouts had come knocking on his door with some pretty spectacular offers. Even the St. Louis Cardinals, his favorite team, had selected him in the first round of the amateur draft.

Ben was also a gifted speaker, and why not? He was a preacher's son. His mother, Halley, had shared stories with Michael about him as a small child.

"On Saturdays when we were at the church preparing for Sunday, Ben would go up to the sanctuary, push one of the platform chairs to the pulpit, and begin to preach his favorite sermon," she had recalled.

"Repent!" his four-year-old voice thundered. From birth, Ben was a diamond in the rough, but his destiny did not lie on the diamond.

As the "In the beginning, God" debate raged on, Michael remembered an evening four-and-a-half years ago when just after dinner his phone rang. "Sure, Halley, I'll be right there." Immediately, he had driven to the high school. When he pulled up in front of the baseball field, he sat for a few minutes, taking in the sight. Ben and his dad, Jim, were out on the field. Jim was in full catcher gear and Ben, with his electric left arm, fired rockets at him. What a Norman Rockwell moment: father and son playing catch.

Halley, who was sitting in the bleachers, caught Michael's eye, and he went over and sat down by her.

"They're working it out," she said. It was draft day, and they had received the news from the Cardinals. The offer was staggering: every parent's—most parents'—dream for their little boy, especially an only child. It would have made them all rich. But the Wallace family was already "rich." Sure, the money would have been great, as it turned out, maybe even life-saving, but their riches went beyond "diamonds and dollars." Ben had decided to go into the *fam-*

ily business. He had been working on more than fastballs. He had been working on that sermon.

Halley had tears in her eyes when she turned to Michael. "He's a good son. We are so proud of him." She sat silently for a few moments. "He's going to turn the offer down. He's going to Roe next year to major in Pastoral Ministries. We would like you to talk to him. We want to make sure this is what he wants, that he's not just being a good son."

"Sure, Halley." Michael put his arm around her. She dropped her head and began to sob. After a few moments she spoke again.

"There's something else you should know. I am sorry to just blurt this out, but…Jim has cancer. Ben doesn't know. We were afraid that telling him right now might alter his decision. The treatment will be expensive, maybe too expensive. We just want him to make his choice without this hanging on him."

She went on to explain a little more about the cancer and the options available. They had no time frame, but the odds of recovery were not good. This would probably be the last father-son catch. In fact, Halley was amazed at Jim's ability to stand the pain he must surely be experiencing as the game of catch roared on, but with a pause and a look, both Halley and Michael understood the incredible love between father and son.

The loud pop of the ball hitting the catcher's mitt brought their attention back to the field. They watched for a few more minutes until the two ballplayers walked over to the bleachers.

Michael remembered how Jim and Halley had excused themselves. Knowing the pain he saw Jim endure over the past few years, he marveled at his composure that night: no sign of pain, only strength for his son. Ben and Michael sat on the bleachers for hours, talking about baseball, about college, about life. Ben did most of the talking. Michael did most of the silent admiring.

Although it would seem sacrilegious to say, he could not help but hear the words from the Bible spoken about Jesus from his heavenly father, "This is my son in whom I am well pleased."

"Yo, Doc, what up?"

Michael looked at the clock on the wall. "Out of time. See you all next time." While the class stood up to leave, the debate continued to rage out into the hall.

"Ben, you doing okay?" Michael worried for the young man still seated.

"He's a fighter, you know. Why doesn't God just take him home?"

There were no easy answers. Many thoughts ran through Michael's head as he searched for an answer to Ben's question.

Why do bad things happen to good people? Is God in control? Does he let bad things happen? If there were no valleys, would we have mountains? If there were no rain, would we appreciate sunny days? Doesn't the rain sustain life?

"Would you like to walk for a while, Ben?"

No more words were spoken. They left the classroom and walked. When they stopped, they were standing in front of Ben's front door, so Michael went in and visited with the family. Jim was on hospice and not doing well at all. In fact, he did not recognize Michael. Ben sat in a chair beside the bed and held his dad's hand, as he did for hours most evenings. When Michael finally realized the time, he had missed his political science class. It was the last time he visited with Jim Wallace on this side of heaven.

Thank You, Lord

"By the seventh day God had finished the work he had been doing: so on the seventh day he rested from all his work. Then God blessed the seventh day and made it holy, because on it he rested from all the work of creating that he had done."

Genesis 2:2–3 (TNIV)

"Remember the Sabbath day by keeping it holy. Six days you shall labor and do all your work, but the seventh day is a Sabbath to the LORD your God. On it you shall not do any work, neither you, nor your son or daughter, nor your male or female servant, nor your animals, nor any foreigner residing in your towns. For in six days the LORD made the heavens and the earth, the sea, and all that is in them, but he rested on the seventh day. Therefore the LORD blessed the Sabbath day and made it holy."

Exodus 20:8–11 (TNIV)

"I will open my mouth with a parable; I will teach you lessons from the past—three things we have heard and known, things our ancestors have told us. We will not hide them from their descendants; we will tell the next generation the praiseworthy deeds of the LORD, his power, and the wonders he has done. He decreed statutes for Jacob and established the law in Israel, which he commanded our ancestors to teach their children, so the next generation would know them, even the children yet to be born, and they in turn would tell their children."

Psalm 78:2–6 (TNIV)

"Honor your father and your mother, so that you may live long in the land the LORD your God is giving you."

Exodus 20:12 (TNIV)

"And in other news, the populations in what are being called 'Marshallvilles,' in mock honor of President Marshall's failed social agenda, are reaching astronomic proportions. An estimated twenty million homeless are now occupying makeshift towns on the outskirts of major U.S. cities. We take you live to Leslie Rodriguez just outside Chicago."

"Thank you, Alan. There are an estimated forty thousand people living mostly out of their cars here in this area. As you can imagine, sanitary conditions are beginning to deteriorate rapidly. This 'camp,' for lack of a better word, is comprised of mostly white-collar families who have lost their homes due to bankruptcy and foreclosure. Most of the people I interviewed have well-paying jobs but say that enormous debt, compounded by a failed federal social agenda, has cost them their homes and their middle-class way of life."

"Leslie, this is Charles in the studio. What do the people in the camps need most?"

"Charles, they need hope. Here are a few of the interviews we recorded today. This is Robert Blades, a senior architect at a major firm in downtown Chicago."

"You work your way through college, or rather you borrow your way through. You do so because you think an advanced degree will get you ahead financially. You try to be careful with your budget, but the complete breakdown of health insurance programs, not to mention caring for aging parents with limited income, just becomes too much. We have good jobs. We just have so much debt."

"Alan and Charles, we talked to person after person with similar stories. This is Amanda White. She is a single parent of three kids. Her husband, a police officer, was killed in the line of duty. Here's what she had to say."

"We went to work. We worked hard. My husband...I've cried all my tears. I've screamed at the stars. No one is listening. No one cares. The rich get richer and the poor fade away. Does anybody care? Mr. Marshall said he had a plan. Are these people around here in his plan?"

"Leslie, what are the local officials saying?"

"Charles, things are escalating too fast. Local officials say they need help from Washington, but they see nothing on the horizon. These camps have existed for several years in other parts of the country, and they are starting to spread. People are getting desperate. They are tired of hearing the same old failed political answers. Some blame the government. Some blame themselves, but pretty soon it won't matter who is to blame. We're going to have mass chaos on our hands...helter skelter..."

As the phone rang, Michael snapped out of his fixation on the TV.

"I got it," Lana called from upstairs.

Michael held his breath. He knew the call would be for him,

and he knew it would be about Jim Wallace. After a few minutes passed, Lana finally came down the stairs. "Who was it, honey?"

"Some girl for Ian," she mocked as she came flitting through the living room and into the kitchen. Within moments, she was back. "Suppertime, Dad."

Dinner was ablaze with conversation as everyone anxiously shared their stories about the first day of the new school year. There were new teachers and new friends, new kids at school—some cuter than others, according to Ian. Lana's first day in high school had come with a few locker challenges, but she managed to find all of her classes. She was tardy only once.

"It's too far and I don't have enough time." Truth be told, she, too, had met a few "cute" people on the way. Soon Ian would be teasing her as much about boys as she had always teased him about girls. *I'm not sure I'm ready for this,* Michael thought to himself.

"So, what is your news, Michael?" Allie asked in the most innocent of voices, never anticipating the avalanche of chaos she was about to unleash.

"Oh my gosh!" Michael remembered he was supposed to meet with Dr. McPherson.

As in all things, timing is everything. Allie had managed to ask her question just as Mark was passing the potatoes to Michael. In his moment of surprise recollection, he dropped the bowl of potatoes onto the edge of his plate, which in turn flew into the air. As he tried to grab for the plate, he only made matters worse by knocking it into his glass, which promptly broke and spilled. After a few moments of bewilderment, the whole table erupted in laughter.

"Well, now that I have your attention," Michael recovered, "I'm not sure how to say this, or even how this happened, but...apparently...I am to replace Henry Johnson as Department Chair."

"Awesome!" Lana raised her glass to toast her father, only to remember that his glass was in shards.

"Michael, that's great." Allie was so proud. "How did you find out? Why the 'oh my gosh'?"

"Henry told me this morning in the chapel. I was supposed to meet with Peter this afternoon, but I got sidetracked and forgot."

"What was more important than Dr. McPherson?" Allie looked across the table as she tossed Michael a towel for his mess.

"Ben Wallace was upset in class today. I walked home with him and spent time with the family. Jim is really bad. I thought the phone call awhile ago may have been from Halley. I'll call Peter later. He'll understand."

Michael fielded questions from everyone about the new position for a few minutes, but soon he was asking them about their days and the scattered chatter resumed at the previous pace. Although it was a pretty corny, "Cleaver-like" family moment, Michael caught Allie smiling at him. How in the world did he ever land such an awesome lady?

Thank you, Lord.

What Does a Man Profit If He Gains the Whole World but Loses His Soul?

From the heavens above the stars shine down. From the heavens above, they watch. They see the good and the bad, the happy and sad as ever before their vigilant eye, a day in the life passes by. Not rushing their turn, they patiently wait for daylight to fade and night to abide. Fragile are we under star and sun as we scurry along on our missions of life—so lost, so disconnected…Removing the speck from our brother's eye we, precisely, surgically—cold…Tolerate we the plank in our own, unyielding, unhumble, undone. Answers to questions of ages gone by are sought in moment and one. Wrong questions asked, wrong answers found, solutions that crumble and fade. Under heavenly light, each man seeks what is right in his own eyes alone—each one free to do so…Free to win…Free to lose. From the heavens above the stars shine down. From the heavens above, they watch. Not rushing their turn, they patiently wait for daylight to fade into night, for mankind to adjust his sight, humbly bow…and make things—right.

Things in Hill City settled into their normal routine. Michael had his meeting with Dr. McPherson and graciously accepted his new position. Dr. Harry Terry handled the news with his usual lack of dignity and class. Michael missed Henry. While Henry lived only a few blocks away, the busyness of life seemed to allow few respites for them to visit.

Henry made regular visits to the Wallace house. Jim was slipping away, and despite all of Michael's best efforts, Ben was following suit. The light that had once shone so brightly in Ben's eyes was just a flicker. That "something" was gone.

Michael sat in his home office—the fourth bedroom upstairs, vacated by Ian when he moved to the basement for more privacy.

"Hey, Dad, what ya working on?" Mark strolled in still dripping wet from his evening shower. Michael, deep in thought about his lesson for the next day, did not hear Mark. Not to be deterred on his quest to gather "Dad" information, Mark made his way around the desk. Peering over his father's shoulder, he began to investigate the notes laying on the desk:

The Sabbath Year   *Jubilee–Leviticus* 25

The Lord said to Moses on Mount Sinai, "Speak to the Israelites and say to them: 'When you enter the land I am going to give you, the land itself must observe a sabbath to the Lord.

For six years sow your fields, and for six years prune your vineyards and gather their crops. But in the seventh year the land is to have a year of sabbath rest, a sabbath to the Lord. Do not sow your fields or prune your vineyards. Do not reap what grows of itself or harvest the grapes of your untended vines. The land is to have a year of rest.

Whatever the land yields during the sabbath year will be

food for you—for yourself, your male and female servants, and the hired worker and temporary resident who live among you, as well as for your livestock and the wild animals in your land. Whatever the land produces may be eaten.

The Year of Jubilee

Count off seven sabbath years—seven times seven years—so that the seven sabbath years amount to a period of forty-nine years…Consecrate the fiftieth year and proclaim liberty throughout the land to all its inhabitants. It shall be a jubilee for you; each of you is to return to your family property and to your own clan.

The fiftieth year shall be a jubilee for you; do not sow and do not reap what grows of itself or harvest the untended vines. For it is a jubilee and is to be holy for you; eat only what is taken directly from the fields.

Leviticus 25:1–12 (TNIV)

"*Wow!* What's all that?" Mark's wet hair finally dripped on the page in front of him.

Still finishing the last few notes, Michael gave him that gentle but firm "wait a minute" look. Mark continued to look at the notes until Michael laid his pen down.

"Those are my notes for class tomorrow."

"Does your class have to learn all of that stuff?"

"Yep, and a lot more too."

"Man, I'm not goin' to college."

"You're not? What are you *goin'* to do?"

"Well, I don't know, but that looks hard. Does anybody understand it?"

Michael scooted his chair back and scooped his dripping nine-year-old onto his lap. "Judging from the news on TV, probably not. Obviously you've had your shower. Did you have your snack?"

"Uh, yeah."

"Did you brush your teeth?"

"Uh, no."

"Well, hop to it. Get laying down and I'll be in to say good-night."

Mark hopped off Michael's lap and headed down the hall, probably to make a mess in the bathroom at best and maybe annoy his sister at worst—at least those were Michael's assumptions.

"Get out of here, brat!" Lana's voice punched down the hall right on cue.

Michael went to make peace and see what was going on around the house. He found Allie sitting on the bed with "the grey pouch" lying beside her and papers strewn all over the bed. That could only mean one thing: bills to pay. He tried to sneak back out, but she looked up and slid her glasses down her nose. "Hey, where are you going?"

"Nowhere."

"I heard you talking to Mark. At the rate we're going, I'm not sure any of the kids are going to college." She turned her attention back to the bills.

"That great, huh?"

"You know, it's not rocket science. You only spend what you make. You save when you can. You put some back for a rainy day… days…lots of days…There's too much month at the end of the money."

Yeah, it was bill-paying night—that ritual held in every household across America in the land of the brave and the home of the broke; where the government guarantees the right to the pursuit of happiness, but does not promise to finance it; someone else already has and is now charging thirty percent interest compounded by the minute. Refinance—save hundreds, even thousands a month—sure, save hundreds monthly, but pay that loan off over *years* instead of months. Save hundreds monthly and pay tens of thousands more for the opportunity to *save!* Get our card—zero percent interest—until you *use* it. Buy now, pay later. Buy now, pay forever. Yes, it was that night.

"Get back here, buster. Don't walk away." Allie lured him into the room. "We need to talk about the future."

"We have a future?" Michael walked over to the bed.

"Don't be smart with me. I know where you sleep. You're just a good whack in the head away from me getting all that insurance money."

"We borrowed against that to finish the basement," Michael reminded her.

"Are you trying to cheer me up? Who came up with 'budget billing' anyway? Do we ever get a refund if we pay too much? Who decides?" Allie was a real tiger on bill-paying night. Michael made the budget, but Allie made it work…usually. "You're spending too much on watering the grass. Let it die. We need to eat."

Michael loved his yard, so that comment really hurt. Allie took her glasses off and offered him her arms. He fell on the bed and flipped her over.

"Ooh, get a room." Mark stuck his head in the bedroom.

"Hey, little bit, this *is* my room," Michael blurted as he fell off the bed.

"Yeah, yeah, come tuck me in."

"Hey, Mom, what's Dad doing on the floor? I need lunch money." Lana joined the festivities in the bedroom. "They said my account is empty at school. Oh, and did you sign my choir trip form?

I have to turn in the two hundred-dollar deposit by Friday. Love you." Lana thumped Mark in the ear and darted out of the room.

Under her breath, Allie said, "Too much month at the end of the money."

"Come on, buddy. I'll tuck you in." Michael swept Mark up on his shoulder like a sack of potatoes and carried him down the hall. It could have been one of the coolest dad moves except that he smacked Mark's foot on the door going into his room..."Yow!" After flopping him in bed and making sure his ankle was okay, he kissed him goodnight. As he left the room, he couldn't help but hear Mark start his prayer: "Thank you, God, for Mom and Dad, and Lana and Ian. Please help us to get some money so Mom won't worry. She loves you, God, and I think you should love her too."

"Rise and shine you sleepyheads! This is Sunny Jack on WROE. It's gonna be rainy...and sunny, too, probably—what do the weather folks know? All I know is the sun is rising and you need to do the same. Rise and shine..."

Unfortunately, it was rainy—or fortunately, depending on your point of view. Michael, thinking back on Allie's "watering the grass" comment last night, was happy because he would not have to water today. Michael kissed her good-bye. "See you at noon." He headed off to school. It was mid-September, and the foliage around campus was still green. The rain seemed to accentuate the color. Soon the leaves would begin to change and the mature trees on Roe Campus would transform from their summer green to a fall patchwork of bright yellow and orange—one of the attractions of an older campus. The large trees and stately buildings certainly added to the collegiate atmosphere. The beautiful scenery came in handy on the college publications and recruiting pieces.

After spending some time in the chapel, Michael made his way across the campus. A student carrying a stack of papers ran up to him.

"Here's a flyer about the meeting tonight. Starts at seven."

"Hello and good-bye," Michael said to the back of the young lady as she ran off to hand out more flyers. *And so it begins,* Michael thought to himself. The presidential election pre-season was kicking off in Iowa, as usual. The Iowa Caucuses would take place in January, and the candidates were already canvassing the state for votes. Several politicians, not the least of which was Texas Senator Monroe P. Downs, one of the leading Democratic candidates for the presidency, would be on-campus this evening for a town hall meeting. Michael had been talking about the meeting with his political science class, and they would all attend the event as a class assignment.

After finishing his usual morning office routine, he headed up the steps to history class. They had been talking about the Great Depression for several class periods, and Michael was anxious to move on, but the class was really fixated on the period. They had talked about the factors leading up to the stock market crash and the changes implemented to ensure that history would not repeat itself. They discussed the "Hoovervilles"—small shantytowns made up of the displaced thousands who had lost everything in the Depression. There were many similarities to the "Marshallvilles," as they had come to be known—also shantytowns, or camps of people who had been displaced by a different kind of depression. Nearly one hundred years ago, thousands of people had lost their jobs as the economy crashed. Today, many of those who filled the "Marshallvilles" still had their jobs—even good jobs. They had simply broken down under an enormous burden of personal debt, a debt load that threatened the national economy as literally millions lost their homes with no hope of recovery. It was this connection between the Great Depression of the twentieth century and the current situation facing the nation that fueled the class discussion.

"How can these things be happening again? It doesn't seem like anyone has a plan," came the questions from several in the class.

"What about another New Deal?" asked Shelly Tate, the eternal optimist.

"Senator Downs has a new deal," Robert Washington replied. "He had dinner at our house last night and talked at length about his *new deal.*" Robert rolled his eyes and stretched out his arms. "I mean, at *length.*"

Senator Downs was adept at hobnobbing with the well-to-do and then expressing his undying devotion for the poor and middle class. He was also good at cherry-picking the media moments to make a big splash with minimal effort. He came from old oil money—Texas oil money in the billions. His family had been rich before, but in the early years of the new millennium, when the country was waging an unpopular war on terrorism—at the center of which happened to be Middle East oil—as well as trying to recover from horrible natural disasters, the Downs family made record profits on the backs of record-high gas prices. While middle-class America was giving millions of dollars to hurricane relief efforts, the Downs, along with other oil families, doubled and tripled their family fortunes.

"Senator Downs," scoffed Ben Wallace from the back corner of the room. Michael, though he agreed with Ben's tone toward the eminent senator, hated to hear the anger in his voice. At this point, however, it was the first time Ben had joined the discussion in weeks. "How much will his 'Big Deal' cost us?"

"Okay, class," Michael broke into their discussion, as class time was running short. "December 7, 1941, 'a date that will live in infamy,'" he used his best Rooseveltian voice. "Read about it. Learn about it. Talk about it…next time. See ya."

Before Michael could leave the room, Harry Terry came beaming in, puffed up like a peacock. If not for the annoyance of having to listen to Harry, he could provide, on some strange level, a bit of comic relief.

"Dr. Hamilton, guess what?"

"Wha—"

"I have been chosen to moderate the town hall meeting tonight. Well, actually, I volunteered. Dr. McPherson felt so guilty about not giving me the Department Chair position that he conceded to my demand…err…offer to moderate."

"That's great," Michael replied in his best couldn't-care-less voice. "I'll be there to…to…wish you well. Let me know if you need anything." It was just a polite gesture, not a real offer. Michael couldn't stop the words before they escaped his mouth and immediately went through the mental process of knocking himself in the head.

"Oh, that would be great. Do you think I should wear blue or black? Blue, patriotic…I have a great flag tie. Black, formal, my best color."

"Black, Harry, definitely black. I've gotta run to class. See you tonight." Michael untangled himself with Harry getting out of the room. He was still saying something as Michael left. "Okay, Harry." He nodded over his shoulder.

"Call me tonight!" Harry shouted after Michael in his familiar, pathetic tone. "Please?"

Michael was halfway up a flight of stairs on his way to Religion. *What a disaster. What was Peter thinking?* The thought of Harry sweating to death under all of the media lights made him laugh out loud.

Michael walked into class and, bypassing his usual spot on the edge of the desk, he went straight to the white board and began to write. As he filled the board with the notes that had mesmerized Mark, the class began to buzz. Obviously, many in the class had been listening to the same news broadcasts as Michael, and the economic news was not good. Record numbers of homeless, hopeless families were trapped in a spiraling cycle of debt that threatened to send the U.S. into another depression. The economists and politicians pontificated on talk show after talk show about their take on the issue. Some—mostly Republicans who were currently in power—downplayed the seriousness of the situation. Others—mostly Democrats seeking election—railed on failed policies. No one, however, seemed to care about the people. As Michael thought about the lack of concern for people, he could not help but recall Henry Johnson's advice about caring. As far as Michael could tell, no one cared at all. Memories of Calvary and countless other churches that had closed their doors drifted through his mind.

"Who can tell me about the Year of Jubilee?" Michael addressed the students as he finished writing on the board. The class was full of energy, but no one seemed brave enough to tackle this subject.

Finally, Sarah Johnson spoke up. "Sabbath economics, God's economic plan for his people. On the seventh day of creation, God rested. We are to follow suit…

"Remember the Sabbath to keep it holy. Six days shall you labor and do all your work, but the seventh day is a Sabbath to the Lord your God…For in six days the LORD made the heavens and the earth, the sea, and all that is in them, but he rested on the seventh day. Therefore the LORD blessed the Sabbath day and made it holy.

"Commandment number 4, Exodus 20:8–11."

From there, the class went on a roll. Michael could hardly keep up. As the end of the class period drew close, the white board was full:

- Sabbath-from Hebrew verb-to rest or stop working
- Jacob had 12 sons-Joseph sold into slavery-taken to Egypt
- Joseph interprets Pharaoh's dream-7 years of plenty-7 years of famine
- Joseph raises to prominence-2nd in command to Pharaoh
- During the famine-Jacob and clan of 70 people move to Egypt
- Pharaoh that "knew" Joseph-Hyksos 17th Dynasty-Foreign-primarily Semitic-nomadic "non-Egyptian"

200 Years Pass...

- Then a new king who did not know Joseph came to power-
- Ahmose-18th Dynasty-Egyptian heritage-hated previous dynasty
- Israelites enslaved
- 430 years total in Egypt

- Originally 70 went to Egypt
- 600,000 men-probably 2+ million Israelites left Egypt in the Exodus
    - Israelites-Egyptian captivity-
    - Egyptian economic system-military-industrial (capitalism like)
- Israelites were slaves to Egyptian system
- Like U.S. Capitalism-Egyptian system-surplus = wealth = power

Manna Story

In the desert the whole community grumbled against Moses and Aaron. The Israelites said to them, "If only we had died by the Lord's hand in Egypt! There we sat around pots of meat and ate all the food we wanted, but you have brought us out into this desert to starve this entire assembly to death."

Then the Lord said to Moses, "I will rain down bread from heaven for you. The people are to go out each day and gather enough for that day. In this way, I will test them and see whether they will follow my instructions. On the sixth day they are to prepare what they bring in, and that is to be twice as much as they gather on the other days."

Exodus 16:2–5 (TNIV)

God's economic plan (Exodus 16:16-18):

1. Every family gathers just enough for their needs

    * No surplus

* No shortage

Contrast to Capitalism-Infinite Tolerance for Wealth and Poverty

2. Bread should not be stored up (Exodus 16:19-20)

* Egyptian system-surplus = wealth = power

* Slavery for Israelites-forced labor to build

Store cities for storing the spoils of war

* Egypt-dominant civilization- forcing concentrations of resources and wealth

3. Sabbath-"On the sixth day they gathered twice as much—the Lord has given you the Sabbath; that is why on the sixth day he gives you bread for two days."

Exodus 16:22-30

* Not just a suggestion-"Anyone who desecrates it must be put to death; whoever does any work on that day must be cut off from his people."

Exodus 31:14

* Emphasized dependence on:

i. God

ii. Land as a gift-not a possession

iii. Let the land rest-God in control not man

iv. Man would choose to work 7 days-greed-never enough

v. Seven days of prosperity-6 days of work-God's blessing

* Economy of Grace

i. There is enough for everyone

ii. Don't hoard

* Manna-Hebrews asked, what is this?

4. Sabbath extends to Years-Seven years of "food" for Six years of work

* Let the ground rest in the Seventh Year (Exodus 23:10-11)

* People and animals may eat whatever grows

* Allows for balance-equilibrium for poor

5. Canceling of debts

At the end of every seven years you must cancel debts. This is how it is to be done: Every creditor shall cancel any loan they have made to another Israelite. They shall not require payment from anyone among their own people, because the LORD time for canceling debts has been proclaimed. You may require payment from a foreigner, but you must cancel any debt one of your people owes you. However, there need be no poor people among you, for in the land the LORD your God is giving you to posses as your inheritance, he will richly bless you, if only you fully obey the LORD your God and are careful to follow all these commands I am giving you today. For the LORD your God will bless you as he has promised, and you will lend to many nations but will borrow from none. You will rule over many nations, but none will rule over you.

Deuteronomy 15:1–6 (TNIV)

The Year of Jubilee

Count off seven sabbath years-seven times seven years-so that the seven sabbath years amount to a period of forty-nine years. Then have the trumpet sounded everywhere on the tenth day of the seventh month; on the Day of Atonement sound the trumpet throughout your land. Consecrate the fiftieth year and proclaim liberty throughout the land to all its inhabitants. It shall be a jubilee for you…

Leviticus 25:8–10 (TNIV)

Michael was exhausted. The discussion was brisk, and he barely kept up. Everyone in the class had contributed, but the main charge was led by Larry Finner and Sarah Johnson. Larry was a brilliant student, and Sarah, well, let's just say, the apple did not fall far from the tree—in this case, the grandparent tree. Henry would have been proud. Walking out of the classroom, Michael thought about the news on TV and the discussion in class. Shaking his head, he thought to himself, *What does a man profit if he gains the whole world but loses his soul?*

Does It Spin on Greed…or Good?

As Michael walked home to meet Allie for lunch, he noticed the action around the campus theater. All the major TV networks were arriving with their news teams. Tonight would be the first event of the 2028 presidential election campaign. Suddenly, the thought of Harry Terry representing the college on national television did not seem so attractive. *What would the Admissions folks think about that arrangement?*

The media continued to arrive on campus all afternoon. The political science class was excited about the evening, as well as their professor's agreement to cut the class short in exchange for their assigned attendance at the town hall meeting.

"Doc, do you think Hoover got a fair shake? What did he do that was so bad? Things didn't really change *that* much after FDR got elected in '32," Danielle rifled questions from her seat in the back of the room.

"Mostly nothing, Danielle. That was the problem. Hoover thought everything would be fine, so he did nothing, and there was a lot of history to support his…patience. Just let the economy correct itself." Michael had been seated in his usual position on the edge of the desk, but he made his way over to the Smart board. He touched the screen and it sprang to life.

Roaring Twenties

- Traditional values challenged
- Jazz Age
- Americans buying on credit

  -Cars

  -Household Appliances

  -Speculating in the Stock Market
- American Business booming

  -Only 8% increase in average wage

  -Imbalance of rich and poor

  -0.1% of population earning 42% of the income

  -Increased production

  -Rising personal debt

Great Depression

- Black Tuesday, October 29, 1929
- Stock Market Crash
- Banks fail/businesses close
- 15 million unemployed (15% of workforce)
- Worst economic collapse in modern history
- Spread worldwide
- Precursor to World War II
- 1929–1940s

Herbert Hoover

- Underestimated crisis—"a passing incident in our national lives."
- Will be over in 60 days
- Government should not intervene
- Trickle-down economics

  -Help banks and businesses

  -Business preferred to layoff workers

  -Diminished demand for goods
- Hoover Flag–empty pocket turned out
- Hooverville–shantytowns

Franklin Delano Roosevelt

- Rich
- Governor from New York
- New Deal Platform
- 1932–Landslide presidential victory
- First 100 Days

  -4-day bank holiday

  -Emergency Banking Relief Act–stabilize banks
- New Deal

  -Political Alliance

    * Labor Unions

    * Minorities

    * Farmers

* Intellectuals

-Government providing relief for people

Results of the Great Depression

- Increased employment opportunities for women
- Increase in social services
- Increased personal prudence and savings
- Increased expectations of government

  -Care for needy

  -Regulate economy

Robert Washington was the first to respond. "Whoa, Doc. Shouldn't people take care of themselves? Why is it the government's responsibility to care for the needy?"

"Isn't that one of the big differences between Republicans and Democrats?" Shelly Tate posed. "Republicans want to leave the power with the states, power with the people and let them take care of themselves…smaller government, less tax, less regulation. The Democrats want to centralize power in Washington. Give us the power and the resources and we will take care of everything. More social programs, more government, and more taxes. Hoover was a Republican. Roosevelt was a Democrat."

Michael left the Smart board and grabbed a dry-erase marker. "Tell me about the parties." He began to write:

Democratic Party

- *Thomas Jefferson-1790s-emerged to oppose the Federalist Party*
- *supported by southern planters and northern farmers*

- John Quincy Adams (1825-29)
- Andrew Jackson (1829-37)
- Martin van Buren (1837-41)
- James Polk (1845-49)
- Franklin Pierce (1853-57)
- James Buchanan (1857-61)

- Very powerful 1825-1860
  - Grover Cleveland (1885-89)
  - Woodrow Wilson (1913-23)

Republican Party

- 1854 party emerged-main opposition to Democrats
- Little support in the south
- 1856-John Fremont-1st presidential candidate-defeated by Buchanan
- 1860 Abraham Lincoln defeated Stephen Douglas
- Powerful after the Civil War
- Supported protective tariffs
- Supported by industrialists in the north

Northern and Midwest farmers and most immigrant groups

- Names
    - Ulysses Grant (1869-1877)
    - Rutherford Hayes (1877-1881)
    - James Garfield (1881)
    - Chester Arthur (1881-1885)
    - Benjamin Harrison (1889-1893)
    - William McKinley (1897-1901)
    - Theodore Roosevelt (1901-1909)
    - William Taft (1909-1913)
    - Warren Harding (1921-1923)
    - Calvin Coolidge (1923-1929)
    - Herbert Hoover (1929-1933)

"So that brings us back to Hoover," Michael said as the class period came to an end. "We'll talk more about him next time. How are you coming with your assignment?" Michael had given the class the assignment of developing a presidential election campaign strategy.

Assignment-"Operation Mr. Smith Goes to Washington"

- *Develop a presidential candidate*
- *Choose a party*
- *Develop a platform and election strategy*
- *Assemble a campaign team*
- *Arrange the financials*
- *GET ELECTED*

His question was met with mixed responses, but there was no time left to discuss it. "I'll see you tonight. Save me two seats, please."

As afternoon wore into evening, the excitement on campus continued to build. By the time Michael and Allie walked across campus to the theater, the atmosphere was electric. There were dozens of media trucks and trailers outside the theater, with countless numbers of cameramen and reporters positioned to catch the perfect Midwest sunset as they taped their segments for the early evening news. Security was tight, so it took a few minutes to get into the theater.

"Are you meeting your class?" Allie fidgeted as they waited in line outside the theater.

"Yes. They should have a couple seats saved for us,"

"Are you okay? You seem distracted." Allie looked into the eyes of her usually calm husband. He seemed a bit restless.

"I'm fine," Michael replied unconvincingly. "I just don't like this Downs very much."

"Senator Downs?"

"Yeah. He's going to be the front-runner, and he is all wrong for the country. He thinks everything is fine, and maybe things are fine if you're sitting on billions, but seven years ago things were *fine* and our church closed its doors, along with countless others. Millions of people are homeless. Does anyone care? Does Senator Downs have any ideas, any answers? Is he even asking the right questions? Accumulate, accumulate, accumulate…more wealth…more power…more…" his voice trailed off in frustration.

"What about Delaney or Smithson?" Allie asked about the other candidates participating in the town hall meeting.

"They're not bad men, but they have no vision, no fresh ideas. Everyone is touting the same tired answers. Either they beat the 'everything's okay' drum, or they just throw dirt at the Marshall administration. Certainly, the president has become an easy target. Like Hoover before the Great Depression, he's on the 'just ride it out' campaign."

"Can I see your bag, ma'am?" A security officer extended his white-gloved hand toward Allie. Allie obliged, and soon they were moving into the theater. The place was filling up. The theater was one of the older buildings on campus. Michael loved the classical atmosphere it provided, but he wondered why they were not using one of the newer, more modern facilities on campus. There were cameras everywhere.

"The world is certainly watching." Michael nervously sighed to Allie.

"Dr. Hamilton, down here!" Shelly yelled at him from the front row.

Great, Michael thought, as he was not a "front row" guy. He was more comfortable in the back—especially at events like tonight, but destiny has a funny way of ushering the unlikely to the forefront.

Michael noticed Dr. McPherson pacing the stage as he and Allie made their way to the students.

"Michael, have you seen Harry?"

"Not since this morning. He's probably still powdering his nose," Michael quipped through a wry smile.

"Not funny," Peter snapped. "We start in thirty minutes, and he has not been out here to go over the schedule with the producer."

Michael laughed. "Good old Harry."

"Don't laugh. If he doesn't show in ten minutes, you're taking his place."

Michael had no idea how much trouble he was in, for Harry would turn out to be a no-show. On his way to the theater, Harry had seen all of the media trucks and cameramen. Allowing his vanity to get the best of him, he ducked into the student center to check his look. As fate would have it, Harry was on a collision course with a practical joker. Earlier in the evening a student made his way into the first-floor men's restroom in the student center and christened each of the toilet seats with a fresh coat of baby oil—normally pretty harmless—but tonight…

Harry walked right into, rather sat right on one of those chosen seats. While this would have represented a minor setback for most people, Harry was not the norm. He managed to get baby oil all over himself, his suit, his hair, his…He was a mess. The more he tried to clean himself, the worse he looked. Too embarrassed to show his face, Harry spent the better part of the evening in that first-floor student center restroom, leaving Michael to destiny.

"Twenty minutes, Michael. It's going to be you." There was no arguing with a college president on a mission in front of a soon-to-be national audience. "Come with me."

Michael glanced back over his shoulder at Allie as Dr. McPherson led him away. She was shaking her head and grinning from ear to ear.

"You go, Doc," came the enthusiastic, if not mocking outcry from his poli-sci class, all twenty-three occupying the front two middle rows of the theater. *They must have arrived at noon to get those seats,* Michael thought.

Maybe it was better this way. Michael would have been a nervous wreck, but there was no time. Peter whisked him off to the dressing room where a lady named Christine waited with all manner of makeup, spritzes, sprays, and stuff Michael did not want to know about. Time was short. Michael looked at Christine and then at Peter.

"I'll be right back." Peter darted off and Michael sat down in the makeup chair.

"Be kind," he said as he eased back in the chair without looking up at Christine.

"You're in good hands, honey. I'll take good care of you."

Perhaps to avoid thinking about his impending doom on national TV, Michael struck up a conversation. "Where are you from?" That was all it took. Christine did not take a breath until Peter came back and interrupted her.

She was from the NBC affiliate station in Kansas City, married with three kids—Andrea, 17, Ella, 15, and Josh, 12—working on the road a lot, and she missed her family. They were living the American nightmare, as the American dream had become for many of the middle class. They lost their house a few years ago when the interest-only mortgage did not pan out so well. The housing market bottomed out, and instead of the value of their house appreciating, it depreciated. Like many Americans they had stretched themselves thin with credit, and their house of cards came tumbling down. Andrea got sick and the medical bills—even with their insurance—finished them.

"These guys don't care," she fumed at the politicians who would be participating in the debate.

Michael's heart went out to her. He wanted so much to tell her that things would be all right, but who could say for sure? She was right. These guys did not care about her. They were only concerned about getting elected. They had to be all things to all people, which really meant they would end up being nothing for anybody. They would have to promise overnight solutions to decade-old issues. Fearing to stray too far from the crowd, they would propose the same solutions couched in different language, ultimately leading down the same old paths the nation had been on for years. Einstein once said, "We can't use the same ideas to solve problems that we used to create them."

We are a nation gone insane, Michael thought. *We keep doing the same things, expecting different results.*

Peter came back into the room with a man in khakis, a plaid shirt, and sweater vest. "Michael, this is Dane. He's the producer tonight. He'll tell you what to do."

Michael, feeling pretty stupid about the makeup, extended his hand to Dane, who, with a dead-fish handshake, took only half of Michael's hand. Michael shuddered inside. *Shake like a man,* he thought to himself.

"Okay. Here's the deal." Dane took charge. His handshake may have been pathetic, but his presence was formidable. In two minutes he gave Michael the lay of the land. "Make sure you do this...Don't ever do this...Your job is to be invisible. Just let the big boys shine."

"Invisible, got it." Michael shuddered again, thinking, *If you only knew how invisible I would like to be.*

Dane handed him a script and several index cards. "Here are the bios and intros for the candidates. Take a few minutes to familiarize yourself with them. It will help you when you're trying to read the teleprompter."

Great, Michael thought sarcastically.

Dane began to leave, but turned back abruptly. "You coming?"

Michael formed the word "no" in his mouth, but somehow yes came out.

"Do you have a tie?" Dane asked in a rather condescending tone.

"Sure, I carry one in my wallet," Michael smarted back. Until now, he had not even thought about how he was dressed—denim blue shirt and khakis. *Great.*

"Don't worry about it. We gotta go."

Michael looked back at Christine as he rushed out of the room behind Dane and Peter. No words came out of his mouth.

"Good luck." She smiled as she tossed the brush back onto the counter. "You'll do great."

"Great" seemed to be the word of the hour. Coming from Christine, however, it sounded much less sarcastic than it had in Michael's thoughts.

They rushed down a hallway toward the stage. Michael could hear the buzz of the packed house. From just offstage, he could see the bright television lights. *How in the world did I ever get here?* he thought. *Harry is dead meat. Where is he?*

He remembered the cards in his hand and quickly glanced through them. There were four candidates altogether, and they were all Democrats. President Marshall would surely receive his party nomination for re-election, so there were no Republicans in attendance.

- Card 1: Senator Monroe P. Downs–Texas
- Card 2: Representative Joseph Delaney–Massachusetts
- Card 3: Representative Frederick Smithson–Utah
- Card 4: Senator Harold Lawrence–California

A man wearing a headset tapped him on the shoulder and asked, "You Michael Hamilton?"

Michael nodded, and the man fitted him with a wireless microphone. Just as they finished, Dane motioned to him from the stage. The lights were blinding. He could barely see Allie and the students in the front row. Dane helped him get acclimated to the stage, pointing out the teleprompter and the multiple cameras.

"Don't worry about the cameras. Just be natural. I heard you used to be a preacher. There's your pulpit." He pointed to the moderator's podium. "Your congregation is the nation tonight."

No pressure, Michael gulped.

The candidates were busy taking their places.

"Two minutes," came a voice from offstage.

"All right, Michael, I'll be right there by the teleprompter." Dane checked the mic and rolled his eyes at Michael's clothes. "I'll give you your cues. Just watch me and the teleprompter and you'll be fine. Any questions?"

Michael laughed at the thought. *Any questions…How about a thousand? How about…*

"Thirty seconds."

Dane patted him on the back and they both took their places.

"Three, two, one…"

Dane pointed at Michael, and he began to read from the teleprompter. "Good evening from the campus of Roe College in the heart of Iowa. Welcome to the first of five town hall meetings that will be held around the state over the next few months as part of the Iowa Caucus process. Tonight you will meet four of our presidential hopefuls. They will have a chance to introduce themselves and share their visions for the future of our nation. And now, let's meet the candidates."

Michael seemed to gain confidence with every word. While the teleprompter took some getting used to, his days in the pulpit served him well as he stood before the audience. This was a much different format than the classroom, not so different from the sanctuary. He felt a sense of reverence come over him. This was the great American election process in motion—something he had taught many times, and now he was part of it. *While this nation may have its flaws,* he thought, *it is still the greatest nation on earth.* The election process in the United States represented the greatest transfer of power in the world, and while it was not perfect, it would be peaceful.

He introduced each of the candidates, and then it was their turn to speak. He had survived the opening. He gave Dane a "how am I doing?" look, but the producer only pointed at the teleprompter. "Stay focused," Dane mouthed to him as he returned his attention to the candidates.

He glanced out at Allie. She gave him a reassuring look, as she had done so many times on Sunday mornings past.

This shouldn't be too hard, he thought to himself. *Just watch Dane for the cues—read off the teleprompter.* Seemed pretty simple.

The candidates each spoke for about five minutes, mostly elaborating on the introduction Michael had given them. At the end of their comments, Michael thanked them.

"When we return, I will ask each candidate a series of three questions. They will have two minutes to respond to each question." With that, there was a break for television commercials.

Dane made eye contact with Michael. "You doing okay?"

"I'm good," Michael replied.

"Just read the questions off the teleprompter. It will tell you which candidate to address. When they finish responding, thank them and read the next question. Stay focused."

"What if they go too long?"

"They won't. Don't worry. If they do, just watch me."

"Ten seconds…Three, two, one…"

"Welcome back. Tonight's questions will deal with the military, the economy, and the general state of the union. Once again, candidates will be given two minutes to respond to each question. The order of response was determined before the meeting. Gentlemen, are you ready?"

Michael began to ask each of the candidates the questions as they appeared on the teleprompter. All in all, his role in the evening seemed pretty mindless. Just read the prompts…be invisible… seemed simple. Michael paid more attention to watching the time each candidate was taking than he did to their actual responses. Each candidate answered questions about the military. No one exceeded their time. *So far, so good.* Michael continued to relax. They moved on to the economy.

Each candidate received a different question, but all of the answers sounded alike. Michael, in his invisible role, said very little between candidate answers. His job was simply to thank the candidate and read the next question. Three of the four candidates answered their economy questions. Had Michael been paying more attention, their answers would have angered him, but he was focused on invisibility. As Representative Smithson finished his response, leaving only Senator Downs to respond, Michael noticed Christine standing just offstage. For the moment, the sight of her snapped him out of his mindless moderator role. He wished he would have had some words of encouragement for her back in the makeup room.

As his thoughts came back to the stage, he noticed that no one was speaking. "Thank you, Representative Smithson," he stammered, hoping that only a few seconds had passed. He gave a quick look at Dane, who was just looking at him with one eyebrow cocked.

He quickly asked the final economy question. "Senator Downs, the Marshall Administration has come under considerable attack in recent months for their lack of response to the mounting tension caused by the millions of displaced Americans living in what have come to be called 'Marshallvilles.' The economy has been spiraling down for some time now, with many drawing attention to parallels between the current state of our economy and events leading up to the Stock Market Crash in 1929 and ultimately the Great Depression—"

"Oh, bull!" the senator interrupted. "You would think the sky has fallen with all of the naysayers going off these days. Debt, debt, debt, that's all you hear, as if everyone is in over their heads. Truth is, one-fourth of the population has no credit cards at all, and one-third of those who have cards pay them off every month. Some people don't know the difference between their needs and their wants. That does not mean the whole state of the economy is in jeopardy. In the grand scheme of things, there is only one lost sheep and the ninety-nine are fine. We don't need to go crazy with the economy. We are the strongest nation on earth, and our economy can withstand any storm. People said outsourcing jobs to other nations would be the end of us, but we survived, and we're stronger as a planet, not just a nation. People said the downturn in the housing market would spell doom, but again, we're fine!"

"*Fine,* sir?" Michael was no longer invisible. Before he could think beyond the blood rushing to his head, he went on. "Do you think the twenty million homeless living out of their cars think we're fine? Do you think they will be inspired to vote for you and your couldn't-care-less agenda?"

"You are out of line, sir. I have been caring for and serving the *fine* people of this nation for forty years. I know what I am talking about. We see things from Washington that you cannot imagine. I know—"

"The people don't care how much you *know* until they *know how much you care!*"

The room erupted with applause. The whole world was spinning for Michael. Dane...where was Dane? The teleprompter was blank. The red light on the camera was still on. There was no way to bring the room under control, so Michael did the only thing he could think of: He looked at the camera and said, "We'll be right back."

Senator Downs was immediately in his face screaming. Michael was not listening. *Invisible...Just read the teleprompter...Simple... What was so hard about...?*

Dane stepped in between Michael and the senator. "Great TV!" he shouted. "I didn't think you had it in you, man! Where did that come from? All right, get ready. We're coming back in thirty seconds. Take your place and watch the teleprompter."

The room was still going crazy. The students led the cheers as a chant for their beloved professor began to rise in the room.

"Hamilton for President! Hamilton for President!"

Senator Downs was still fuming, but he was back at his station.

Michael was too busy watching the teleprompter and wondering if any words of wisdom would be provided. The answer was no.

"Three, two, one..."

"Welcome back," Michael started. The teleprompter was still blank. The chant in the room had grown deafening. Thinking on his feet and hoping the teleprompter would follow him, Michael pushed on. "And now for our last category, the state of the Union." He breathed a sigh of relief as the teleprompter came back to life, and he did his best to become invisible. The chant subsided, and for the moment things settle back to "normal." Michael wanted to look at Allie, but he was afraid he would lose his concentration. He addressed the question on the teleprompter to Senator Lawrence of California and wished to himself that the night would be over. The senator took the bait and launched into his answer. Michael looked at Dane, who gave him a big smile. He looked over at Christine; there were big tears running down her face. *Oh, I don't need this right now,* he thought, but he felt good about finding the words for her and the countless other families suffering across the nation. His timing was bad, but his intentions were good. Another crazy thought ran through his mind: *I wonder if I still have a job? Where is Peter?*

The rest of the candidates answered their questions without incident—even Senator Downs. As the last question was asked and answered, the responsibility of closing the evening fell to Michael. Polite applause rose in the room as Michael invited the audience to join him in thanking the candidates. The teleprompter gave Michael his closing remarks. *Just stay invisible,* he thought. *Keep it simple.* But his eyes found Allie. He thought about his family.

"America is a great nation. It was founded by men with certain ideals in mind, men who, 'in order to form a more perfect union,' held certain truths to be self-evident. They believed that men should be free. Countless thousands have died for those truths over the life of this nation. They did not die for monuments or medals, not for profit or loss, not for right or left, Republican or Democrat, not for rich or poor...They died for people. They died so people could be free. If we stop caring about people, how long will we be free? God bless and good night."

The room was silent. No one moved, not even the candidates. They all seemed to be frozen in time—just for that moment. Michael looked at Dane. He was staring back. The teleprompter was blank except for the blinking cursor...blink...blink...blink...The red light on the camera finally went out.

Suddenly, Michael was surrounded by his class. They were all speaking at once. He looked over his shoulder and saw the candidates being escorted backstage. Before he could turn around, there were cameras and microphones coming from every direction.

"Dr. Hamilton, have you ever run for office? Are you going to run?"

"What's your party?"

The questions were flying faster than he could think. "I'm just the moderator," he managed to say. He did his best to answer the questions, but everything had become a blur—a media feeding frenzy. His students were being interviewed right and left. Allie was trying to make her way to him, but she also had a microphone in her face. Dane finally came to the rescue. He gathered Michael and Allie and escorted them backstage to one of the dressing rooms. He left them there for a moment. When he came back, he motioned for them to follow, and he led them to one of the big trailers outside the theater.

"Well, mate, so much for invisible." Dane grinned as he stepped into the trailer.

"'Hamilton for President'?" Allie just looked at him, not knowing whether to laugh or panic.

"I know, I know...Just keep it simple...just be invisible...How hard can it be? Just read the teleprompter. Downs is a—"

"Michael, what about the kids?"

"They'll be okay. They're seniors, mostly—"

"No! Our kids."

"They'll be okay," Dane assured her. "The media can be a nuisance, but they're not dangerous. Where do you live?"

"About a block away." Michael looked at Allie. "Are you ready?"

Dane stuck his head out of the trailer. Most of the media were still in the theater interviewing students and the other candidates, so the coast was clear. Michael and Allie made their way across campus. At first, they were almost running, but there was no one following. It was a gorgeous fall evening, and they were crossing through one of the beautiful campus gardens. As they slowed to a walk, Allie took Michael by the hand and pulled him to a stop. They were standing on stone pavers surrounded by landscape walls with vines growing on them. There were plants of all kinds; the fall mums were especially pretty. The Roe College groundskeepers were masters of their craft.

"So, Mr. President, may I have the pleasure of this dance?" She curtsied to him.

Michael bowed low and took her hand. "Yes, you may, my lady."

While Ginger and Fred they were not, they were two people who loved each other very deeply. Allie was more beautiful in Michael's eyes tonight than she had ever been—not just because of the moonlit moment, but more because she knew his soul, and she was taking care of him with every dip and twirl.

The evening had thrown Michael. He did not know what would happen next; so many thoughts were running through his mind. Had he disgraced his school? What would Peter think? Do? Were his kids—all of them, the ones at home and the ones still back at the theater—okay? What would tomorrow bring? One thing, one very important thing was not in question...Allie.

Michael stumbled over one of the pavers and almost fell down. They both stopped, looked at each other, and began to laugh.

"What in the world just happened?" Michael whirled his eyes to the sky. "How could I be so stupid?"

"It's okay. You spoke from your heart. You were right. They didn't have anything to say."

"Yeah, but at least it was their turn to speak. Who says that I have anything to say?"

"Well, a theater full of people. Hamilton for President!" Allie shouted at the sky.

Michael, coming back to the urgency of the moment, remembered the kids. "We need to get home."

"I'm proud of you." Allie took him by both hands and pulled him over to one of the stone benches in the garden. They sat down, allowing the fullness of the moment to surround them. Michael looked down at the plaque on the ground.

In loving memory of
David Larson–Class of '98
He gave his life for others 9/11/01
Ladder Company 88 World Trade Center

Michael thought about the countless number of heroes there had been on that fateful day when the world seemed to change. For a short time after the Trade Center fell, the nation seemed to be a kinder, gentler place to live. Priorities were shifted.

"It's about people, right? Does it always have to be about the almighty dollar? Isn't there enough for everyone, or do the Downs of the world have to have it all? Mine, mine, mine…money, power…The world goes round and round. Does it spin on greed…or good?"

See You at the Hollow

Roe Campus was filled with a mix of new and old buildings. For the students' part, no building could compare with their favorite hangout, The Hollow. It was essentially a great big cave. Discovered in the nineteenth century, it ran for miles back into the bluffs surrounding Hill City. In the mid-1950s, the college had constructed an entrance to the cave that resembled an enormous oak tree. Two huge doors opened inward to a cylindrical stone-floored tunnel, about ten feet around and thirty feet long, leading to the first of two large rooms. The first room was an area about sixty feet wide by eighty feet deep and served as the coffee shop area. It was filled with rustic chairs and couches, tables, and several big-screen plasma televisions. It may have been rustic, but it did not lack for technology. There was a large oak bar running along the north wall. Students could buy sandwiches, pizzas, snacks, sodas, and all kinds of coffees, not to mention the famous Hollow cinnamon rolls. The combination of cinnamon and coffee made for a wonderful-smelling room. It was near impossible to visit The Hollow and pass up something to eat or drink.

A second cylindrical tunnel about twenty feet in diameter exited the outer room in the northeast corner and ran for about a hundred fifty feet down to the second, or inner room, which was larger than the outer room. While this second tunnel had been finished with stone pavers to make the walk easier, the inner room remained in its natural condition. It was a round room with a circumference of about two hundred feet that formed a perfect indoor amphitheater. The floor terraced its way in concentric circles down to a large "stage" area that consisted of a stone surface. The flat stage had a circumference of about thirty feet and was surrounded by a moat. The ceiling was over a hundred feet high and had a thirty-foot opening in the center that allowed rain to fall into the room, and in the spring, rainwater filled the moat area around the stage. Several wooden bridges had been constructed to allow access to the stage.

While there was no electronic sound system in the room, it was perfect for acoustic music performances, stand-up comedians, and speakers. The college campus was full of budding musicians, comedians, and poets, so there was no shortage of performers. Several times a semester professional performers were brought in to entertain. All in all, The Hollow was quite an attraction.

Tonight it was filled with students talking about the town hall meeting. The poli-sci class was hanging out in the back corner. Their excitement was different. While most of the students were dealing with the events of the evening from a distance, Dr. Hamilton's class was at the epicenter. They were swapping interview stories, slamming down slice after slice of pizza, and loading up on caffeine while positioned in front of a fifty-four-inch plasma screen. The cable news networks were focusing on a riot raging in one of the Marshallvilles outside Los Angeles, so the only news regarding the town hall meeting were little blurbs running across the bottom of the screen. It was five minutes to ten. The students were restless but hoped they would see themselves on the ten o'clock news. They were debating their choice of network to watch but finally settled on WNN. There was no great philosophical reason behind the decision. The reporter had been cute, so the guys, wanting to please the girls, gave in to their choice.

Shelly slid a chair up to the TV and changed the channel. "Still on commercials," she moaned as she moved her chair back.

"Welcome to World Network News. This is Steve Jenson reporting."

The first story was on the riot outside of L.A.

"Oh, come on!" Larry screamed at the TV.

Finally, after about five minutes, a shot of Roe College appeared on the screen.

Shelly shushed the group. "Here it is!"

"Tonight, sparks flew in Hill City, Iowa. What had all the makings of a boring town hall meeting to kick off the 2028 Presidential Campaign season turned into an all-out war of words between Senator Downs from Texas and, of all people, the meeting moderator, a Dr. Michael Hamilton."

The picture on the screen switched to the scene inside the theater when tensions had broken out between Dr. Hamilton and the senator. "People don't care how much you know until they know how much you care!" The audience erupted. It was déjà vu for the students.

"There we are!"

"Shhh! Listen!"

Steve Jenson was now interviewing the reporter.

"He's so cute."

"Shhh!"

"Steve, we have been seeing a lot of tension around the nation. You have been reporting on a riot outside of L.A. all evening. People want to know where the politicians stand. The politicians here tonight did not seem to have any fresh ideas or solutions. I think

Michael Hamilton just got fed up with it all. His words struck a chord with the audience, and they responded in a big way. We caught up with Dr. Hamilton after the meeting."

"I don't know...I'm just the moderator."

"Dr. Hamilton, what do you think caused the audience reaction? They were ready to crown you king."

"I think people just want to know that someone cares, that someone is willing to stand up and face the hard facts. Things are not okay. Millions of people are living out of their cars. Millions of people have no health insurance, and many of those who have insurance still end up with major bills that are not covered. We have been greedy for too long. The average CEO makes three hundred times more than the average worker. Five percent of the people in this nation earn eighty percent of the income, and these gaps are growing! Where does it stop? Where is this nation without the middle class? When will the *haves* have *enough?* There's nothing evil about money or even being rich. There is something wrong with greed."

"That's all we got, Steve. Dr. Hamilton was led away with his wife, and we have not seen him since."

"Who is this guy, Evan? Do we know anything about him?"

"Evan, that's his name!" Ginny whispered loudly.

"Shut up!"

"Well, Steve, we interviewed several of his students, and to be honest with you, they love the guy."

"There we are!"

Shelly was the first one on camera. "We've been studying a lot about the Great Depression and the events leading up to the Crash in '29. There seem to be a lot of parallels. Hoover thought everything would be fine in sixty days. The Depression lasted over a decade."

"He's taught us a lot the last few years." Larry's face filled the screen. "He's not just a nine-to-five guy. He spends time with us. He cares."

"He cares, Steve. That seemed to be the sentiment of each one we interviewed. I'm sure the analysts will tell us over the next few days just who he is…or was. I have a feeling things are going to change for Michael Hamilton."

"See if we're on another station."

For the next few hours, the students flipped from station to station. Roe College and Michael Hamilton were everywhere.

Michael's picture was on the front of the *Morning Herald.* The reporter was right—Michael's life was about to change. He was also right about the media analysts. By afternoon of the next day, which just happened to be a Saturday, Michael's biography was playing on every channel.

Michael watched a little as he read about himself in the morning paper and laughed. *What a boring subject,* he thought. No secret mistresses or shady backroom deals; no flags burned or major protests in college; only two speeding tickets in his whole life. With no dirt to find, he wondered if the media would create something…something just to make the story interesting.

One by one the students began to wake. With their class project taking on new meaning, the poli-sci group had a mission now and a noon rendezvous at the library. After too much news, too much pizza, and too much caffeine, they had come up with the idea to make Dr. Hamilton their class project candidate. At first, it was just a name to fill in the blank, but it had grown with the passing hours.

There is no period in life like the time spent in college. College is not for everyone, so some never go. Some breeze through in four years, some in five, and some, like Danielle Winters, make college a career. At twenty-seven, she was in her ninth year of college. She had majored in everything from business to Bible, finally settling on biblical studies with hopes of becoming a missionary. Like many a lost cause, Dr. Hamilton had taken her under his wing and tried to steer her down a productive path. He was not convinced that the jungles of South America were ready for Danielle, but she seemed determined, and at least she was on course to *finish* her degree.

Danielle was the one who suggested they use Dr. Hamilton as their candidate. Like many college students, she was a dreamer. College just seems to be the time of life to dream. Even the brightest students don't seem to know that they don't know everything. Therefore, anything is possible—even getting your college professor elected President of the United States. By two o'clock in the morning, they were in full-fledged primary planning.

Since Danielle was a student worker in the library, she volunteered to reserve one of the study rooms for the Saturday rendezvous. She took good care of them, reserving a room complete with computers and Internet access. Shortly after noon, the sleepy group began to arrive.

"Hey, where's Ben?" Sarah hoped he was just running late.

"Thing for Ben, have ya?" they teased her.

"No. He wasn't at The Hollow or the town hall meeting. What's up with that—?"

Shelly interrupted their banter. "He's not the only one who can lead. Let's get busy. We have a lot to do. Who knows about the Iowa Caucus system?"

"I do," Larry offered.

"Of course," the group responded sarcastically. They gave Larry a hard time about being the brain, but they also had a great deal of respect for him. Larry truly was brilliant.

He described the necessary steps to get Dr. Hamilton entered into the Iowa Caucus and eventually into the New Hampshire Primary. Assignments were made, and they felt pretty good about their plan for the first two stages of the campaign process.

"What about Super Tuesday?"

"Who woke you up, Lenny?"

Lenny had been napping in one of the corner reading chairs but joined in with a daunting question: *What about Super Tuesday?* One day, multiple states.

It was one thing to plan a mock candidacy, but the students were actually thinking about entering Dr. Hamilton into the election process. Where would they get funding? Would anyone take them seriously? How would they get out of class? How would they tell Dr. Hamilton?

"Don't worry about it," Shelly pushed them on. "Let's just take care of these first steps and see what happens. Robert, you're the money man, you check out funding. Sarah, you check out Super Tuesday."

"We need a Web site," Larry added. "I'll take care of it."

"Ladies, ladies," the voice from the reading chair rumbled as once again Lenny roused from his slumber. "What's our…you know…our thing, campaign thing? What's our message? Are we Republican or Democrat?"

"Touché. One question at a time," Shelly bellowed, still playing the lead role. "Let's talk party first. We know the Republicans will nominate Marshall, he's the incumbent, so I say we should be Democrat."

"Don't you think we should check with Dr. Hamilton?" Danielle winced at the thought of being rejected.

"N-n-n…no. It's our assignment," Shelly staggered, trying to sound confident and in charge. "Anyway, the Republicans were in power just before the Great Depression, and a Democrat got elected in '32. I think we should go with that."

Danielle continued to press her point. "We don't even know Dr. Hamilton's preference. Don't you think that is important?"

Ginny finally brought some sense to the debate. "If Dr. Hamilton is Republican, we don't have a chance to be elected. Marshall is the incumbent, end of story. He has to be a Democrat. Besides, he just blew Monroe out of the water last night. That would be his biggest competition."

"Okay, it's settled. Democrat." Shelly made a note on her pad of paper.

"Power to the people," chanted the smooth Californian in the corner.

Shelly grabbed the floor back. "Let's talk about message, our platform."

"Maybe we should talk about the issues first."

"Good thought, Sarah J."

They tossed around the issues for the next hour. They gathered data from the Internet. They made millions of notes. Even Lenny was out of his comfy chair and working hard. Eventually, Larry stepped back from the action and admired his friends. Everyone was involved. Everyone was contributing and being respected for their contributions, and he thought back to freshman year when they had all met for the first time. Back then, they spent most of their time arguing and fighting, usually about nothing. That, however, had been an important part of their friendship process. All the eggshells were smashed long ago, so there were no more egos to manage. Everyone had been reduced to their most basic personality—their true selves. They had grown comfortable with each other knowing that there were no secrets. Some of the things they knew about each other were scary, but they had long since moved past those imperfections. They were ready.

"Jubilee!" he finally shouted into the mix. He had to shout it three more times before he had their attention. "Jubilee. All of our classes connect. Look..." Larry went to the board and began to write:

RELIGION	HISTORY	POLI-SCI
Egypt-	U.S.-	Democrats
Industrial/ Military	Industrial/ Military	Republicans
Wealth = Power	Wealth = Power	Southern
Accumulate = Store Cities	Credit	Plantations
Slaves	U.S.-Slaves	Civil War
Moses-Freedom	Lincoln-Freedom	Emancipation
Jubilee	Capitalism	Unions/ Stock Market
God	Man	Greed

Plenty	Shortage	Depression
Forgiveness of Debt	Accumulate Debt	Crumbling Economy
Promised Land	Homeless	World War/ Helter Skelter

JUBILEE!

"We need a Year of Jubilee."

They all stared at the board for a minute. Shelly was the first to speak. "What are you saying, Larry? Forgive all the debts? Free all the slaves?"

"We don't have slaves anymore." Robert rolled his eyes.

"Yes, we do." Sarah stared back at Robert, who shrugged his shoulders. "A slave is a person who works for someone else, who does not control his own destiny and has no hope of ever doing so. Our nation has become enslaved to debt. People go to work to pay their bills. They no longer dream of a better life, they just hope that life doesn't get worse, that no one in their family gets sick, that no catastrophe hits them. Lotteries and casinos promise riches. The credit industry shouts: 'Buy now, pay later…low rates!' An unwitting public marches by the millions into the snare. They trade their freedom for a moment's pleasure. They are caught. They are slaves. They are beyond hope."

"Well, too bad. Let the buyer beware," Robert snapped. "Sure, forgive all of the debt, but what is that going to do to our economy? What about the banks and the credit card companies?"

Larry joined back into the discussion. "I don't know for sure, Robert. I am sure we could calculate the total debt of America. I've seen figures of 2 trillion dollars. That is a huge number for sure. But what is the cost of not forgiving the debt, of just ignoring it?"

One by one, the group began to weigh in on Jubilee. Robert held his own and continued to ask good questions. His family was very wealthy, so it was hard for him to imagine the struggles that many families faced.

"Let me pose this to you, Robert." Larry looked his friend deep in the eye. "In May of 1931, the KreditAnstalt, Austria's largest bank, collapsed. The U.S. and several European nations had been working on a plan to help the bank. If the plan had been implemented, the bank could have been saved, but the French resisted. They were greedy and wanted to know what was in it for France. The delay caused the window of opportunity to close, and the Austrian bank collapsed, which in turn started a domino effect that led in part to the rise of Hitler and eventually to the Second World War. Tens of millions of soldiers were killed, six million Jews, Europe demolished. How do you even begin to calculate that cost?

"Why did the audience respond to Dr. Hamilton's words last night? Why did we? Because for a moment, he gave us hope. For a moment he made us believe that someone cared, cared enough to take a stand, to think differently, to speak up. How much will it cost when the millions living without hope in the Marshallvilles around the country revolt? Look at L.A. Jubilee may be crazy, but it's not as crazy as doing nothing."

Robert was done fighting. He didn't mean to oppose his friends. He just couldn't see how Jubilee could be the answer.

"Okay, everyone, it's getting late." Shelly looked at the clock on the wall. It was after six. "We all have our assignments. Let's get back together on Wednesday. See you at The Hollow."

Go Find Your Calling

The phone had been ringing nonstop at the Hamilton home all day. Michael was tempted to unplug it. News media, talk shows, newspapers, and magazines all looking for a scoop, a story to sell. *There is no story,* he kept telling himself. *Ignore it and maybe it will go away.*

Ring...Ring...

Ignoring the phone had become as hard as remaining invisible last night.

"It's for you, Dad." Lana brought the phone to Michael.

"Who would have guessed?" His patience was running thin.

"No, it's Mrs. Wallace. I think she's crying."

"Hi, Halley."

"He's gone, Michael."

"I'm so sorry. What can I do?"

Nothing could be done. Jim was gone. He had fought a good fight, but the cancer was too much. Halley gave Michael the arrangement details and asked him to do the eulogy.

"You know I will. How is Ben doing?"

"He's not good. I am really worried about him. He's talking about leaving school."

"I'll talk to him."

"Thank you, Michael."

Sunday morning services were solemn. The excitement of Friday night had grown cold with the passing of Jim. The lights and cameras seemed a distant memory. After church, the Hamilton family turned off the TV and the phones and spent a quiet day at home. Michael toiled most of the day in his study, working on class notes and preparing a few remarks for the funeral service scheduled for ten o'clock the next morning.

At Halley's request, Michael and Allie headed to the funeral home an hour early for the visitation. They spent some time with her, mostly talking about the arrangements for the next morning. After a bit, Michael excused himself and went looking for Ben.

He found him in one of the small chapels the funeral home provided for grieving families. It was a beautiful room: a tiny sanctuary with six pews, stained glass windows, and an altar area in the front. Ben was seated in the second row with his head bowed. Michael went in and sat down behind him. Neither one spoke for a long time.

"I can't do it." Ben looked up at the ceiling but did not turn around. "I can't take his place."

"No one is expecting you to, Ben."

They were silent again for a while.

"I'm just a little lost, Doc. I am going to school to become a pastor, and right now I don't think…I can't take his place."

"I know you and your father were close. He loved you so much. Did he give you any advice?"

"When he coached me in little league, he always told the kids, 'Go as hard as you can for as long as you can. That's all anyone can ask.' We played our hearts out for him. He asked the same things of the workers at church. He believed people should give their all, nothing more, nothing less. It was okay to fail, as long as it was your best. Things always came so easy for me. I didn't always have to give my best. He raised me better than that."

"Ben, what are you expecting of yourself? You are senior class president, carry a 4.0 GPA, volunteer for community service, and you serve in your church. I know your dad was proud of you."

"The Cardinals called again. I don't think I'm ready to pastor. I'm leaving, Doc."

A thousand things went through Michael's mind. *What about your mom, your senior year, graduation that is so close? Why are you running?* But he did not verbalize any of them. Ben was obviously hurting. He didn't need another guilt trip.

"Have you told your mom?"

"We talked for a long time last night. We've been talking a lot, just sitting around with Dad. He hasn't been awake for the past few weeks so…so we've been talking. I just can't take his place, Doc, so I gotta go."

"When do you leave?"

"In a few days."

"I'll take care of school for you."

"Thanks, Doc."

They stood to their feet. Michael couldn't help but respect the strength he saw in the young man's eyes. His heart was broken and his spirit was searching. All Michael could think of was how much he loved Ben.

Michael extended his hand. Ben took it and they pulled each other close. One man cried for his father, the other for his best friend. After a few moments, they stepped back looking each other in the eye, their hands still clasped.

"Let's check on your mom." Michael motioned toward the door. They gathered themselves and walked back to the main chapel.

The receiving line was a mile long. Halley stood for hours talking to one visitor after another. Ben never left her side. Michael and Allie sat in the front row and did all they could, but that was precious little.

Michael cancelled his Monday classes. He and Allie went to the church around eight thirty to prepare for the ten o'clock service. Michael had performed his share of funerals back at Calvary, but this would be very different. At Calvary, he was the pastor. This service would be for his pastor, his close friend. No words seemed adequate. He prayed for God's wisdom and, especially, His grace. "Please reach out your arms and hold Halley and Ben, Father. Please hold them close."

At about nine thirty, a familiar face came through the door, and Michael went to the back of the chapel to meet him. "Henry, I'm so glad you are here."

"Hi, Michael. You've been on quite a rollercoaster ride these past few days."

They talked for a few minutes, but soon it was time for the service to begin. Michael shook Henry's hand and started to walk away, but Henry did not let go of his hand. Michael stopped and looked back at Henry. There were no more words spoken, but Michael recognized the look in Henry's eyes. It was the same look Michael had given Ben the night before in the small chapel.

"Thank you, Henry." Henry let him go to take his place by Allie.

Receiving a nod from Halley and Ben, Michael made his way to the podium and started the service. "Good morning, friends. On behalf of the Wallace family, thank you for coming, especially on such a beautiful day. You may think it strange for me to call this a beautiful day," it had been raining all morning, "but I think our brother, Jim, would have loved this rainy day. How often did he hope for rain to water his precious yard? He was the king of watering. And yes, I, of all people, would be a hypocrite to rib him about watering. His lawn and gardens were his passion. Every blade and petal were carefully manicured, every stone perfectly placed. Jim had an awesome vision for beauty.

"The love of his yard, however, did not hold a candle to the passion he had for you, his congregation, his friends, his family. He always had time to talk, to teach, console…always ready for a round of golf, a hard-fought game of Scrabble…a catch. I don't think I ever heard him say the word 'no.' He challenged us as people to be better friends, better neighbors, better fathers and husbands. It was easy to watch him in the pulpit after watching him in the trenches. No matter the hour…no matter the task…no matter the person…"

Halley caught Michael's eye and his words stuck in his throat. The tears in her eyes did not diminish her strength. In fact, he thought she looked like a pillar of strength. Her tears came from a well of memories, a lifetime of partnership and love. Neither the passing of that partner nor the passing of time would rob her of those memories.

"He loved you, Halley," he finally managed in a whisper that he forced with all his strength. She nodded at him and he gathered himself. A funny thought came to him, and he chuckled as he wiped the tears from his eyes.

"Can you just see him now, standing just outside those huge doors that lead to the throne room? The doors open, and he makes his way in for an audience with the Almighty. Who do you suppose would speak first?" He chuckled again. For the moment Michael was transported to heaven, standing just behind his friend, watching as he made his way up to God.

"I think Jim would speak first, just to put God at ease like he always did for us. 'Hello, Father. Could I tell you about my wife and son?' He's home, friends. He ran the good race. He marked the path well for us to follow. It's someone else's turn to take the baton and carry on. Our friend has passed through the valley of the shadow of death and now stands in the gaze of his God. He is the perfect picture of blessed assurance, perfect submission. All is at rest. Jim, in his Savior, is happy and blessed.

"Father, thank you for this precious life...for this awesome man...We will remember his life until we ourselves have no more life with which to remember. Amen." Michael led them in a song and the service concluded.

The next day, Ben stopped by Michael's office at the college to say thank you.

"Where are you headed?" Michael still had hopes that Ben would change his mind.

"Tucson, Arizona. Fall League. It's been four years since I was drafted. I need to pitch myself into shape. I'm a lefty, so they were willing to give me a shot."

"Do you need anything?"

"Please look after Mom. I told her I would call, and I will, but I'm not very good on the phone."

"We'll take good care of her, Ben. Here is my cell number. Call whenever you can."

"Thank you." They hugged and Ben turned to leave. After a few steps, he turned around. "Do you think I'm wrong?"

Michael sighed. "I wish I could say yes. I wish I could ask you to stay. There seems to be wisdom in finishing school when you are so close. But no, I don't think you're wrong. I think you should know this, though. Each one of us has a calling on our life, a purpose for which we are best suited. You have a strong left arm. You also have a strong faith and a strong voice. This journey will test it all. Go find yourself. Go find your calling."

Days of Rain

It was raining as Michael peered out of his first-floor office window at Ben making his way across campus. There were so many things to do—lectures to organize, e-mails to read, phone calls to return. Michael turned off the lamp in his office, leaving only the dim gray light from the window to fill the room. The weather matched his mood as he sat down in his chair and stared out over the campus for a while. The soft rain on the window was soothing and a little hypnotic. This was a rainy day full of grace. Sunny days demand happy thoughts, but rainy days seem to say, "It's okay to be sad. It's okay to be still." We can get so busy. Sunny days say "work." Rainy days say "rest…think…renew."

As the moments passed, he reflected on many things: the events that had led him to the college, a new life, and new friends, especially the Wallace family. He thought about Henry and about his own family. Silly Mark, of course he would go to college. What lay ahead for Lana, *high school memories, dances, boys*…He smiled to himself, thinking of how she had grown into a very special young lady. She was the image of her mother—smart, creative, and full of life, absolutely beautiful inside and out. Ian, halfway through high school, *driving*! Where does the time go? What would time hold for Ian? Would he be successful? Would he have a family? Would he be a vagabond wandering the earth? Children…*God love them,* he thought, and then echoed that thought in a prayer. He let his mind wander to Allie. Usually, thoughts of her would have been enough to bring him out of his melancholy, but sometimes it's good to feel…rainy. Sometimes the "rain" slows us down and we take time to look at life a little deeper, a little longer, with a spirit that is quiet and still.

A clap of thunder stirred Michael from his thoughts. His mind's eye looked out instead of in, and he watched the rain for a few moments. *It's raining on the homeless,* he thought, *and not just drops of water, but drops of life.* How many millions had lost everything? How many "Marks" would not be going to college? How many "Lanas" were on the street instead of in the classroom? How many "Ians" truly were vagabonds wandering through camps of broken families? How many husbands and wives had split as they watched their lives fall apart? So much pain…his heart broke…so much rain.

More thunder rolled, snapping him back to his gaze out over the campus. For a minute, he felt stupid. *Who are you to let your heart break for a nation? You are a failed pastor, a marginal professor, an idiot who can't keep his mouth shut on national television. Who do you think you are? Some grand crusader from the past, Mr. Fancy History Teacher? Face it, you are nobody. Cry your tears for a world gone mad. Let them fall like rain, and then get on your knees and be thankful for what you have. Who are you to see metaphors in the rain? What are you going to do about it? You had your fifteen seconds of fame, but you are no senator. Downs eats people like you for a snack.*

Lightning flashed and thunder shook his office. Rain was falling in sheets.

"What?" he screamed at the sky. "What am I supposed to think? Understand? Do?" He slammed his fist on the desk. "I am nobody!"

Lightning! Thunder! Rain! He sat with his back to the window looking into a dark room. The light from the window was almost gone, as the clouds were thick and the storm in full fury. He sat in the darkness, letting his mind wander to the place he had always gone for answers.

Be still. Know, don't just think, know that I am God. Noah was six hundred years old when he started the ark. He worked on it for one hundred and twenty years. He was a nobody.

The rain slowed a bit.

Moses had his forty years of fame as an Egyptian prince. He failed. He killed an Egyptian and fled for his life into the desert. Forty years later he stood in front of a burning bush—a nobody who did not speak so well. I don't need great men or women. I only want obedience. Be still...Know that I Am God...

Soft rain...Distant thunder...He had come and gone, yet His presence remained. God is not bound by time. The words Michael heard in his spirit that rainy day he had read in Scripture as a child. There was no mysticism in the storm. He conversed with God daily as he prayed and read from the Bible. Michael was a nobody by himself, but he was in the hands of God. He pulled a sheet of paper out of his desk and began to write:

Days of thunder, days of rain
A time of wandering through days of pain
Childish dreams, reality stains
You planned to prosper till the thunder came
Days of thunder, days of rain
A time of wandering through days of pain
Questions asked again and again

Days of thunder, days of rain
Into the busy, you plunge from the still

Darkness from daylight, morning from night
Day after day changes ever so small
Give up your soul for the good of it all
Memories of memories, returning to mind
It's hard to answer when you don't know your lines
For all of your efforts, successes, and gains
Your present's oppressive and your future's in chains
Days of thunder, days of rain…

Pathways are crossing, the answers are strange
Wisdom is wasted and the trusted have changed
For the child in your soul that is dying to see
Cover his eyes from the reality

Is there an answer to the questions at hand
Is there a shelter—does the rain ever end
Is there a Savior—please cover my shame
'Cause I am deafened by thunder…
And drowning in rain

Sign of the times, shine in our eyes
The market is calling, but it's so full of lies
Light of this world, won't You shine for us now
We have fallen so far, but You still know who we are

Days of thunder, days of rain…

Out of Sodom and into Tomorrow

The seasons were changing—not just from summer to fall, and now late fall, but the seasons of life. Seasons are more than just the changing of the sun's angle, or the temperature, or even of nature around us. People have seasons. There are seasons when we grow and seasons when we die; seasons when we follow and seasons when we lead. Institutions, like Roe College, also have seasons. It is inevitable, because they are more than brick and mortar, landscape and location. They are blood and bone, people who live and move and breathe within their structures and designs. Like their people, they grow, they follow, and in the right season, they lead.

The Hollow was in peak season as the poli-sci class descended on her. Surrounded by fall color, her massive doors welcomed the wide-eyed group of dreamers. They had been through seasons of following, of learning, and growing, and now, they, in their pure, if not naïve hearts, were ready to lead the charge for the humble professor. They gathered as planned, each sharing the results of their labors. The table in front of them was covered with all the necessary items to successfully launch any campaign: paper, pencils, laptops, cell phones, caffeine, and pizza. They wrote and typed and talked, all with greasy fingers and full mouths. They were excited and loud. Several other students hanging out at The Hollow came over to see what was going on but, upon learning it was school-related, quickly fled, leaving the class to their scheming.

Amidst their jubilation, Shelly took over and asked for reports from those who had been given assignments at the library. "Larry, talk to us about the Web site."

"The site is up. It's pretty crude right now, but I'm working on it. The site is www.theyearofjubilee.com. I got it up and running last night, and there were already a few hits by this morning. I think people are looking for information on Doc."

"That's good." Robert put his laptop down. "We're going to need a boatload of cash. Serious candidates raise millions. I think this whole thing is crazy. At this point, we can't even afford an ad in the school newspaper."

"Good job, Robert. We'll get back to you." Shelly chose to ignore the obvious hurdles and concentrate on the possibilities.

"I think Super Tuesday is going to be tough as well," Sarah added as she flipped a few pages onto the table. "I'm still working on it, but we are going to need money for ads to get our name in front of the public."

"This is the Presidency, gang," Shelly bellowed. "Let's talk about what we *can* do, shall we?"

"I think we should talk to Dr. Hamilton," Danielle mumbled through a mouthful of pizza. "What if he says no?"

That brought Lenny to life. "Say *no?* Oh, what are the odds? Let's see. Give up his nice, cushy teaching job to have his personal life torn apart under a microscope by politicians and reporters who only care about winning and getting a story, to run all over giving speeches, shaking hands, hugging strangers and kissing butts, to share some crazy idea about forgiving all the debt in the world that will destroy any credibility he's ever had and make him the laughingstock of the political world? Oh, how could he say *no?*"

Everyone pounced on Lenny at once. After a few minutes of bedlam, Ginny got everyone's attention. "Shhh! Look at the news."

"The police have restored order, but tensions are escalating out of control." The reporter stood in front of a scene of burning buildings and total chaos.

"Where are they?" Larry grabbed a notepad.

"Kansas City," Ginny said as she tossed him a pen.

"Four people were killed in the riots that we know of, and several others are missing. This is Robert Benton reporting for WNN."

"He can't say no because someone has to say *yes.*" Sarah tore her pages in half.

They untangled themselves from Lenny and decided to pay a visit to their teacher. Making their way across campus, their optimism was renewed by Larry, who told them about the possibilities the Web site could bring. It would be a way to get their message out to people all over the nation. There were issues to be sure. How would the homeless hear their message? But at least the discussion put them in a positive frame of mind as they stepped onto the Hamiltons' front porch.

"What time is it?"

"Ten o'clock." As discussion broke out about it being too late, the porch light came on and Ian opened the door.

"Hey, man, is your dad home?" Lenny stepped to the front.

Ian showed them into the family room where his dad was watching the news. For a few minutes, they all just watched as the reporters covered the Kansas City riots. Unfortunately, KC was not the only city having riots tonight. They were becoming more widespread and frequent.

"What do you make of this mess?" Michael surveyed the group and invited them to find a seat.

One by one they shared their thoughts. They talked about the news and the events of the town hall meeting. By now the students were seated all over the family room, and even though they had descended on the Hamilton household after ten o'clock, there was no chastisement from their professor. In fact, he made them feel so welcome that they forgot the time. Allie had made some hot apple cider earlier in the evening and served it to the group as they talked. Ian and Lana sat on the steps leading up to the second floor, and Allie sat on the arm of Michael's chair. The students sipped their drinks and wondered how to deliver their message.

Michael finally asked the obvious, "So, you heard we were serving apple cider tonight?"

"Yes, sir," Lenny cracked. "The news is all over campus. Have you been busy tonight?"

After everyone murdered Lenny with their eyes, Sarah took the floor. "Dr. Hamilton, we've been working on our assignment... well, poli-sci." She fumbled for a moment, which was unlike her. She was always very confident, but this had become a matter of the heart—a matter with which Sarah had less experience. "It's you, sir. We want it to be you."

In their usual all-talk-at-once style, they bombarded Michael with requests to say yes. "We have it all planned...They need you...Please?"

Michael looked at Allie. "I think you lost me. Say yes to what?"

Larry took over and became the voice of sanity, even if the request *was* insane. "Dr. Hamilton, most of us have been with you for four years. I know you're just our teacher, but we heard your words last Friday at the town hall meeting. The whole world heard your words. They don't know you like we do, sir, but we want them to. We want you to be our candidate."

"Well sure, Larry, you can make me your candidate. It's just a class project."

"No, sir. We want you to be a candidate, to really run."

Michael looked at Allie. "Oh, guys, I—"

"Please don't say no, sir. Please," Shelly begged her professor. "You're different. You had something to say last Friday. People believed."

How does one respond to young minds and hearts who, though naïve, truly believe that all things are possible? That "Mr. Smith" really can go to Washington? That a broken nation can be healed? That a man—a simple man whom they have listened to and learned from—can make a difference? Michael had no delusions about becoming President of the United States. He did not, however, know how to answer his students.

"Let me talk to my family. We'll talk about it in class on Friday."

There was a hushed excitement around the room. "He didn't say no," was the prevailing whisper. One by one they thanked Allie for the cider and headed for the door.

Sarah was the last to leave. She lingered at the door until everyone was gone. "Dr. Hamilton, is Ben okay?"

"He's searching, Sarah. He left yesterday morning for Tucson. I asked him to stay in touch."

"Will you let me know when you hear from him?"

"I sure will."

Sarah left to join her friends as they scampered back across campus, celebrating their victory. The absence of a "no" was as good as "yes" to them. The rain had stopped. Seasons were changing.

The next morning, Michael stopped by the chapel on his way

to the office. It had been a few weeks since his last visit, and although he wanted to stop, he always seemed to be in a hurry. He also missed Henry. The chapel seemed empty without him. This morning, however, the chapel was not so empty.

"Good morning, Michael." Henry looked up from his Bible as Michael sat down beside him in the pew.

"Good morning."

They sat without speaking for a few minutes. It was nice just taking in the atmosphere of the chapel, the peace and quiet, the familiar sights and smells. *"Be still and know that I am God,"* Michael thought.

"I hear you have a decision to make." Henry nudged Michael.

"How did you know?"

"Sarah called me last night."

"It must have been pretty late."

"Yes." Henry chuckled. "Yes, it was, but my phone does not ring very often." He shifted his glasses down his nose and looked at Michael. "It was good to hear her voice. She believes in you, Michael, as do I."

"Thank you, Henry. You know how much those words mean to me, but run for office?"

"Do you have time for a walk this morning, Michael?"

"I need to get to the office, but I could walk for a bit."

Henry led Michael out of the chapel and up Fairmont Street to Elm. They turned left and followed Elm for a couple blocks until they came to Valhalla.

"Valhalla, land of the dead. Some would say it is a morbid place. Unfortunately, when you reach my age, you have more friends here than any other place. I come here to visit once in a while. I visit Joe Stanton over there on the ridge and Martha McKinney down by the concrete bench. Once a month I bring flowers for Grace. It will be twelve years next March since she passed. We had a great life. I still miss her."

"Henry, I—"

"Be quiet, son. Let an old man talk. I'm not used to anyone talking back when I'm here. Some would say I'm crazy for coming here and talking to my friends, to my wife, but people have thought worse things about me. I like to read the headstones. I like to imagine what the lives of those who reside here must have been like. Some of the stones predate the college itself. Some who lie here were pioneers crossing the wilderness for free land. They opened up this territory. They were brave souls. I wonder where we would be if they had not come. I wonder what drove them to climb in a wagon with all of their belongings and travel west into a vast unknown.

"Can you imagine all of the firsts? The first night out on the trail, the first camp, first river crossing, the first broken wheel or illness or…loss of life. I bet there were times they thought about going back. What do you suppose drove them on? How about seeing a brand new nation spreading out before them with limitless possibilities? For some, the trail ended right here in Valhalla. Others went on to cross more rivers and mountains." Henry began to laugh at himself. "Sorry, it doesn't sound so corny when you're talking to yourself or these other stiffs around here. They don't seem to mind." He drifted back into his thoughts.

"Michael, things are tough for our nation…for people right now. They face new 'rivers' and 'mountains,' and they don't know how to cross. They are crying out for leadership. They are rioting for it, and soon they may do worse. How many of our government buildings bear the words 'Where there is no vision, the people parish,' yet how many of our leaders understand that phrase? Their vision has become nearsighted at best, if not blind. They listen without hearing and speak without caring. Some start out with good intentions, only to be swallowed up in a sea of me, myself, and I. We have worshiped the almighty dollar, forsaking the laws of nature and God. We have chosen gold over good, profit over people, and passion over compassion. There is not, nor will there ever be, enough. We have gorged ourselves, yet we starve. We drink until drunk, yet we thirst. We fill our banks and our storehouses, yet we are empty. Our population explodes, yet we are utterly alone. Who will fix the wheels of our wagon? Who will look out into the next great unknown and guide an unwilling, unappreciating, unknowing people out of Sodom and into tomorrow? Will our next president lead us there, the next governor, senator? Don't run for president, Michael, but don't run from it."

Sarah's Words

By Thursday evening, Larry Finner had his hands full. The Web site was going crazy with e-mails. People wanted to know how to support Michael Hamilton.

"Where is he speaking?"

"How do we get involved?"

"Where do we send money?"

Somehow the news of Dr. Hamilton had made it to the communities of homeless who were spread all over the nation. So many of these people had lost their homes, but they still had their jobs. They still had access to the Internet.

Larry began to search other sites on the net. Hamilton sites were popping up all over. There were chat groups and blogs talking about Hamilton. The press had put out so much information about him that his life was an open book and people could not get enough.

On Friday, the class passed their information on to their professor. Everything was happening so fast. He asked them for a few more days and promised an answer on Monday.

The class needed some capital to make things happen, and Robert had access to some funds. It wasn't much in political terms, but it was enough to get a bank account established, along with all the necessary functions to receive and process campaign funds. They all spent Saturday replying to e-mails and getting their message to the masses. It may have been premature, but "Hamilton for President" was taking shape—even without a confirmed candidate.

By Saturday, Michael had all but made up his mind to take Henry's advice and throw his name into the hat. He would take the opportunity to spread a message of hope, and he would challenge the other candidates to change the nation's course. He had no delusions of grandeur. Odds were that he would make very little difference, but he decided that saying yes to his students was important. He was mowing the yard when Allie brought the phone to him.

"Hello."

"Michael Hamilton, this is Sydney Porter. You are one big newsmaker."

"I'm sorry, Sydney, do I know you?"

"No, I am the campaign manager for Senator Downs. We would like to invite you to the town hall meeting scheduled for two weeks from yesterday in Des Moines."

"Oh. No more moderating for me, Mr. Porter. No, thank you."

"No, Michael. We would like you to be part of the debate. What do you say?"

It's hard to see yourself as presidential when you are standing in the middle of your yard, wearing your mowing clothes, and dripping with sweat. It also made Michael think really hard about his commitment to the students, which, until now, had been somewhat abstract. This made it crystal.

"Come on, Michael, what do you say? Are you in?"

"Yes…Yes, I am."

"Great! We will see you at six o'clock for preparations a week from next Friday evening at the Hotel Fort Des Moines on Grand

Avenue. Wear a suit this time. You're playing with the big boys now."

"I'll be there."

Sydney Porter's tone had changed after Michael agreed to participate. The last words seemed to be more insult than invitation. Whichever, Michael was committed.

Michael's instinct had been good. The last words were more setup than welcome.

"He's in, sir."

"Well, how nice." The senator spun his chair around and gazed out over the D.C. skyline. "Let's see how the reverend preaches from *this* pulpit."

As the weekend passed, Michael began to feel good about his decision. In fact, he was a little excited about the news he had to share with his class as Monday arrived. He listened to their whispers through religion class. He smiled at them squirming through history, but he knew they would be waiting for him in poli-sci.

He walked into class, took his usual spot on the edge of his desk, and looked around the class. Twenty-two students were on the roll for the class; only one was absent. He stood up, walked over to the window, and without looking back at the class, he simply said, "Yes."

Chaos erupted—books, paper, desks all in motion, cheers, hugs, and tears in some cases. Even too-cool-for-life Lenny was excited.

"There's more," Michael brought them back to earth. "We're going to Des Moines a week from Friday. We're in the debate."

Again, chaos reigned supreme.

"Okay, tell me what you have so far." Michael made his way back to his desk.

Larry did most of the talking. "We've been responding to e-mails and letters since last Friday. So far, we have received $3,432.00. There are 'Hamilton for President' groups popping up all over the country." Larry went on to bring everyone up to speed on the evolution of the Web site. Several of the computer geeks had helped him improve the function and look; the graphics were hot, according to Larry.

Each student reported on his or her area of responsibility. They were becoming a pretty formidable team.

"Sir," Shelly grabbed the floor, "we need to talk about our message."

"That would be good," Michael mused at the thought. "What is our message?"

"Jubilee, sir."

"Jubilee?" Michael replied with one eyebrow cocked. He stood up from the edge of his desk and walked for a moment as he pondered their response. "Forgive the debt?" He looked up at them with his arms folded.

"Yes, sir," Ginny responded.

"Sabbath economics," Sarah followed.

"It's all broken anyway, sir," Lenny added.

"Was that Lenny?" Michael scanned the room, surprised. "Even Lenny's in on this?"

"Everyone is in, sir," Shelly replied as the leader.

Michael felt like he should salute, but he just smiled. They had been listening this semester.

They talked for a while longer, and then Michael started to give them some assignments. He stopped short just as the words were about to leave his mouth. They were no longer his class. They had become a campaign staff, and he decided to treat them as such. "Okay, what's the next move?"

"We have a speech to write for the debate, and we have research to do on the other candidates." Robert confidently joined the conversation.

"Do we have any writers?" Michael again looked over the class to see what hidden talents would surface from unexpected sources.

"I'll write with you, Dr. Hamilton." Sarah warmed his heart.

"Sounds good, Sarah." Michael smiled.

Everyone else volunteered for assignments. Class was over. The campaign was on.

They spent the week working in teams. Some worked with Larry responding to all of the contacts from the Web site. Sarah and Danielle led another team researching information for the debate. Others were busy making contacts for campaign visits and speeches.

"Okay, we need to get organized, people!" Shelly yelled above the commotion around the Hamilton living room. It was Monday evening, and they had four days to prepare for the debate in Des Moines.

Larry's team gave their report first. Along with countless contacts and requests for information, money continued to arrive—over twenty thousand dollars at last count. They had reimbursed Robert for his contributions and were beginning to make some funding headway. In truth, other candidates were raising millions, but the students were still excited.

Sarah went next with her information. "Debt has been a serious issue in our nation for a long time. We saw its effects during the Great Depression. During the first decade of this, the twenty-first century, credit card debt alone climbed to over eight hundred billion dollars, with an average household debt of more than eight thousand dollars. Over a quarter of the population reported problems paying their monthly bills, with only about half being able to pay off their credit card balance at the end of each month. A problem that has long been considered an issue for the poor began to drastically affect the middle class.

"Even with record profits, banks laid off thousands of workers to cut costs. At the same time, credit card companies were sending applications by the billions to the American public, sometimes in excess of five billion applications per year. Even children were solicited. The marketing efforts were phenomenal. Cards were marketed based on sports teams or special interests. 'Have a favorite color? Hey, our card can be that color.'

"New practices known as 'universal default' came into vogue. Credit card companies would raise the interest rates on all cards if a customer was late on payment for one. Rates reached into the thirty percent range. Bankruptcies soared, increasing over eighty percent from one decade to the next. While debt was increasing, average median income was actually decreasing.

"Many people turned to home-equity loans to stave off the looming doom of their unsecured debt. New mortgage products were created: interest only and negative-equity loans. Adjustable-rate loans became very popular during a stretch of time when interest rates dipped for a while. The adjustable rates, along with the other new mortgage products, also spelled doom when rates began to rise and the housing market, fat with over-priced houses that had seemed affordable because of the low rates, began to collapse. Increases in interest rates from one percent to six percent raised monthly payments between nine hundred dollars and eighteen hundred dollars. Over five million households were affected nationwide and that was just the beginning. Where did the Marshallvilles come from, you ask?

"Politicians, hopelessly lost in a cycle of gridlock, continued to see life through rose-colored glasses. Along with the economists, they postured that while individuals and families would suffer, the debt levels would not hurt the ten trillion dollar-a-year U.S. economy. After countless studies of the worldwide housing market over several decades, they concluded that it would take at least a twenty percent drop in housing values to create a serious problem. Well, housing values have fallen more than twenty-*five* percent. Multitudes of people are now homeless. Maybe now it will matter that individuals and families are hurting, now that they number in the millions."

Silence filled the room. There were few dry eyes. The television, which had been on with the sound turned down, was showing pictures of a Marshallville outside Birmingham, Alabama. The pictures made Sarah's words all the more real.

Grace Where We Fail, Hope for Tomorrow

After a short week of preparation, Michael, Allie, Sarah, Larry, and Shelly loaded into the Hamiltons' van and headed for Des Moines. For a while they all quizzed Michael on his points, but for the last twenty minutes of the trip he asked them to let him think.

There were so many thoughts whirling in his brain—why did he ever say yes, for one. *Oh sure, I'll just run for president. What was I thinking? I am going to make an utter and complete fool of myself tonight!* That line of thinking began to fade as he thought about Sarah's words and the millions of people who would be sleeping in their cars—or worse. He began to think about Christine and wondered if she would be there tonight. *She'd better be,* he thought. This whole thing was her fault. None of this would be happening if she had not been standing just offstage at the town hall meeting. The thought of her made him want to smile and cry at the same time. She was a good reminder that none of this was about him. It was much bigger. Finally, he thought about Henry's words. He was not running for president. He was just taking the opportunity to speak for millions of people who had lost their voice, their presence in the system, their hope. *Who cares if you make a fool of yourself tonight? Speak from your heart and care about people.*

As he turned on Grand Avenue, they were getting close.

"Are you ready?" Shelly leaned forward from the backseat.

"You've all done a great job getting me ready, Shelly, so…yes. I'm ready to speak for those who will not get the chance to speak for themselves."

As he spoke those words, they pulled up in front of the Hotel Fort Des Moines. There were fancier hotels, but this hotel had charisma—and history. She had seen her share of the who's who from days gone by: Mae West, Charles Lindbergh, Jack Kennedy, and Richard Nixon had all passed through her hallways. The hotel's motto, "We treat you famously." Michael was not seeking fame, but he truly hoped he would not achieve infamy.

The bellman welcomed them and took their bags inside while the valet parked the car. There were members of the media looming, but Michael was pleasantly surprised at their ability to make it through the lobby and check in without being noticed. With the assistance of Sydney Porter, they had reserved three rooms and everything seemed to be in order. It was four o'clock in the afternoon when they reached their rooms. That gave Michael a couple hours to relax before he had to be downstairs for preparations.

The Hamiltons' room, or rather *rooms,* were amazing. Sydney Porter had made the arrangements and spared no expense. There was a large room complete with a big-screen and three overstuffed couches, a bar area, and a formal dining area. The bedroom was huge with a California king and lavish furniture. The bathroom was a marble masterpiece, and there was fancy artwork everywhere.

"We're not in Kansas anymore, Toto." Allie took in the details of the rooms.

"Don't be callin' me no dog now, woman," he teased with her.

"Do you think the closet will hold all of our clothes?" She smiled as she gestured toward their only bag.

Michael didn't hear her because he was busy exploring in the bedroom. When he emerged back into the living room, he had his cell phone in hand and was talking to Lana.

"That's right, marble." He laughed. "Yeah, we'll try to look important." He handed the phone to Allie, and she talked to all of the kids in turn. It was all pretty exciting.

Allie said good-bye and walked the phone over to Michael. As she handed it to him, she took him by the hands and looked into his eyes. She held his eyes until he finally asked, "What?"

"Mr. President, I do believe the distinguished senator from Texas would like you to be distracted. It's going to be hard to identify with the homeless while your standing in the penthouse, don't you think?"

Michael took inventory of the room and all its amenities and then returned his gaze to Allie. "I have an idea." He dropped her hands and went into the bedroom.

"I don't think that's a good idea," she called after him.

He came out of the bedroom carrying their suitcase, a big smile on his face. "Come with me." He took her by the hand. They went down the hall to the girls' room and knocked on the door. "Hey, Shelly." He grinned when she answered the door. "Would you trade rooms with us?"

She gave them a funny look. "Sure."

They waited as the girls gathered their things, and then they walked them back to the fancy room. Needless to say, the girls were a little surprised. "Are you *sure?*"

"Have fun, kids." They left them to explore. The regular room was still nice, but it provided a better reality check for Michael. He and Allie ordered sandwiches from room service and ate an early dinner. At five o'clock Michael hopped into the shower to begin his preparations for the evening. Allie flipped on the television to see the news. It turned out to be a wise move.

"John, I'm not sure this news was totally unexpected. The bank had been seeking federal assistance for several months." The newsman in the studio addressed the reporter on the scene.

"What bank?" Allie asked the empty room. "What's going on?"

"Steve, what brought them down?"

"Well, John, we've seen over five million families lose their homes, one trillion dollars in loan defaults. Not all of that with First National, but they had a large share of the bad loans. Their growth over the last couple of decades had been in alternative financing, interest-only loans especially, and the downturn of the housing market really caught up with them."

"What is the impact on the economy, Steve?"

"For a long time, the economists and politicians have been saying that these types of numbers would not hurt the economy, that individual families may suffer, but the overall economy would be fine. Well, things seem to be getting a little farther out of hand than they anticipated. Mortgages and falling housing prices are only part of this picture. Credit card debt is reaching record highs, over eight thousand dollars per household. People who once used the equity in their house to refinance their credit card debts have been faced with two issues: where their equity used to be growing with a healthy housing market and a conventionally amortizing loan, equity has now been shrinking with the falling housing market, and many have already refinanced away all of their equity. The old ads said, 'Save hundreds, even thousands a month on your bills,' but they failed to mention the term of the loan. People did see their monthly payments go down, but that smaller payment extended out over twenty or thirty years and cost them thousands upon thousands in extra interest. They may have paid less per month, but they have and will pay a great deal more over time. Now most people are out of options. The credit industry that has profited from naïve and/or desperate consumers is now reaping the crop from those deceptive seeds."

Allie lost track of time. She suddenly realized Michael was standing right behind her. "Have you heard any of this?"

"A little." He continued drying his hair with the towel. "Are you surprised? I thought the kids sounded a little crazy with their talk about Jubilee, but it may actually be the only way out of this mess." He laughed a little to himself. "Imagine that, God actually having a good plan. At least it'd better be a good plan. I'm getting ready to sell my soul for it."

Allie laughed. "At least you'll be selling it to the right side. Oh man, what time is it? I still have to get ready."

It was almost six o'clock, time for Michael to be downstairs for preparations. They agreed that he should go on down and she would follow as soon as she could get ready.

"Check on the kids when you get a chance," Michael called to her as he headed out the door.

"Which ones?"

"All of them." The door closed as he rushed down the hall.

A reporter was lingering in the lobby as Michael exited the elevator. "Dr. Hamilton, could I have a word with you?"

"It'll have to be quick."

"What do you think of the bank collapse?"

"I think it is very sad, and—"

"Will this affect the economy?" the reporter interrupted him in mid-sentence.

"Yes, I think it will, but—"

"Thanks." With that, the reporter was off to get his next sound bite.

Michael made his way to the prepping room as he had been instructed. He was pleased to see Christine motioning him over.

"I know, I know, be kind." She grabbed her comb as he walked over.

"How is your family? I heard about the riots in Kansas City, and I wondered if they had affected you." He sat down and she began to work her magic.

"We were never in real danger, but we could hear the shooting. It was very surreal. I thought things were bad when we lost our house, and I couldn't imagine them getting worse, but each day seems to bring a new low. Sorry, you have bigger things to think about right now."

"Nothing is bigger than real people who are suffering through these days of chaos."

"You're a kind man."

Michael was not comfortable with the makeup, but he was glad for the chance to spend time with Christine. "Is Dane here?"

"Oh yeah. The whole crew is here."

"If I could have your attention, everyone…" It was Sydney Porter. He spoke for a few minutes, giving instructions for the evening. The rules would be the same as they had been in Hill City. There were three candidates : Senator Downs, Senator Lawrence, and Michael. Representatives Delaney and Smithson had been called back to Washington. *Must be something big for them to miss this opportunity,* Michael thought. He was incredibly naïve about the political process. The two congressmen had been called back to Washington, but for reasons designed more by Senator Downs than actual necessity. This race would be dirty, and Michael had no idea what lay ahead for him.

Allie and the students finally made their way in to see Michael.

"Nice blush," Allie teased. He introduced them all to Christine. Dane made his way over to them and they chatted for a brief moment.

"Good luck, mate. Watch your back. These guys are playing hardball. You threw them a curve last time, but they're ready for you tonight. Any surprises up your sleeve?"

"Oh, let's just say it should be a jubilant night."

"Five minutes!" came the call. "Places, everyone!"

Allie kissed Michael and wished him luck. Then she and the students took their place in the audience. Christine stayed at her post backstage to assist with any makeup issues that might arise.

Michael followed the other candidates to the stage. To this point, the other senators had ignored him, but they had him in their sites as they stepped up to their podiums. Downs was in the center, with Lawrence stage right and Michael stage left.

Downs looked at Lawrence and then back at Michael. "What say you, Harold? Do you think the professor is ready for a lesson tonight?" Senator Lawrence did not respond. He just looked down at his podium.

"Three, two, one..."

"Good evening and welcome..." The moderator kicked the evening into gear. *The game is afoot,* Michael thought. The rules were given just as they had been in Hill City. The pre-selected questions had been changed because of the bank failure earlier in the day. Topics for the three questions would cover health care, debt, and the economy. Each candidate would be given a different question on each topic.

No being invisible tonight, Michael said to himself. *Best come straight at it.*

"All right, gentlemen, are you ready?" The moderator for the evening was Derrick Jet, a young African American flying through the ranks of the cable news arena. Receiving a nod from each candidate, he proceeded. "Each candidate will make a brief statement lasting no more than five minutes. By random selection, Senator Lawrence will go first, followed by Senator Downs, and then Dr. Hamilton. The floor is yours, Senator Lawrence."

Michael was thankful to be last in the first round. Actually, he would have preferred to be last in each round, but the order would vary. The senators each stayed with the tried-and-true statements they had used at the first town hall meeting. Michael thought they were uninspiring, but as seasoned debaters, neither gave anything away. Finally, it was Michael's turn.

"Thank you, Mr. Jett. Good evening, America. It is my honor to share the stage with these two distinguished senators. They have each served our nation for many years, and they should be praised for their efforts. I am but a simple college professor whose résumé does not include United States Senator, Fortune-500 CEO, oil baron, or governor, as do my auspicious colleagues here tonight. My résumé reads scholar, pastor, professor. I am a student of history and of my faith. I am a professor of hundreds over the years, a father of three, and a husband of one. I am a simple man. I have not held one of the hallowed seats in Congress representing thousands of my fellow citizens. I have not listened to their many needs or pled their cases on the sacred senate floor. With all due respect, however, I ask you this evening to take inventory of your life. How are you doing? Is there bread on your plate? Is there a roof over your head? Do you have a job, benefits, retirement? How does your future look? If your answers to these questions are exceedingly positive, and you look at your neighbors and see the same for them, then I suggest you follow and support the leaders who have led you to this point, for they have served you well. If, however, you face a daunting present with a clouded future, and you see no help or hope coming from your leaders, I suggest you look for new ideas and new faces to lead in a new direction. I am just a common man, like most of you. I think it is time for us to stand together. Thank you."

"Thank you, gentlemen. When we come back, we will move into our first topic, health care."

"Pretty big talk for a 'common' man." Senator Downs smirked at Michael as soon as the camera was off. "I hope you have some magic up your sleeve tonight because you're going to need it." He turned to speak to Senator Lawrence before Michael could respond.

Michael was thankful. He preferred to use his time thinking about his responses to the upcoming questions rather than bantering back and forth with the stuffed-shirt senator from Texas. He looked out into the audience, but he could not locate Allie and the students. He admitted to himself that the whole scene was pretty intimidating, but he thought about Henry and his wise counsel. He was just a common man, but that was okay. How could these billionaires understand the plight of the homeless, the struggling, and the hopeless? The rising tide of despair would have to reach pretty high before it touched their ivory towers.

"Three, two, one..."

The first question on health care was given to Senator Downs. He expounded on the great advances in medicine and the miracles that were taking place.

"We continue to find cures for many of the deadliest diseases that have plagued our world. Advancements in medical technology leading to new surgical procedures mean surgeries that once kept patients in the hospital for days or weeks are now performed as outpatient procedures. I have a long-standing record on the side of health professionals, something I cannot say for my colleague from California, and, oh yes, our dear professor has no record or experience at all with these matters."

He took his full two minutes making some impressive boasts about his personal contributions to the field of medicine, including funding for a heart clinic bearing his name in southern Texas.

The moderator turned his attention to Michael. "Dr. Hamilton, you have been outspoken about the lack of concern the leaders of this nation have shown for its citizens. Please share your thoughts on possible solutions to the problem of shrinking benefit programs and health care plans in the United States. You have two minutes, sir."

"Derrick, shrinking benefit programs and health care plans are a serious issue in our nation. Most entry-level jobs offer no benefits, so while our graduating students face a new phase in their lives, filled with student loan payments and the many expenses of getting their private lives started, they also face high health care costs or high risk with no insurance. A medical bump in the road can spell financial doom. While we continue to see miraculous advances in medical science, just as Senator Downs has described, those advances serve a diminishing portion of our population. Health care costs continue to outpace average hourly earnings three to one. And yes, new technologies and procedures do provide a higher quality of care, but they come with a higher price tag. The issues seem to be twofold, runaway cost and disappearing coverage. Some of the cost increases could be slowed by bringing medical malpractice suits under control. To be sure, doctors and health professionals should be held accountable for their work, but some amount of sanity should be brought to bear on the courts. Disappearing coverage, especially for new entrants into the workforce, should be reversed by making sure that all sectors of workers receive a fair share of company profits and benefits. Average CEO pay exceeds average employee pay by over two hundred percent and should be reviewed. Practices that allow huge bonuses to some while costing others their benefits are simply wrong in a civilized nation. We—"

"Thank you, Dr. Hamilton. Your time is up. Senator Lawrence, your state has seen the closing of several of its largest medical facilities in the last few years. Please give us your thoughts on the causes, effects, and solutions."

"I would be happy to, Derrick. First, let me say that I have opposed Senator Downs on several health issues because I felt like the legislation he supported did not fully address the issues we are facing. It probably did not further my political career to oppose him, but we need solutions for all of our citizens, not just the wealthy.

"Several of our medical facilities in California closed because of rising costs and a health insurance program that has been decimated. We serve so many who cannot afford insurance. The facilities that closed were trying to serve the underrepresented and the poor, even the middle class without insurance. They failed." He looked at Michael and started to say something to him, but he stopped short. This was, after all, a debate, and the stakes were too high to show any solidarity with another candidate.

During the commercial break, both senators visited with their campaign managers. Michael looked out at Dane, who gave him a "thumbs-up" sign of encouragement. He also found Allie and the students in the audience. They were just out to his right, but the stage lights made it difficult to see them. They all cheered him on.

The next round of questions focused on debt, and Michael would be first to answer. This was his question, the reason he was part of this event. *Don't swing and miss,* he thought.

They came out of break, and immediately Derrick threw the

first question to Michael. "What does the collapse of First National Bank mean for this nation?"

"Hopefully, it means that our nation, especially our leaders, will take this issue seriously." Michael shared the statistics Sarah had provided. "For too long we have swept this issue under the rug. One hundred years ago, President Hoover presumed the recession of the late 1920s would last less than sixty days. Looking at the historical trends and listening to his advisors, he plodded along, doing nothing. That proved to be his greatest mistake, and we slipped into what would become the Great Depression. Maybe First National will be the wakeup call we need. Maybe as a professor I am more comfortable with this phrase than our statesmen will be, but if we do not learn from history, from the mistakes of the past, then we are doomed to repeat them."

"Thank you, Dr. Hamilton." Derrick then turned his attention to Senator Downs. "Senator, it is customary to give each candidate a different question on each topic, but obviously this is the topic and question of the day, so I will ask you the same question. What does the collapse of First National Bank mean for this nation?"

"Well," the senator started with a mocking smirk as he looked at Michael, "I certainly do not share Mr. Hamilton's view. No, sir, *not at all!* I do not find any positives in the collapse of one of the nation's largest financial institutions, not to mention the jobs that may be lost. The professor seems to think we are pretty dumb in Washington, that only he has his finger on the pulse of this nation. How presumptuous. It is a long way from Iowa to D.C., and the professor has no idea how complex the issues are that face this nation. He would have us believe that debt is the only issue, and, by the way, have we heard any real solutions from him yet? I think not! I will offer you all a solution. Leave the teachers in the classroom to pontificate and postulate all they want, but let the true leaders of this nation do what they do best...lead."

The crowd was beginning to grow restless. Michael had not necessarily stirred the hearts of the crowd on the positive side, but Senator Downs, with his condescending attitude, was beginning to stir their angst. A few boos began to float up to the stage as the audience shifted in their seats. Feeling like he was the only thoroughbred in this race, Downs scoffed at the audience, but that seemed to only incite more anger from the crowd.

"Obviously, this is a topic with a touchy nerve," Derrick interjected as he tried to maintain control. He pitched the same question about First National to Senator Lawrence.

"First, let me speak to the families who are directly affected by the action taken by First National today. Please know that your government has taken notice, and we will do all we can to find solutions to the issue of debt in this nation. The figures are staggering. Over 2 trillion dollars in consumer debt, mortgages in chaos with millions left homeless, not to mention the incredible burden of health care costs. I have my prepared answers tucked in my back pocket. They would be safe. They would be worthless. I do not stand before you with real answers, but I pledge to search for answers that will make a difference, answers that will change our course, leading us away from another recession, or Depression, as the case may be." He looked at Downs, who was shaking his head in disgust.

"You're a fool," Downs flipped at Lawrence emphatically. The audience reacted fiercely. "Oh, go on!" he shouted back at them. "These bleeding hearts will not solve your problems!"

"Gentlemen!" Derrick shouted back over the crowd. "This will not be a repeat of the last debate. I would also caution the audience to maintain your sense of decorum. We are here to exchange ideas, not harsh words. Senator Lawrence, you still have the floor."

"Statesmen do not instill confidence with apologies, so I will offer you a pledge in its place. I know this sounds hollow, but we will find solutions, and we will do whatever it takes to care for the people of this nation."

The crowd rumbled as they broke for commercial, but they did not lose control. Tension in the room was extremely high as Michael looked at Dane. "I know, great television." Something Michael had not noticed before, however, were the secret servicemen gathering just offstage. It was a good reminder that this was serious business, as if the bright lights, cameras, and rowdy crowd were not enough.

"Welcome back, America. This will be our final round of questions for the evening. Our final category is the economy. Senator Lawrence, we start with you. You have pledged to find solutions for our struggling economy. If there is one thing you could change tonight, what would that be, and why?"

"Well, Derrick, I think one of the greatest issues facing politicians and our political system is that people expect us to come up with quick fixes, like 'one thing I could change tonight.' We live in a world of sacred cows, things about our heritage that are untouchable. For example, throughout most of our nation, K through 12 public school systems run on a nine-month calendar with roughly twelve weeks off in the summer. Why is that? Most studies show that our kids would learn better if we adopted a twelve-month school year with several shorter breaks. In fact, several other countries have adopted a year-round system and have experienced great success, success that rivals ours, yet we do not change. Why? It is our heritage, 'we've always done it that way.' If I could change one thing tonight, it would be our perspective. If we're going to change our course, we're going to have to look in a new direction. We're going to have to turn the steering wheel. If we want change, we're going to have to change."

"Thank you, Senator. To you, Dr. Hamilton, what one thing would you do tonight?"

Time seemed to stop. All eyes, not just those physically present, but *all* eyes seemed to be on him. He could hear his own heart pound with the passing of each second. This was it. This was his question. It was as if he had lived his whole life just to step to this podium and say…"I would forgive the debt."

The crowd was immediately back in the game. They had been interested in Senator Lawrence's soul-cleansing speech, but this… this had meat. This had headline written all over it. From the teleprompter, Dane thought, *That's my boy!*

Senator Downs shouted, "What?" at the top of his lungs.

Senator Lawrence just wished he had been so bold.

"I would work out a plan to alleviate American families from their unsecured debt, especially credit card debt. I would split the cost between the Federal and State Governments and the companies holding the debt. Only a fraction of the nation is paying their bills anyway. I would eliminate the *credit* card system and move to a *debit*-only card system. With their debts forgiven, families would be free to rebuild their lives, which in turn would jumpstart our stagnating economy. While I would not forgive mortgages, I would strongly urge Congress to pass laws eliminating many of the hybrid loans, especially the interest-only and negative-amortization loans. I would also push for a stabilizing of variable rates to stop the increasing monthly payments that are costing people their homes."

The audience was spellbound. Everyone, including Derrick Jett, was on the edge of their seats. Allie and the students were silently going crazy.

"He did it!" Larry blasted to Shelly in the most excited whisper he could find.

Downs was glaring at Sydney, who was feverishly taking notes.

Michael continued. "Is this a crazy idea? Maybe, but it's not nearly as crazy as doing nothing. There are twenty million people living in their cars tonight. They are spread all over this nation. Sanitation is breaking down, and tensions are increasing. Riots are becoming more common. We have a time bomb on our hands, and this is no time to be sitting on those hands."

"Do you have a name for this crazy plan?" Downs chided from his podium.

"Yes, sir. It's called *Jubilee.*"

"Well, *Jubilee* it is." Downs' response was extremely sarcastic and condescending.

Undeterred, Michael continued to make his case. "Yes, sir, Jubilee. 'On the seventh day, God rested...after seven years, let the land rest, free the slaves, cancel the debts. Count off seven Sabbath years, seven times seven years. Consecrate the fiftieth year and proclaim liberty throughout the land to all its inhabitants. It shall be a jubilee for you—'"

The crowd erupted just as they had done at the college. They were on their feet cheering, and this time they would not be stopped. Despite his efforts, and the fact that Senator Downs was screaming at him, Derrick could not restore order. After a few minutes, Senator Lawrence left his podium, crossed the stage, and extended his hand to Michael. He looked him straight in the eye and shook his hand. "Thank you, Dr. Hamilton. Maybe your idea is just a dream...maybe it will never happen, but it feels good to dream tonight." And with that, Senator Lawrence left the stage.

The debate was over. There were no closing remarks, not even from Derrick. After a few more minutes, the light on the camera went out and the reporters rushed the stage. Michael was looking for Allie and the students. He was also hoping for a little bit of Dane's magic to help them escape from the crowd again. For the moment, however, all he saw were microphones and notebooks.

"Dr.... Mr.... Hamilton... Who? What? Why? Where? When?" They were mobbing him. Outside the ring of reporters were countless numbers from the audience, all wanting a piece of the newest celebrity in town. *It would be easy to run,* Michael thought to himself, *but the battle has begun. Why not stay and finish it? They might as well get the straight scoop from me rather than mess it all up on their own,* he thought.

He started by telling the reporters closest to him that he would stay and answer their questions, but he requested their assistance. It took a few minutes to get everything settled down, but he managed to get the crowd to allow Allie and the students to make their way to him. At the same time, he made his way back to one of the podiums and grabbed the microphone. He motioned for the crowd to back up, and in another few minutes he had most of them sitting down—some in chairs and some on the floor surrounding him. *Preaching in the round,* he thought.

"Folks, I will stay as long as you want and answer as many questions as I can." Before they could start asking questions, he asked one of his own, "Is Jubilee crazy? At least I think that is about where we left off. I realize that we all come from different backgrounds and may have many different beliefs. I am not trying to force mine on anyone in this room, or this nation, for that matter, but I believe our nation was founded on Christian principles. I believe my proposed solution is consistent with the vision our founding fathers had for this country. We are a land of limitless possibility, a land where we are free to reach for the stars, dream big dreams, attain miraculous accomplishments, and yes, fail miserably. With great possibilities come great risks. The time has come to balance the scales. If we do not, the 'American Dream' will cease to exist."

He shared his thoughts on Jubilee while they sat around him. This place had almost become sacred, and the experience would long be described by even the most jaded in the crowd as religious. Not in a Baptist, or Catholic, or Jewish, or any other "religion" kind of way, but a simpler, purer—just people caring about each other, searching for answers to the questions they saw all around them—kind of way.

The chaos that had existed was now stillness. The panic set off by the bank failure was now peace. There were possible answers where there had only been hopeless questions. Eventually, someone brought Michael a chair and he sat down. He gave answers to each question he received.

"Where will we get the money?" a well-dressed lady asked.

"Where does the money for war or natural disaster come from? Where do the funds for countless pork projects that get added at the last minute to congressional bills come from? There are those who will say that people in debt have caused their own problems. I will not totally disagree, but let me look each of you in the eye. Which of you are completely secure in your tomorrows? Which of you know the future? Are the hospitals filled with the well? Which of us will fill them tomorrow? Will tomorrow's sky be blue or black? Which of us gets to decide?"

"How will we live without credit?" asked a man sitting on the floor at Michael's feet.

"How does the alcoholic live without the next drink, the gambler without the next bet, the addict without the next fix? First of all…he *lives.* He lives better, because all of those things, when they get out of control, bring him down, even kill him, just like debt kills our dreams. In the same way, we will live better lives without revolving credit. We will live within our means, we will have to. Marketing strategies will need to change. Live by the sword, die by the sword…Live by credit, die by credit, and not just the consumer, but also the lender. Credit used must continually be extended. At some point it is overextended and eventually collapses. At first, it collapses on the consumer, but eventually, as we have seen with First National today, it collapses on the creditor as well. Credit is not limitless. To believe so is to deceive ourselves."

A red-headed little girl stood up from the floor and walked over to Michael. She stared into his eyes for a moment. "Does this mean my dad will love me again?"

He picked her up and sat her on his lap. For a minute he let his eyes move from person to person. The pain of a nation's breaking heart was on their faces.

"How long have we been broken?" he finally pushed past the emotion. He looked past her red curls and into her beautiful green eyes. "I don't know, sweetie…but I know we will never give up hope."

As he sat her down to go back to her mother, his eye caught a glimpse of Dane standing just offstage. Allie, Larry, Shelly, and Sarah were with him, and they were all trying to get his attention. He had been speaking and answering questions for over two hours. While some had left, there were still over a hundred people in the ballroom.

"This evening is coming to an end, but I have a feeling the adventure is just beginning. They say whoever chooses the beginning of the road chooses the destination. Well, not to be too trite, but I would say that we, and I truly hope this is a *we,* have chosen the road less traveled. It is also my hope that we will arrive at a new and better destination. This is still a nation of 'We the People,' and we the *people* need to start taking care of each other, regardless of our station in life, or the lack thereof. We need to reach across all boundaries and grasp every hand. Those at the top need to lift and those below need to reach. May God hold us in His arms, may He lead us, may He give us grace where we fail and hope for a better tomorrow. Goodnight, everyone."

I Am Just a Weed

Reward for obedience:

> If you follow my decrees and are careful to obey my commands, I will send you rain in its season, and the ground will yield its crops and the trees their fruit. Your threshing will continue until grape harvest and the grape harvest will continue until planting, and you will eat all the food you want and live in safety in your land. I will grant peace in the land and you will lie down and no one will make you afraid...I will look on you with favor and make you fruitful and increase your numbers, and I will keep my covenant with you. You will still be eating last year's harvest when you will have to move it out to make room for the new. I will put my dwelling place among you, and I will not abhor you. I will walk among you and be your God, and you will be my people...I broke the bars of your yoke and enabled you to walk with heads held high.
>
> Leviticus 26:1–13 (TNIV)

"Well, bless my soul, Hill City, this is Sunny Jack for WROE. How about our own Dr. Hamilton? You go, Doc! You certainly have the whole nation stirred up. Some love you. Some hate you. Here's a sample of the headlines:

"New York, *Mad Professor Plays God with Nation's Debt.* Boston, *Forgive It All?*" Jack scrolled through some of the other headlines. "Let's see here, Washington, D.C., *Even Congress Can't Outspend the Professor.* Here's a kind one, Cincinnati, *Professor Preaches Forgiveness.* Hey, Doc, my pocketbook likes this one, St. Louis, *Salvation for the Middle Class, Forgive the Debt!* Let's see what the Texans have to say, Dallas, *Bankruptcy for Some vs. Bankruptcy for All.* Vegas, Doc, they're even talking about you in Vegas, *Professor Rolls Holy Dice with National Debt.*" Jack laughed the deep laugh of a professional announcer. "These guys are cracking me up. Oh, here's the City of Angels, Los Angeles, *Jubilee, Stop the Riots.* Yeah, it's been 1968 all over again in the streets of L.A.," Sunny Jack's voice grew suddenly somber as he let the images of a nation in trouble roll through his mind.

"You go, Doc!" His voice broke a little as he cued the next song. *God, help us all.*

It was a little after eleven o'clock in the morning when the Hamilton troop drove away from the hotel and headed for home. About an hour down the road, Larry's phone rang. "Slow down, I can't understand a word you're saying. Yeah. Yeah. No way!" After a few more minutes, he hung up the phone.

"No way *what?*" The girls were both pounding on him in the backseat.

"The Web site is going crazy. Some of it is good and some is not, but it's definitely busy. I'm not sure our site can handle the volume."

They had all been rather quiet on the ride home until then, but the call seemed to stir their excitement. Was this really happening? They talked about the debate and what it meant for the future. One person would barely finish a sentence and another would begin talking. They were a pretty naïve bunch. Little did they know the impact they were having on the other candidates.

While Downs was making the news show rounds, his brain trust was busy scheming. Sydney Porter laid out several scenarios for discrediting Michael. He distributed assignments and sent his wolves out in all directions. Some were sent to gather dirt on the Hamilton family, while others were sent on missions of intimidation. The Downs arm could reach far and wide, and the professor and his band of merry college punks would be stopped.

Sydney called Downs, who was en route to his third interview of the day. "Yes, sir, it's going well…Yes, sir, we did locate him…No," he laughed arrogantly, "he came cheap." There may be nothing worse than the wrath of a scorned woman, unless it is the bitterness of a frustrated Christian.

Michael's name was everywhere. Some were hailing him as a genius, a free-thinker, a savior, while others thought he was the Antichrist. Many of the same experts who had made their way across the network and cable news stations with Michael's bio just weeks before were now expounding on Jubilee. They all gave their version of the text from Exodus and Leviticus. Experts who had not darkened the door of a church in decades were giving their best exegeses on a subject they obviously did not understand. By the end of the day, Jubilee was a twisted nail in the coffin of the middle class. Senator Downs was also everywhere, on every news program imaginable, blasting Michael and Jubilee. Senator Lawrence, on the other hand, was curiously silent.

Over the next few weeks, the Hamilton campaign team did their best to keep up with the growing demands on their time. Michael did interview after interview—at times flying all night from one place to another. It was becoming increasingly difficult to keep up with his teaching duties, but it was late November and winter break was coming soon. The students were also busy returning phone calls and e-mails. Donations were pouring in from all over the nation—mostly from people who did not have a dollar to spare. The stories received in the letters along with the donations drove the team on. They were all reaching the point of exhaustion, but the stories of families being split apart as kids were sent to live with relatives rather than in the Marshallvilles where their parents were eking out an existence pushed the students to return one more e-mail, write one more letter, make one more phone call. Reading the stories, the students could not help but think of the differences between Jubilee and capitalism—one philosophy based on plenty for all and the other based on shortage; one providing for all, the other promoting great wealth, hoarding, and abject poverty. Finally, one late night, as they were all hanging out at The Hollow, their own debate began to percolate.

"There's nothing wrong with working hard, being successful, and making a lot of money," Robert defended his wealthy family.

"That's right, Robert," Larry reassured his friend. "There is nothing necessarily evil about wealth or capitalism. It's simply a system in which each person is free to work hard and be successful, nothing wrong with that. The problems come with greed. When is enough, enough? When is it okay for a very small portion of the population to reach a point where they control eighty to ninety percent of the income and wealth, especially when they are not willing to use those resources to help the less fortunate? How do any of us tolerate starvation at any level, from the children we see in other nations to those in our own backyards? How do we say it is fine for the CEO of a company to receive a multimillion-dollar bonus on top of their multimillion-dollar salary and then cut benefits to those who actually did the work to make that salary and bonus possible? For too long we have been a 'me-centered' society. We look at glamorous magazines and TV shows about the rich and famous, and we dream of joining those ranks. It's the 'American Dream,' anything is possible, and it is, but we have lost the ability to see beyond our noses. What can I get? Where's my stash? I can do anything I put my mind to... Whatever happened to 'I can do all things through Christ?' Madison Avenue says, 'Sure it costs more, but *I'm* worth it.' Where is 'Love your neighbor as yourself' in all of this?

"Our 'neighbors' are starving. They are living out of their cars. They are watching their children leave with friends and relatives. Our neighbors are dying in decaying shantytowns where riots rage and diseases loom. Typhoid is beginning to break out in several of the camps. As sanitation breaks down, rodents and fleas have been attracted, and there are reports of plague in some camps. Plague! Remember the lessons from class—capitalism, ultimate tolerance of wealth and poverty. That same attitude of tolerance now seems to extend beyond wealth and includes tolerance of the worst in human suffering. We should become all that we can become, dream big dreams and shoot for the stars, and if we get rich in the process, great! But it should not be done on the backs of our neighbors, at the expense of our neighbors, with no concern for anyone but self! Whatever happened to *we* the people?"

"Who feels like the choir here? Anyone? Anyone?" Lenny rebutted in his smooth California tone. Lenny was not always the sharpest knife in the drawer, but he knew how to cut through tension. Larry's point was well taken, but he was preaching to the choir, and this choir was doing their best to sing a new song with new harmonies even though they faced a world of dissonance.

Thanksgiving came and went. Across the nation, the effects of the declining economy were beginning to play out in many different ways. Grocery stores that normally sold millions of turkeys were left with huge numbers of unsold merchandise. There were some benevolent efforts to get the excess to the Marshallvilles, but even those efforts had little success and, in some areas, led to more health issues as hungry people pushed the limits on spoiled food that had not been properly refrigerated. Many people became sick, and with a lack of resources to seek proper medical attention, sickness that would have once been easily treated became a major issue. Health insurance had become a thing of the past for all but the extreme upper middle class and above.

By Thanksgiving, the Christmas shopping season had been in motion for several weeks. The malls, however, were empty. By mid-December, storeowners were getting desperate. They offered incredible sales, but tactics that had worked over the past quarter-century were no longer valid. There was no more room on the credit card. Christmas had saved the mall for decades, but there would be no salvation this year. Thousands of stores, like the churches before them, closed, and the era of the mall was seriously changed forever.

Michael had given his last exams for the semester, graded all of the papers, and turned in his grades. On a Saturday evening in late December, he flew to New York to be a guest on one of the

Sunday morning news shows. Sydney greeted him as he arrived at the television studio.

"Good morning, Sydney. I didn't realize the Downs team would also be here today."

"Well, we can't let you have all the fun, Professor."

Their conversation was brief, if not curt, and Michael was pleased when they were interrupted by the preparation staff. There was makeup to be done and directions to receive. Michael learned that he and Downs would indeed be sharing the "couch" for the interview.

Downs was on the attack from the beginning. Michael traded jabs with him for a while, but eventually he remembered the fancy hotel room in Des Moines. It was a good reminder that he should stick to his game plan. Downs was taking him down roads where he did not belong. Michael decided to keep things simple. *Just be yourself. Let people see that you are different from Downs. Let them see that you care.* Downs was busy tearing Jubilee to shreds with the usual comments about bankrupting America and the credit card companies. He seemed to have a negative response for everything. He provided no real solutions; he simply stood on his statesmanship and dared Michael to knock him off Capitol Hill.

"Dr. Hamilton, how can you possibly understand what this nation needs? I have been blessed to serve in her top offices for decades. It is the knowledge of men like me that will find the answers to these complex issues facing our nation. We have the brains and the knowledge."

"A man is not rewarded for having brains, Mr. Downs, only for using them, and it doesn't seem to take a wise man to figure out that this generation of leaders has failed."

Downs was enraged, and he railed on Michael for several minutes, including a tirade on Michael's personal life and his family. Michael was enraged inside but reminded himself to stay cool.

"Great minds discuss ideas. I've heard no good ideas from you today. Good minds discuss events. I hear you discussing only negative events. Small minds discuss people. You may discuss me and my family all you want, but I do not think that will resolve the very pressing issues of the day." Michael had pushed the senator's buttons.

"Dr. Hamilton, you are just a weed. You sprang up with your holier-than-thou words and schemes, and a whole nation grimaces at your irresponsible proposals…a weed."

Michael looked the senator in the eye and replied, "'A weed is just a plant whose virtues have not been discovered.'[a] I am happy to be a weed in this garden of complacency, in this garden of stagnation. I am glad to be a weed standing next to your beautiful flower, a flower that only looks good, but provides no sustenance for life, glad to be a weed climbing the walls that keep the less fortunate out, climbing the white marble walls of Washington where the politics are for the rich and the status quo is maintained for the profit of the few at the cost of the many. I am just a weed, but weeds live through the famine far more often than flowers. While everything else is turning brown, the weed is still green. Unlike the flower that spends its energy sustaining its looks at the expense of its life, the weed spends its energy on life itself. If I am just a weed, a thorn in your side…good."

As the program came to a close, the moderator gave Downs the last word, and he used the time to blast Michael again. As Michael left the studio and made his way back to the airport, he noticed two men following him. Things were becoming a bit more intense—maybe even dangerous. On the plane, he let his mind wander back over the morning, and he wrote these words down on a napkin:

I am just a weed, just a thorn in your side
Blowin' in the breeze, messin' with your mind
Wonder what I am, wonder what I'll be
I am just a weed, won't you set me free

Who Is this Hawk?

Ben arrived in Tucson in mid-October. He would be playing for the Tucson Fall Boys in the Arizona Fall League. Most players in the league had spent the regular season playing at the double- or triple-A minor league levels. Ben would be one of the very few who had not played all year—probably the only one who had not played in four years. Fortunately for him, left-handed pitchers were always in demand, so the Cardinals were sending him to the fall league to evaluate his possibilities.

The manager of the Fall Boys was Donny Jones, an ex-major league pitcher. Donny had done it all—starting pitcher, post-season play…He was a character in his day, but he had mellowed with age and girth. Ben was not sure what to expect, but Donny was cordial.

"Come on back to the office, son." He walked up the tunnel leading under the stadium and back to his office just off the locker room. "Let's get you squared away." He opened up a binder that was sitting on his desk. "You'll be rooming with Joe Donnel. He boards with the Millers. Haven't met 'em, but the family sponsors are usually pretty nice. You'll get eight hundred dollars a month. Don't spend it all in one place. You'll get your meals on the road, but the rest is on you. Here's a schedule. I don't have many rules, but don't be late. I hate late. Any questions?"

"No, sir."

Donny stuck his head out of the office and yelled, "Hey, Joe! Can you step in here?"

Ben watched as Superman himself strolled over to the office. Joe was built like a Greek god, standing about six feet six. Ben was over six feet tall himself, but he was still a little intimidated by the chiseled professional athlete.

"Yeah, Coach?"

"Joe, I want you to meet Ben Wallace. He'll be rooming with you."

"Hi." Joe shook Ben's hand. "I'm ready to go when you are." It was a polite welcome, but not a warm one.

Ben looked at Donny, who nodded his approval for them to leave. Joe grabbed a bag from his locker and led Ben out of the stadium. They got into Joe's car and headed up into the hills surrounding the stadium. No words were spoken as they made the ten-minute drive to the Millers.'

Ben knew that he would have a roommate and that they would be boarding with a host family, but he had not been given any information about any of them. Joe pulled up in front of a modest ranch-style house.

"Home sweet home." Joe hopped out of the car.

"Wow, he speaks." Ben followed him into the house.

A blond-headed little boy in a diaper met them at the door. "What's up, brat?" Joe stepped around him. The smells of Southwest cuisine filled the air as Ben stepped into the house. It was small but clean. Joe disappeared into the kitchen.

"What's your name?" Ben looked at the little boy staring up at him.

"Billy."

"Is your mom or dad here?"

"Mom!" He ran into the other room. A few seconds later, a tall, slender lady who appeared to be in her early thirties came out of the kitchen.

"Hi, come on in. My name is Sue."

"Hi, Sue. I'm Ben."

"Let me show you to your room." She led him through the kitchen and down the steps to the finished basement. It had a family room, two bedrooms, a bathroom, and an unfinished area that housed the washer and dryer. Sue walked past the closed door of the first bedroom and into the second one. It was a small room with a bed, night stand, and dresser. There was a lamp and an alarm clock on the night stand and a closet at the end of the room.

"Looks like you're traveling light." She checked the room for toys in case the boys had left any behind. "The bathroom is at the end of the hall if you need to freshen up. There are towels in the hall closet. Supper will be ready in ten minutes."

"Thank you." Ben dropped his bag on the bed.

He met the rest of the Millers at supper. John Miller was a concrete worker in his late thirties and had worked on the construction of the Fall Boys stadium. When an announcement was made about opportunities to house players, he had volunteered. It was a chance to pick up a little extra cash for his family without having to be away on a second job. He was already working thirteen-hour days to make ends meet, and after a long day in the hot sun, he was exhausted. Sue had an in-home business managing billing records for three medical offices. It had the promise of a good future, but she was still in the early stages. She was hoping to pick up business for a couple more doctors soon, which would ease some of their financial pressures, but the business allowed Sue to be at home with the two kids. Billy, who Ben had met, was two, and Jeremy was four. Donny was right; they seemed like a really nice family.

As soon as Joe finished eating, he looked at Ben. "Be ready at seven in the morning. We have to be at the stadium early to catch the bus." With that, he left his dishes on the table, shot out the door, and would not return until well after one o'clock.

Ben was used to helping his mother with everything around the house. She had been so busy caring for Jim during his illness. When he finished eating, he started to clear his plate, but Sue stopped him. "I can get that."

"Sorry, ma'am. I'm just used to doing it myself." Ben walked his dishes over to the sink.

"I'll bet you put the seat down too." Sue marveled at her new tenant as he returned to the table.

The kids finished and went into the other room to play. Sue cleared the rest of the dishes and cleaned the kitchen while John and Ben sat at the table and talked. Before they knew it, Sue had the kids through their baths and tucked into bed.

"You better go tell them good-night, John." She sat back down at the table. It was about eight o'clock. "Donny said you were going to be a preacher. Why did you change your mind?"

"I'm not sure. Maybe I still will be someday." He told her the story about his father, and they talked about life for a while. John rejoined them after getting the kids to sleep.

"Life can be tough, kid." John shook his head. "It's no picnic playing ball. Most of the guys we see fade away pretty quick."

The next morning, after a big breakfast, Joe and Ben drove down to the stadium. The team was arriving and the bus was being loaded. When they were ready to leave, Donny stood up in the front of the bus and barked out orders for the trip. They would be gone for a week, traveling to three cities. Some nights would be spent in motels and a few nights would be spent in homes. Their game tonight was in Scottsdale.

Ben took a seat by himself and, for the time being, was happy to have a few minutes alone to sort out his new life. After riding for a while, he realized he had not called his mom to let her know how he was doing. He pulled out his cell phone and dialed. She was doing well, at least she said so. He wondered if she was just trying to be strong so he would not worry about her. He, too, had made his new arrangements seem a little rosier than they felt. They talked for about twenty minutes. Ben told her his schedule and agreed to call her in a couple days.

The next few days rolled by with little fanfare. Ben was not scheduled to pitch until later in the week. He filled his days with workouts that included a fitness regiment and sessions with the pitching coach on the sidelines. The team itself seemed to be pretty average. They won a few games and lost a few. As it turned out, Joe really was Superman. He played first base and could hit the ball a country mile. There were a few other players on the team who seemed to have major league potential, but most were just guys trying to get noticed. Ben thought John was probably right; most of these guys would fade away pretty quickly—himself included.

Although Ben was working hard at his game while they traveled, he was taken more by the people and things he saw along the way. There were temporary towns outside each of the major cities they passed through—Marshallvilles, he presumed. They seemed so distant on the television news, but seeing them in person was much more alarming. These were real people living out of their cars and makeshift shacks. Ben wondered about the kids. How did they get to school? Did they even go to school anymore? What effect did all of this have on the communities where these people used to live? How would these people ever be right again? What would happen when their cars began to break down? What would happen when there was no more hope? How did they have any hope now?

Over the next month, he got to pitch a few times. He did fine, considering he had not pitched competitively in so long, but he was definitely beginning to wonder if leaving school was a mistake. At a home game in Tucson, he met a man named Hawk. Hawk was Indian, and that was about all Ben knew, other than he appeared to be about sixty years old and was providing food and supplies to a group of families living on the outskirts of the Saguaro National Forest. Each time the team was in town, Ben went with Hawk to the "camp," as Ben referred to it.

At the close of the Fall League season, Ben bid farewell to the Millers and went with Hawk, who lived close to the camp in an incredible log cabin that he had built himself years ago. This quiet place was perfect for Ben to clear his head. He spent his days helping with chores around what turned out to be a small farm. Hawk had chickens, a few milk cows, and several fields of vegetables. Every Tuesday morning a cargo truck pulled up outside a big barn on the property and dropped off cases of canned goods. Hawk was using his farm and the canned goods to supply the camp with food. It was a pretty rugged life, but it suited Ben very well.

They made trips to the camp three times a week. Hawk had what used to be a large rental truck that was old and worn out, but it ran well and worked perfectly for transporting large quantities of food and supplies. Several times a week, they drove to Tucson to pick up supplies. Hawk never talked about his business, but each time they went to town, they stopped at a storefront operation that was a cross between Goodwill and the Salvation Army. It was located in an older section of the city and was staffed mostly by Hispanics and Native Americans. There were shelves full of odds and ends for sale in the front and a huge warehouse area in the back where several men and women restored donated items. There was also an area for washing and restoring clothing. It did not look like a very lucrative business, and Ben often wondered how the twenty or so employees made a living. Each visit they loaded the truck with clothing and other items and made deliveries to several poor communities in the city and the camp.

Between keeping up with the farm and their deliveries, they stayed very busy. Hawk and Ben spent a lot of time talking in the evenings. They were too tired for anything else, and there wasn't much to do at night anyway. After several weeks of talking shop, Ben finally got Hawk to talk a little about himself while they cleared the dinner dishes.

"I'll wash." Ben carried the last glass over to the sink. "You never told me your last name."

"Last name no good. Blow on wind to friend and foe. Better have no last name."

"What?" Ben turned on the faucet as they both laughed. "Why the 'Indian' thing?" Other than his obvious heritage discernable from his physical features, Hawk had never broken into anything other than perfect English.

"Sorry, just seemed to fit the question. Me Hawk. You Ben."

"Come on, quit teasing. You know all about my family. Tell me about yourself. I really want to know."

"Start washing and I'll tell you a story. About one hundred years ago, a baby was born into the Pascua Yaqui tribe not too far from here. The family was poor, and times were hard, especially during the 1930s. As soon as he was old enough, Tom, we'll call him, joined the navy and was sent to the South Pacific. Being a minority in the service was not easy in those days. Tom was always pulling grunt duty. He went about his work without complaint though, because even the life of a grunt in the navy was better than life at home.

"After World War II broke out, he was assigned to the PT boat division in the South Pacific and served as a mechanic. For the most part, his life was not that exciting. He didn't get to go out on the missions, but rather was left behind to work on the boats when they came back from battle. Once again, it was hard work, but old Tom got pretty good at repairing and patching and generally keeping the boats running.

"One night a call went out across the camp for men to get to the boats. There was a lot of confusion in the camp. Men were running everywhere. Tom ran down to the docks to see if he could help, and in the commotion of the moment, one of the officers threw a jacket to him and told him to climb onboard. Being a dutiful sailor, Tom jumped on the boat, cast the ropes back to the dock, and they took off into the black night. Wind and spray were rushing past, and Tom's adrenalin was flowing. This was his first mission, his first action of any kind, and he didn't know whether to be excited or terrified. Terrified ended up to be the correct choice.

"They had been running for about twenty minutes when the boat engines cut to half-speed, and then to a complete slow. They were idling through black water on a black night, and Tom wondered how the captain could navigate. There had been other boats around them before, but now they could only hear what sounded like the engine from a single boat. Tom barely saw the metallic glint as the Japanese boat sliced through the darkness with all her guns blazing. Seconds later, the PT boat blew apart, and before he knew it, he was thrown into the water and began swimming for his life. Shots rang out all around, so Tom dove down under a part of the sinking boat to avoid the bullets. Once underwater, he felt someone frantically tugging at him. Feeling his way through the blackness, he determined that the man was caught in some of the wreckage. After a few moments of sheer panic, he freed the man and they both swam for the surface. As they crested the water, a single shot caught the man in the shoulder. Before he could scream, Tom grabbed his mouth and shoved his head back under the water to muffle the sound. When they resurfaced, they could hear the Japanese boat leaving.

"As Tom surveyed the face of the man in his arms, it was the officer who had pulled him onboard back at the camp. He was bleeding badly from his shoulder, and he was having difficulty swimming. The man was not very coherent, but he was able to communicate that his leg was a mess, probably broken.

"Most of the wreckage had sunk, but they rested for a moment on a piece that was still afloat and tried to gather their bearings. The officer was in and out of consciousness. Tom thought he could hear waves washing ashore to his left, so he decided to swim for it. He used the small piece of the boat to stabilize the officer, and he pushed him through the water toward what he hoped would be a safe beach.

"It took about fifteen minutes to reach the shore of the island, and luckily there were no enemy troops patrolling. Tom moved the officer up the beach and into the cover of the trees. He did what he could for his wounds, but the officer was not in good shape. Several times through the night he heard patrols pass, but they went undetected. He fought the urge to close his eyes through the night as he lay covering the officer with his body to keep him as warm as possible. Finally, fatigue won the battle and he fell asleep.

"When he awoke it was early dawn. He knew the boats usually left camp about this time, but he did not know where they went. He listened intently, hoping to hear an engine. In the stillness of the humid morning air, he heard a faint sound in the distance and began to wonder if it was safe to break their cover. Deciding their only hope was to attract attention, he made his way out to the beach and hailed the PT boat as it came into sight. Men from the boat loaded the officer onboard and they rushed back to camp.

"It was several days before Tom learned the fate of the officer. Early on a Sunday morning, he was awakened and summoned to the camp medical tent. The officer had just regained consciousness and was asking for the 'Indian.' Tom never shared the name of the officer, but he was apparently from a well-to-do family, some say a mob family. While the details are somewhat gray, Tom was well taken care of by the officer's family when they returned to the States."

When the dishes were done, Hawk and Ben went into the living room to continue the story. A blazing fire made the moment seem significant. Hawk reached up on the mantle and removed a rectangular acrylic object and handed it to Ben as they both sat down. It was a small piece of a palm branch encased in a clear acrylic sleeve.

"My father gave this to me when I went off to college. He told me it was his most prized possession. He passed away during my freshman year at UA."

"Arizona?" Ben looked up from the palm branch.

"Yes. My mother died just after I passed the bar."

"You're a lawyer?"

"Let's just say I passed the bar. It was my father's dream. He meant well, just wanted me to be somebody. He had money, but he kept the secret of its source as tucked away as the branch within that casing. I gave up my practice along with my last name a long time ago. I have been free ever since."

"How did you get started with your...business?"

Hawk laughed. "You're a great kid." He let his head fall back and he looked up, as if searching for the answer in the shifting shadows created by the fire's glow on the ceiling. "I have listened to your professor speak, to his ideas about Jubilee. It was for the same beliefs in fairness and an economy of plenty that I chose my work. My parents left great wealth to me. It never seemed to make them happy. One day I lost my train of thought as I sat at my desk in the law office. I pushed my chair back and decided to go for a walk. I walked a great distance, and soon I was no longer among the fancy buildings of the well-to-do, soon I was among the less fortunate. Suddenly, my suit and tie seemed out of place.

"As I walked, I came upon the storefront you have seen many times. I went inside and, after looking around out front, I made my way back to the warehouse. A kind lady stopped me and asked why I had come. When I told her I did not know, she smiled and bid me to come with her, so I did. She led me to the office area and introduced me to a man named Jesse. He was the oldest person I've ever met. He told me to take off my tie and go to work out in the warehouse for the day. I took off my tie and went with the lady. I worked in several areas of the warehouse, and I went back the next morning. After a few days of working in the warehouse and going out on the truck to make deliveries, Jesse called me into his office.

"'What did you see?'

"I saw kindness, I told him. He said, 'I will call you Hawk, for your eyes are good.'

"I have worked there ever since."

"Did you ever get married or have kids?"

"I was married for a while. My wife wanted to be married to a lawyer, so she left me when I stopped practicing."

"I'm sorry."

"Jesse was right. I do have good eyes. I saw you."

The fire crackled deep into the night as they sat and watched the flames dance.

Ben stayed in touch with his mom as best he could. She was a little concerned about him, but she trusted her son and was proud of his work. She did wonder though, *Who is this Hawk?*

Family Album

An Alberta Clipper swept out of Canada, sending the whole Midwest and part of the South into a deep freeze. Record-breaking snowfalls brought the nation to her knees with power lines downed, and hundreds of thousands left in the dark. Although the power outage paled in comparison to the hardships faced by the homeless, it gave the fortunate a taste of life's bitter side.

The Hamilton family, snowed in with the rest of the nation, decided to spend the day gathered around the fireplace looking through family albums. At first, they were all looking at the same album—the wedding album—which brought lots of laughs about how young Mom and Dad looked.

"You were beautiful, Mom." Lana was taken by the youth of her mother in the picture.

Michael started to respond to the "were" part of the statement, but seeing the admiration on his daughter's face for her mother, he simply said to her, "I see a lot of that beauty in you."

"Oh, mush!" Mark flopped back onto the couch.

Little by little, they each grabbed a different album and retreated to their own corners of the room, at least those that the heat from the fireplace would reach. Hours passed as they looked and giggled and awed. A few questions and comments were exchanged, but quiet prevailed for most of the morning.

The power came back on at exactly 12:32 p.m., Ian calculated as he ran around the house setting all the clocks to the correct time. After eating lunch, they all decided to play with their family Christmas present: a new piece of computer software that would allow them to re-record their family videos into a more "movie-like" format. They spent the rest of the day taking turns playing producer as they rolled one family memory after another across the screen. They watched babies and birthdays and countless little league games. There were Thanksgivings and Christmases past with countless "who's that?" comments about forgotten faces from their distant memories. There were pudgy pictures and skinny snippets of everything from first days of school to crazy Halloween costumes. There were scenes from the old church, of the kids' baptisms, of old friends, and of the old house. Some things brought laughter and some tears.

As afternoon turned into evening, they each made a trek through the kitchen for a snack or a plate of holiday leftovers, but there was no official dinnertime. They were too enthralled with the pictures of their lives. It was nice to retreat from the cares of the world and take a walk down memory lane.

Allie, with the ever-sensitive "eye for a special moment," snapped pictures and shot video all day. By late evening she was reclined in a comfy chair, watching her family. Clothed in her favorite pajamas and robe and draped with a blanket, with a plate full of cookies and a mug of hot cider, she was happy. As her eyes wandered the room watching her family bubble with excitement over the pictures and videos, she noticed a box of photo albums that had gone untouched through the day. Reluctantly, she roused herself from the comfort of the chair to investigate the box. She scooted it over by the fireplace and sat down on the hearth. The albums were older than the others, containing pictures of her parents and grandparents. Some of the pictures were faded with age, but the memories they held came back fresh in Allie's mind. She laughed at the expressionless look on the faces. It was a different time. People were different, more serious. Finding a favorite picture of her mother, she laid everything else down and studied it for a while. Her mother had passed away when she was just seventeen, a year before she left for college. While it was a sad memory, she remembered the lessons her mother instilled in her young heart.

"No bitterness," she had said as she lay in the hospital. As an only child, Allie was especially close to her mother. The loss could have been devastating were it not for the strength and encouragement she received from her in those last few days. There was no self-pity, no "why me?"

"My love will be with you always." She had taken Allie's young face in her hands. "Take that love wherever you go, and in that way, I will go with you." She passed just a few hours later.

"Thank you, Mom," Allie whispered to herself as she sat on the hearth looking across a room filled with a beautiful family enjoying a beautiful day. She put the pictures back in the box and returned to her comfy chair. She covered herself with the blanket, picked up a cookie, and smiled.

No More Water from the Past

While most at Roe College relaxed on their winter break, the poli-sci class was hard at work. Some went home for a few days around Christmas, but they were all back now. It was one week until the Iowa Caucuses, and there was a great deal to do. Despite their hard work, there was no real way to tell how they would do. The polls had Downs and Lawrence way ahead, but at least Dr. Hamilton was beginning to show up in the numbers. He needed to receive at least fifteen percent of the vote to be considered a viable candidate and continue in the process. He was currently polling at about eight percent.

When the night of the caucuses finally arrived, Iowans from over two thousand precincts gathered in public buildings, schools, and homes around six thirty in the evening to cast their votes the old-fashioned way—by show of hands. As part of the process, participants gathered themselves in groups according to the candidate they were supporting. They pled their case for an hour or so, trying to sway their neighbors from one side to the other. According to the vote, delegates from the precinct caucuses would be elected to go to the county caucus in March, district caucus in April, the state convention in June, and ultimately the national convention in July.

The results from the precinct caucuses would not be nearly as important as the later caucuses or the upcoming state primaries, but they would at least give the Hamilton campaign a sense of their viability. The students, along with the Hamiltons, gathered at The Hollow to watch the results. The news stations were busy with analyses and commentary throughout the evening. Most of the attention was given to Downs and Lawrence, but Michael received more attention than Congressmen Delaney or Smithson. It seemed that Downs' plan to eliminate the congressmen from competition had worked.

"Evan, this is Steve Jenson in the studio. It's been a few months now since Hamilton burst onto the scene. What do you make of his chances?"

"Well, Steve, we have crews out all over the state, and they are reporting a lot of talk about Hamilton. Just last week he was polling in the eight percent range, so we thought he was fading, but I think we may see some surprising results tonight. Exit polls from sites have shown him up in the fifty percent range. Those were definitely the minority of sites, but who knows?"

"Evan, are we looking at a phenomenon like Jimmy Carter?"

"No, I think we're looking more at a Pat Buchanan situation. I don't think Hamilton has any real staying power throughout this campaign because of his radical ideas, and he simply does not have the financing like the major candidates. He is, however, raising the level of awareness about several key issues in this nation, very serious issues that none of the major candidates seem to be able to solve—"

"Evan, let me interrupt you for a moment. We are receiving

some of the initial results. This is with about forty-two percent of the precincts reporting. Let me put them up on the screen:

- DOWNS 34%
- LAWRENCE 30%
- HAMILTON 22%
- SMITHSON 8%
- DELANEY 5%
- OTHER 1%

"Those are pretty much what we expected from Downs and Lawrence, but you have to be impressed with Hamilton, Steve. He's becoming a major part of this campaign."

"Woo!" screamed Shelly, and the rest of the group followed her lead. The crowd in The Hollow turned to look at the group, but by now everyone was well aware of who they were and why they were there. Many students came over to congratulate Dr. Hamilton.

"It's still early," he would say as he thanked them, but the numbers changed very little as they eventually reached the one hundred percent reported level over the next few days. In fact, as it turned out, Michael's numbers in Iowa only got better as the process moved from stage to stage.

"On to New Hampshire!" Larry screamed above the pandemonium.

Several reporters were also at The Hollow, and Michael answered their questions. Soon he began to show up on the news reports they were watching. The group went nuts each time they saw themselves on TV.

With their success came a new wave of support from around the country. People were volunteering to run local campaign headquarters. Michael was becoming something of a folk hero in the Marshallvilles. It became apparent that continuing the campaign and maintaining his full-time schedule as a professor would be difficult. He met with Dr. McPherson, and they worked out a plan for Michael to teach an elective political science class. His current class was welcome to enroll. It would reduce all of them to part-time status, but it was a way to continue the campaign. Most of the fall poli-sci class signed up for the elective as well as a few on-line classes. New assignments were given, and a group of seven students, along with Michael and Allie, headed off to campaign in New Hampshire.

Although the team arrived very late compared to the other candidates, who had been campaigning in the state for several years, they were very well organized. Hundreds of volunteers greeted them as they pulled into Manchester aboard their Silver Eagle. It was January seventeenth—ten days before the primary—and an entire state before them. After a brief meet-and-greet session at their downtown storefront campaign headquarters, they hit the road. By the end of the first day, they had covered countless miles and shaken thousands of hands. Everyone was in great spirits, but they were wondering if it was possible to make up for so much lost time. Downs seemed to have a stranglehold on the Democrats in the state, while Marshall, despite all the chaos around the nation, was still firmly entrenched with the Republicans.

As they gathered for an early breakfast on the second day, the Hill City group consisted of Larry, Sarah, Shelly, Robert, Danielle, Lenny, Ginny, Allie, and Michael. While they ate in a local diner, several other buses pulled up out front. A familiar face climbed off the bus and stood on the curb, surveying the town.

"It's Ben!" Sarah rushed out to greet him. "Where did you come from? How did you find us?"

"Whoa, slow down, missy. You are running a national campaign here, aren't you? It's not like you're traveling incognito."

Michael, who was expecting Ben, was not far behind. "It's good to see you, son." They had talked a few times over the past several weeks. Ben had two busloads of Arizona folks with him, and he was expecting several other busloads of volunteers from states they had visited along the way.

It took a while to get everyone fed, but they made good use of the time. Plans were distributed for the day, and everyone hit the campaign trail. They were to meet that night in Concord.

Michael visited several schools, went door-to-door, and did whatever his campaign team put in front of him. There were a few hecklers along the way, but Michael was so nice to them that even when they disagreed with his politics, he still won their hearts. They crossed paths with the other candidates several times throughout the day. At one point, Senator Lawrence invited Michael to share his bus for a while. The conversation was a bit forced, but Michael liked Lawrence, who seemed sincere. By the time they met for a late dinner in Concord, everyone was bushed.

Ben shared a table with Michael, and they talked for a long time.

"It's bad out there. Winter is wreaking havoc on the Marshallvilles. People are sick, and there aren't enough supplies to go around. There were a lot of suicides during the holidays. Lots of people wanted to come with us, but we didn't have the resources or the room on the buses."

As the days rolled by, more and more volunteers continued to arrive until Michael lost count of the numbers.

"Do you think it's always like this?" he asked Allie as they lay down to sleep at the end of the last day before the primary. As he thought back over the past ten days, there were countless faces and towns and memories rolling through his mind. They had been extremely lucky with the weather, as the past week and a half had turned out unseasonably warm. He had been to Jefferson-Jackson dinners, traveled through counties like Hillsborough, Rockingham, Belknap, and Carroll, through towns like Nashua and Derry…He would never forget the past ten days.

Early on January twenty-seventh, the first votes were cast by tradition in Dixville Notch. One by one, members of the campaign team began to meet back at the local diner in Manchester where they had started their adventure. Later, they would head to the ballroom at the hotel to wait for the results. The day seemed to drag on forever, but eventually it was time to turn on the TV and watch the coverage. All of the Hill City crew, including Ben, were camped out in Michael and Allie's room. They had opted for a large room this time to accommodate the group. It was not as fancy as the Hotel Fort Des Moines, but it was spacious.

The first results came in around six o'clock in the evening.

"With only about ten percent of the precincts reporting, the vote looks like this so far," Steve Jenson reported from World Network News.

Everyone froze as they waited for the graphics to appear…

- DOWNS 37%
- LAWRENCE 32%
- SMITHSON 12%
- DELANY 7%
- HAMILTON 4%
- BEACH 4%

- LOWELL 3%
- OTHERS 1%

"Pretty much what we expected, Steve," came the stuffy commentary from the network political expert.

Everyone was stunned. Michael walked over to the television, turned it off, and addressed the group, "I think we need some dinner. I know it's not tradition, but what do you say we go downstairs and eat with the group?"

Allie was quick to follow his lead, and within a few minutes, they were all headed to the ballroom. The ballroom was filled with hundreds of people already, and there seemed to be no end to the line of supporters still arriving.

"Wow." Larry was amazed as they walked into the room.

"There he is...He's here!"

Shouts came from the back of the room where Michael had entered. The crowd turned and began to collapse on him. The DJ, catching a sense of what was happening, announced the arrival and pumped up the volume on the music. The crowd went nuts. Michael shook hands for over an hour as he led his team toward the front of the room. It was about 7:40 when a huge roar went up around the room. New returns were being displayed on the huge video screens at the front of the room.

Forty Percent Reporting...

- DOWNS 32%
- LAWRENCE 31%
- HAMILTON 21%
- SMITHSON 7%
- DELANY 6%

- OTHERS 3%

The screen changed to a shot from a camera in the room that was trained on Michael. He waved to the crowd, and they yelled even louder. He continued to make his way around the room, shaking hands, hugging the necks of volunteers, accepting their kind words of encouragement, and listening to their stories from the campaign trail. At 8:04, another huge ovation went up—more results:

Seventy Percent Reporting…

- DOWNS 30%
- LAWRENCE 29%
- HAMILTON 27%
- SMITHSON 7%
- DELANY 6%
- OTHERS 1%

The political analysts at WNN were starting to take notice.

"Wow. Hamilton is really starting to surge." Steve Jensen was searching the faces of the political experts for answers, but none seemed to be forthcoming.

"He's probably peaked," Stan Peterman said, trying to minimize Michael's numbers, but Steve was not buying it.

"Let's go live to New Hampshire where Kelly Todd is standing by." Steve threw the coverage to the reporter on the scene. "Kelly, what are you hearing from the exit polls?"

"Steve, we're hearing that the numbers for Downs and Lawrence are soft and the surge from Hamilton is real. It seems like some voters were just trying to send a message to the status quo, and in doing so, they may be tipping the scales toward the new kid in town, Michael Hamilton."

The returns continued through the evening, but at 10:05, the crowd raised the roof…

Ninety Percent Reporting…

- HAMILTON 34%
- DOWNS 30%
- LAWRENCE 28%
- SMITHSON 3%
- DELANY 3%
- OTHERS 1%

Within a few minutes, Senator Lawrence was on the screen from his campaign headquarters congratulating Michael.

"He has captured the hearts of the American people." Steve Jensen looked for a response from the experts, but they were too busy scratching their heads.

Michael waited for another hour. Despite the numbers, Downs all but claimed victory from his headquarters, refusing to give the Hamilton campaign any credibility. When Michael finally went to the podium at 11:15, he did not get to say a word for five minutes, and as soon as he uttered, "Hello," the crowd erupted again for another five minutes.

"Thank you all so much. I can't even begin to tell you how overwhelmed we are this evening." He turned to thank the students, who were standing onstage with him, and the crowd went crazy again. Michael noticed that Ben was not on the stage.

"Where's Ben?" A group of people to his left roared and shoved Ben forward. "Get up here, son." He acknowledged his kids at home and then turned to thank Allie. That was more than he could take, and his emotions took over for a few moments. She came to his side, and they embraced as the crowd cheered and the music thumped.

"We are a crazy bunch," he said as he regained his composure. "This started out as a class assignment, but a crazy bunch of kids had a crazy idea, and here we are tonight! We represent all of America. We are young—where is Sandy Ligget?" He waited for the spotlight to find her. "Ten days ago, despite being nine months pregnant, Sandy was working the phones in the Manchester office. Five days ago she gave birth to Benjamin, who is at home with Grandma. Thank you, Sandy. We are young at heart. Where is Melba?"

Another cheer went up as the spotlight located her in the center of the room.

"Melba rode all the way here from Arizona to help us, and tonight she is celebrating her ninety-third birthday!" The whole room cheered and sang "Happy Birthday" to her.

"Hardship knows no boundaries. Tonight, there are families of every race, every geographic area, young and old, blue collar and white, worrying about tomorrow. Some have not eaten today and may not eat tomorrow. Many are cold and many, despite being surrounded by others who share their fate, feel utterly alone and without hope. Does anybody care?"

"We do!" the crowd shouted back.

"Yes, we do. And tonight our concerns were validated in a very tangible way. Tonight's vote was about change. Talking about change is nothing new. In fact, it's old and worn out. For too long, all there has been is *talk* about change. It's time for action."

The crowd interrupted for several seconds of applause.

"There's an American proverb that says, 'A mill cannot grind with water that has passed.' Our current leaders keep trying to run this mill called 'America' on water that has already passed, on ideas that have long since worn out their welçome and on funds long since spent. We have allowed ourselves to be lulled into a false sense of security by men who talk about the past, using phrases that are familiar to gain our trust, but offer no true answers for the future.

"It's time to think differently. It's time to grind with new water, water that runs red, white, and blue through every town, city, and county in this nation, where people still believe that our future lies over the horizon, not back down a worn-out rut.

"A few months ago, a wise man reminded me of the men and women who forged this nation. Sure there were famous statesmen, famous military and industrial leaders, but most of this great land of ours was explored and conquered by people like you and me. Sandy Liggets who loaded their families, newborns and all, into wagons and headed west for a chance at a better life. I'm sure there were many reasons not to go, and I'm sure lots of people told them so. 'You're too young. You're too old. You're not smart enough. What do you know about wagons, and trails, and…Who do you think you are? You're going to die out there.'

"Those old discouragers are still around today, and no, I'm not talking about Melba."

The crowd laughed.

"Melba is one of the good guys. What do we know about national economics and national debt? Who do we think we are?

"We are a new generation of pioneers who seek a chance for a better life, and not just for ourselves, but for all of our neighbors. We seek to find hope for tomorrow, and we are not finding it in the usual places, the usual answers from the usual suspects. It's time to load into a new wagon, and, despite the critics, it's time to head west into a new unknown, to power the mill with new water, water that flows from the headwaters of courage and character that made this nation great. We may fail, but our failure will not be fatal, just as any success will not be final. There will always be new horizons to look toward, new mountains to cross, and new issues to solve. For too long we have camped at the foot of the mountains facing this generation. The time has come to cross over. I, for one, intend to start climbing, and I invite you to join me. Thank you all very much! God bless you, and goodnight."

Say It Ain't So

"Punishment for disobedience: But if you will not listen to me and carry out all these commands, and if you reject my decrees and abhor my laws and fail to carry out all my commands and so violate my covenant, then I will do this to you: I will bring on you sudden terror, wasting diseases and fever that will destroy your sight and sap your strength. You will plant seed in vain, because your enemies will eat it. I will set my face against you so that you will be defeated by your enemies; those who hate you will rule over you, and you will flee even when no one is pursuing you. If after all this you will not listen to me, I will punish you for your sins seven times over. I will break down your stubborn pride and make the sky above you like iron and the ground beneath you like bronze...I will turn your cities into ruins and lay waste your sanctuaries, and I will take no delight in the pleasing aroma of your offerings...I will scatter you among the nations and will draw out my sword and pursue you. Your land will be laid waste, and your cities will lie in ruins. Then the land will enjoy its sabbath years all the time that it lies desolate and you are in the country of your enemies; then the land will rest and enjoy its sabbaths. All the time that it lies desolate, the land will have rest it did not have during the sabbaths you lived in it."

Leviticus 26:14–35 (TNIV)

"Hello?" Michael woke from a dead sleep to answer his cell phone.

"I'm sorry, Michael," a man's shaky voice warbled on the other end of the phone.

Michael looked at the clock in the hotel room. It was 4:17 a.m.

"Who is this?" he tried not to sound irritated; it was obvious the person on the other end of the phone was distraught. Allie sat up and scooted over next to Michael. He placed the phone so she could hear too.

"Are you still there?"

"Yes, I'm still here. Michael, I'm so sorry..."

"Who is this please?" Michael pressed a little more forcefully than the first time.

"It's Ed Farmer, Michael. I've done a horrible thing. I didn't mean to, but...they offered lots of money and then they threatened us. I just couldn't say no."

"It's okay, Ed. Slow down and just tell me what happened. Are you hurt?"

"I gotta go. They're gonna hear me. Michael, I think they might kill us. Please forgive me."

He was gone.

"What happened, Michael?" Allie looked at her husband in the dark.

"I don't know. It was Ed Farmer from our old church. Sounds like he's in trouble. He kept apologizing."

They sat in bed talking for a while, but they could not come up with any reason for Ed to call in the middle of the night. They had not spoken to him since Calvary had closed over eight years ago. Wide awake, they decided to go downstairs for some coffee. The coffee shop was not officially open, but one of the workers had arrived early and let them in when they knocked on the door.

"Give me a minute and I'll have some coffee for you. Congratulations. Yesterday was a big day for you." The middle-aged woman recognized Michael.

"Thank you very much, and thank you for letting us in. I guess you know my name. This is my wife, Allie." They sat down at one of the tables.

"Good to meet you. My name is Brenda."

"Have you worked here long?" Allie tried to make polite conversation.

"It's the only job I've ever had. My dad passed this place on to me when he retired. That was twenty-seven years ago next month."

She came around from the counter and sat two steaming cups of coffee on the table for them. She went back around the counter and flipped on the flat screen hanging in the corner.

"Let's see what's going on in the world. You kids want some breakfast?"

"That would be great." Allie looked at Michael and shrugged her shoulders. It was early, but who knew what the day had in store?

"Menus are on the table. Holler when you know what you want. Pancakes are my specialty."

"Sounds good," Michael called back without even opening the menu.

When the food was ready, Brenda brought out three plates piled full of pancakes and sausage and placed them on the table.

"Mind if I join you? I haven't had my breakfast yet." Brenda gabbed a blue streak while they sat and ate. She was up and down, keeping their cups full of coffee and waiting on the occasional odd customer that drifted in. Eventually, another worker arrived, and that made it easier for Brenda to tell her stories without interruption.

Michael and Allie had almost forgotten about the phone call when suddenly Allie noticed Michael was on TV. She got their attention, and Lena, the coffee clerk, turned up the sound.

"The facts are still kind of sketchy, Ted, but here is the video we shot last night."

The next shot was of Ed Farmer seated at his kitchen table by his wife, Nell.

"He was our pastor and we loved him. We never expected that he would do such a thing to our son." Ed began to break down with emotion.

"Our son, Brian, has Down's Syndrome," Nell picked up for Ed. "Michael used to take him out to the park once in a while so I could get some shopping or whatever done during the day. We didn't find out for a long time that Michael was abusing him."

"Physically?" The reporter looked incredulous.

Neither Ed nor Nell would look up, but eventually Ed answered, "Yes."

"It's going to be quite a scandal, Ted. Squeaky clean pastor/professor abuses boy from past."

"Oh, Michael." Allie put her hand on his shoulder. "We need to talk to Ed to see what's going on."

Michael pulled out his cell phone and scrolled through until he found the incoming calls menu. Ed's was the last call he had received. He pushed the send button and listened for an answer.

Ring... Ring... Ring...

"Hello."

"Ed, this is Michael. What happened?"

"I'm sorry, Michael. Some men came to our door a while back. They offered us lots of money to…to say stuff. Michael, Nell is sick, and the money…We took the money, but then we changed our minds. We tried to give it back, but…they're still here. Tell me what to do, Michael. I don't know what to do?"

"It's okay, Ed. We'll figure something out."

The phone clicked and Ed was gone again.

"Gee, Doc, I didn't know you were a sleaze." Brenda said as she cleared her plate from the table.

"I'm not. This is dirty politics."

"Michael, we have to deny this."

"It's not that simple, Allie. Ed and Nell are in trouble."

Michael was in shock. After tossing thoughts around in his mind for a few minutes, he found no solutions. A world that wanted to crown him yesterday would be ready to stone him today.

"Who's mad at you, Doc?" Brenda at least seemed to believe him.

"Downs," he seethed as he began to think a little clearer. "Or, actually, Sydney Porter, but it's Downs' muscle. We need to wake the kids. We need to put a statement together before the press comes calling. I can't believe they're not here already."

"Actually, they are." Allie pointed out to the hotel lobby.

Brenda followed Michael and Allie as they made their way to the lobby. There were four reporters with cameramen ready and waiting. The lights were bright and the questions were sharp. Michael was hesitant to defend himself against the lies for fear he would cause harm to Ed and Nell. His hesitation only intensified the feeding frenzy.

"We will have a statement for you later this morning," he said, and with that he and Allie made their way back to their room.

They called the kids in for a meeting. In the meantime, Allie called home to make sure Ian, Lana, and Mark were not in harm's way.

Michael explained the situation to the students and told them they were free to go if they had any doubts. No one doubted, and no one wanted to leave. From there they moved to a discussion on how to respond.

There was more bad news. Robert was on-line looking at the bank accounts.

"We are not out of money, but we don't have enough to pay for airtime and provide transportation for all of the volunteers to get home. I knew we shouldn't be spending all that money on the volunteers," Robert fumed in frustration.

"What were we supposed to do? Let them starve?" Danielle shot back.

Things were starting to unravel quickly. They had all pushed themselves to the point of exhaustion, and the fatigue was showing. They had been to the mountaintop hours earlier, and now they were falling off a cliff.

"It will be okay, guys. We need to make a statement this morning, so let's think about what we want to say." Shelly was no longer just playing the part of a leader, but modeled the resolute confidence of a seasoned captain leading troops through the darkest hours of intense battle. With her direction to be intentional, she shifted the focus from self-pity to perseverance and possibility.

Half an hour had passed when there was a knock on the door. It was one of the campaign volunteers.

"Sir, everyone is gathered in the ballroom. I think they would like to hear from you. Is it true, sir?"

"No. No, it's not true. Please tell everyone that I will be down in just a few minutes."

The man nodded, and Michael thanked him as he turned to leave.

The team had been unsuccessful in drafting a statement. Michael was torn between the campaign, which represented many people, versus Ed and Nell.

"Let's go," he said as he gathered the group. "We need to speak to the people downstairs."

The ballroom was packed, but the mood was much more somber than it had been last night. They all watched in silence as Michael made his way to the front of the room. The large sound system was gone, but someone had provided a microphone that was plugged into the house system. Michael checked to make sure it was on and began to address the group.

"The people you saw on the news this morning are Ed and Nell Farmer. They were members of a church we used to pastor. The words you heard were coerced with money and threats. Our adversaries were not happy with the results yesterday, and they wasted no time in getting even. I would like to invite the members of the press in the back of the room to come forward and ask your questions. This will serve as our press conference."

As the press made their way through the people, Michael began to address the main issues of the accusation.

"I did spend time with the Farmers' son, Brian, just as Nell described. I did so to give Nell a break once in a while. I did not ever, under any circumstances or in any way, abuse Brian. The facts being what they may, however, we do not currently have enough funds to battle this out in the media. It is the intention of the campaign team and myself to leave here in about an hour. We will board our bus and head for Missouri with the hope of campaigning for a few days before Mini-Tuesday. You are welcome to come with us. Please know that whatever you choose to do, we will make arrangements for your transportation. Robert and Larry will remain here in the ballroom to assist you until we are ready to leave."

He took questions from the media for about fifteen minutes. The questions were not extremely mean-spirited, but it was obvious the press did not believe Michael. The group of volunteers seemed to be split, and only a small portion remained in the ballroom. While Allie and several of the students went back to their rooms to check out, Michael stayed in the ballroom with the volunteers. He went from group to group and answered any questions that were asked. He was actually more concerned with the questions that were not being asked, but he was thankful that at least some of the people stayed. True to his word, after about an hour a caravan of seven buses pulled out of Manchester and headed for St. Louis.

It was a long drive to Missouri, but everyone was thankful for the time away from the press. It was an ugly scene across the airwaves, and by the time they reached St. Louis, very few people wanted to support the Hamilton campaign. On February third—Mini-Tuesday—elections took place in Missouri, South Carolina, Arizona, Oklahoma, and Delaware. The Arizona team had gone on home to do what they could, but despite the efforts of the remaining faithful, Michael received less than ten percent of the vote in each of the states. Super Tuesday came a few weeks later with many more states going to the polls, each yielding similar or worse results.

The grand experiment seemed all but over when the students, Michael, and Allie rolled back into Hill City in early April. It was a busy time for the students, as many of them had taken on-line classes while campaigning. There were papers, projects, and finals to complete. The team decided to take a three-week break while they finished their class work, and a meeting was set for April twenty-eighth at The Hollow. As Michael sat on his front porch looking out across the campus for the first time in months, he decided to call Ed and Nell.

Ring...Ring...Ring...Ring...Ring...

A young boy riding by on his bike called out to Michael, "Say it ain't so!"

Martha's Stone

Michael and Allie spent the next few weeks making up time with their kids. Evenings were filled with Mark's little league and Lana's high school softball games. Each of the next few weekends were spent camping, hiking, and biking. Ian had a part-time job and missed some of the action, but he did his best to be there when he could.

The bitterness of politics began to fade with the return to the Hamilton way of life, but the thoughts of real people suffering were not diminished. Despite all the distractions, Michael could not stop thinking of all the faces he had seen while campaigning. He had been to fourteen Marshallvilles and looked into the faces of so many who were hurting. Night after night he awoke with the voices of children crying, gunshots blasting, and angry voices screaming in the midst of riots, all ringing in his head. He stopped watching the news; he couldn't stand the pictures.

For weeks he spent hours thinking in his office, until late one night he decided to go for a walk. It was a cool night for spring, so he threw on a hat and jacket and headed across the campus grounds. He walked past the chapel, and he thought of Henry. He wished his friend were walking beside him right now. He walked past the garden where he and Allie had shared their "presidential" dance after the first town hall meeting. He sat down on the bench they had shared that night and stared at the 9/11 memorial. He was too restless to sit for long, so soon he was moving again. He walked past several of the dorms, eventually cutting through a few yards; he found himself on Elm Street, just a couple blocks from Valhalla.

I wonder if Henry's friends have any advice for me, he thought to himself as he walked toward the cemetery.

Valhalla was pretty well lit, at least well enough for Michael to read some of the headstones at night. He visited the sites of Joe Stanton and Grace Johnson for a while, eventually making his way down to the concrete bench by Martha McKinney's headstone.

"Do you have any words of wisdom for me, Martha?" He reached in his pocket for his cell phone to check the time. When he pulled the phone out, a dollar bill fell out and floated down to Martha's stone. *In God We Trust.* Michael forgot about the time as he sat there staring at the one-dollar bill. *The United States of America…In God We Trust…*

As he looked at the dollar lying on the stone, a whispering spring breeze blew in and swept the bill away. Michael, still taken by the words, did not make a move to retrieve it, and soon it was gone. The breeze picked up a little and rustled some paper that was tucked into a potted lily by Martha's stone. Michael picked up the paper and unfolded it.

For the Lord gives wisdom, and from his mouth come knowledge and understanding. He holds victory in store for the upright, He is a shield for those whose walk is blameless, For he guards the course of the just and protects the way of his faithful ones. Then you will understand what is right and just and fair—every good path, For wisdom will enter your heart, and knowledge will be pleasant to your soul. Discretion will protect you, and understanding will guard you. Wisdom will save you from the ways of wicked men, from men whose words are perverse, who leave the straight paths to walk in dark ways, who delight in doing wrong and rejoice in the perverseness of evil, whose paths are crooked and who are devious in their ways... Thus you will walk in the ways of good men and keep to the paths of the righteous. For the upright will live in the land, and the blameless will remain in it; But the wicked will be cut off from the land and the unfaithful will be thrown from it.

Proverbs 2

Michael:

"Trust in the Lord with all your heart and lean not on your own understanding.

In all you ways acknowledge him, And he will make your paths straight."

Proverbs 3:5

Henry

The breeze that had been picking up as Michael was reading came in a gust and blew his hat off.

Oh great! It's going to... rain... He caught himself in mid-thought, and with one more gust, the breeze seemed to curl through the trees and be gone in the same whisper with which it had arrived... Another heavenly visit?

Michael pulled a dollar out of his pocket. *In God We Trust.* He folded the bill up in Henry's note and buried it just to the side of Martha's stone.

"Thank you, Martha."

Holiday Road

April twenty-eighth finally came, and it was time to rally the troops at The Hollow. It was nice to have some time apart after all the hours on the bus, but now everyone was looking forward to the meeting. There were hugs and smiles all around. Everyone gorged themselves on pizza, soda, and stories.

"Remember when we…"

"How about…"

"Can you believe…?"

The campaign may have been over, but the memories would last forever.

When everyone was sufficiently stuffed with food and memories, Michael took the floor. After spending several minutes acknowledging each student for their specific contributions to the campaign, he pulled a piece of paper from his pocket.

"I received this letter a few days ago, and I would like to share it with you." He found a comfortable spot on the arm of a chair and sat down in much the same position he always took on the edge of his desk in class.

Dear Dr. Hamilton:

It is with a heavy heart that I write to you this day regarding our nation, which is ravaged by debt and despair. For too long we have failed to recognize our impending demise wrought at our own hands. The stench of our greed has reached to the heavens, and history may well record our deeds with unfavorable ink.

We have sailed through our history with an unabashed arrogance, much like the fated Titanic, free from the fetters of doubt or pessimism. Though cruising through ice-infested waters, we throttle full and curse the wind in our face. Invincible! We howl at history's moon over the northern sea. The bump, hardly felt, easily ignored, is slowly taking its toll. Our economy, like the majestic ship, glides to a graceful pause, and there in the chill of the night sits idle and calm and still. No panic was observed that night on the sea, no urgent response...With the lifeboats half full, the unsinkable sinks into the abyss...into history...

I do not wish to repeat the mistakes of that fateful April eve. I would like to recognize our precarious state and move to action before the berg and not after. Sir, I am reaching across party lines to you and am asking for your help. I do not understand Jubilee, but we need answers. I am asking you to bring all of your thoughts and wisdom to bear on the solving of our dilemma. I pledge my support to you, sir.

Sincerely,
Douglas T. Marshall
President, United States of America

Folding the letter, Michael returned it to his pocket and surveyed the students' faces.

"I do not honestly know where we stand in the campaign. It

would seem to be a ship that has sailed without us. There does, however, seem to be a very important mission at hand. I have an idea, but first I would like to share a little history with you. Imagine that, history from me!

"In many ways, history records Herbert Hoover with 'unfavorable ink,' and we have certainly studied his flaws this year. Should he have done more to prevent the Great Depression? You can draw your own conclusions, but take a look at another side of the thirty-first president, a very caring and giving side.

"A well-to-do man by the age of forty, he began to look for things to fill his time. In 1914, he helped over one hundred thousand American tourists return home from war-ravaged Europe. In the same year, he began to assist Belgium as they faced a food crisis after Germany invaded by serving as the head of the Commission for the Relief of Belgium. The Commission had its own flag, navy, factories, mills, and railroads, and ran on a monthly budget of eleven million that was supplied by private donations and government grants. Hoover's actions gave me an idea.

"I responded to President Marshall's letter this morning, and I asked him to secure federal funds for us. In return, I pledged to devise a relief plan for the millions of people living in the Marshallvilles. I also met with Robert and Larry yesterday and asked them to look at ways our Web site could be used to mobilize volunteers across the nation. We need food and clothing, transportation and delivery systems, as well as distribution centers. We also need volunteers to run these programs, and we need a team of people to manage this process.

"Most of you have come to the end of your senior year and are set to graduate in a couple weeks. A new life awaits you, and I would not ask any of you to put that life on hold, but I intend to do all that I can to respond to the president's request, and I would be honored if you would join me. We have enough funds left from the campaign to get started, and I am very hopeful that the president will make good on his offer. I have also been in contact with Ben, and he, along with Hawk, whom you all met in New Hampshire, is already mobilizing their resources out west. You have all gone far above and beyond, and I am proud of each of you."

All but a couple of the students agreed to stay on. Lenny had a job opportunity in California, so Michael thanked him and asked him to stay in touch. Ginny had been accepted into law school. There were tears and hugs as she made her announcement. She told the group that the campaign and its national attention had made all the difference for her acceptance by the school.

Over the next few weeks, after bidding farewell to Lenny and Ginny, the group busied themselves with their new task. It was tough going, especially when funds did not arrive from Washington. Apparently, the president was having more difficulty than he had anticipated. Downs did indeed have long arms, and his political machine was stifling the relief efforts at every turn. The group was also facing continuing issues with bad press and national fallout over the Farmer controversy started by Downs. It was becoming more evident that this was a road they may have to go alone and a task that would not be accomplished by sitting in Hill City.

By mid-May, some federal funding began to arrive. Michael decided to go back out on the road to evaluate the situation around the nation for himself, seeing firsthand just where their relief efforts could be most effective. Ben and Hawk were having some success out west, so Michael decided to head southeast. Several on the team were assigned to various cities around the nation to help coordinate relief efforts from distribution centers they had successfully secured. Shelly was assigned to Houston and Danielle to Chicago, while Sarah was assigned to Denver, where she harbored some hope of seeing Ben. Plane tickets were purchased and distributed, and the team spread out across the country.

Michael decided to travel by bus, and an over-the-road coach was chartered. He planned to travel alone, as the rest of the team was needed in Hill City to coordinate the national efforts. On May seventeenth, a beautiful Silver Eagle pulled up in front of the Hamilton home. With bags packed and loaded onto the bus, Michael hugged each of the kids and Allie and kissed them good-bye.

Mark was the last one standing in the farewell line. Michael bent down to say good-bye when Mark hugged him tight around the neck. Michael stood up with him.

"Oh, I'm getting old." His back creaked and he felt the weight of his growing son. "You're growing up on me, son."

Mark just kept hugging his dad's neck and finally began to whisper in his ear, "Thank you, Dad."

Michael felt little tears moisten his neck. He started to move Mark back so he could see his face, but Mark held on tight.

"Thank you for what, son?"

"For baseball, and chess, and camping, and family movie nights, and..." He finally lifted his head up and looked Michael in the eye. "I'm gonna miss you, Dad." He placed a little metal car in Michael's hand. Mark was a collector of "little things"—little cars, plastic animals, and characters. They had become his trademark.

"Thank you, Mark. I love you, buddy." Michael hugged him tight and then climbed up onto the bus. He stood in the stairwell waving to his family as the bus pulled away.

As he turned to make his way to a seat, he realized the bus driver was the same one who had driven him cross-country as they returned from the New Hampshire primary.

"Hey, Jim," he said as he shook his hand.

"Good morning, sir. We have a few stops to make before we get on the road."

"Okay." Michael made his way to a seat. The bus had a kitchen and living area in the middle, a bathroom on one side, and a bedroom at the very back. The kitchen and living area made into several beds. This would be home on the road for the next month or so. Michael was still looking at the little car in his hand and thinking about Mark's words when the bus slowed and came to a stop in front of a familiar house. Standing at the curb with his bags was Henry.

"Excuse me, sir." Jim opened the door and moved out to help Henry with his bags.

"Where do you think you are going, old man?" Michael shouted out to Henry through the open door.

Henry climbed up onto the bus and gave Michael a big hug.

"I'm going wherever you go, son."

Soon the bus was rolling again, but now Michael was paying a little more attention. Jim and Henry looked like cats that had just swallowed canaries.

"Come on, guys, what's up? Where are we going now?"

Henry and Jim just smiled at each other as the bus rolled down the road, eventually stopping in front of a small ranch-style house just off the southwest corner of the campus. Again, there at the curb stood another man with his bags. It was Dr. Nick. Michael was speechless.

"Good morning, Nick," Henry welcomed him onto the bus. Before Michael knew what to think, the bus was rolling again. Dr. Nick took his seat beside Henry, and they both just smiled at each, other exchanging small talk. Michael was fixated on the road.

"Are there more surprises?" He received no responses. The bus turned on College Drive and made its way across campus. There were a few students milling about, but most of the activity surrounded the landscape where the groundskeepers were hard at work, as usual.

"One more stop," Jim called over his shoulder with a wry smile as he pulled up in front of the presidential mansion. This time two men were waiting with their bags, President McPherson and Dr. Harry Terry.

"Peter and Harry?" Michael scratched his head.

"We're going with you, Michael." Peter reached out to shake his hand. "I'm not sure if we all understand Jubilee, but we understand the seriousness of the times in which we live. We would like to share your journey and provide any support you may need. We know you have dealt with many unfair and untrue allegations over the past few months, and we thought our solidarity and vote of confidence may bode well in the public eye."

"Oh, knock it off, Peter, and sit down," Henry howled at his former boss.

Michael welcomed them, and deep inside he was thankful for their company. This would be a tough trip with some very unpleasant circumstances to confront. The press, especially those controlled by Downs, would be brutal, and the living conditions of those they would try to help had been deteriorating for months. The television broadcasts were horrific. As they pulled off the campus and headed for the interstate, Michael knew it would be no holiday road.

Hamiltonia

It took a little over a week to get everyone acclimated to life on the road—and life on the road did not mean life on the interstate. In fact, they were usually far from it. They traveled the unbeaten paths of America and took a look at what was really going on. They spent several days weaving their way across Illinois and Missouri, visiting farms and small factories, talking to people on the streets of the many small towns that dotted their path.

Little by little, word began to spread about the mission of mercy as they made arrangements wherever they could for aid to reach people in need. Small-town newspapers and radio stations began to question this man Hamilton and the stories they had heard from the smear campaign leveled by Downs. How could he be guilty of the terrible accusations? His band of merry comrades were proving to be very useful, as they did all they could to reinforce the truth about Michael and dispel the lies that had been perpetrated upon him.

Along with a growing momentum, they also began to develop a plan for each town. Efforts were coordinated with the home office in Iowa, and agendas were established days in advance of the arrival of "Hamilton's Raiders," as the press began to call them. Dr. Nick met with senior citizens in retirement homes and with various veterans' groups. Henry held meetings with the church communities, Peter with the education communities, while Harry, God bless him, did a great job communicating with women's groups...who would've know? Michael spent his time meeting with the politicians and continued to evaluate relief efforts with the local volunteers and distribution centers.

The president kept his word, and federal funds flowed to Hill City for distribution through the Hamilton network, which came to be known as the Manna Network.

Besides the distribution of food and clothing, Larry also worked out a deal with several major pharmaceutical companies for the distribution of medicine, especially to the areas that were hardest hit by communicable diseases.

Despite all of these efforts, however, the nation continued to stagger, slipping into a full-blown recession and closer and closer to all-out depression. Martial law had been declared in several of the Marshallvilles around New York and Los Angeles, along with Chicago, as the nation teetered on the brink of disaster.

Back on the national campaign trail, Downs was pulling away from Lawrence, as Senator Lawrence had abandoned his safe business-as-usual message, but failed to find a new one to take its place. While the vast majority of people knew that change was needed, they were afraid of the unknown. Downs had the name and the political machine. He controlled newspapers from coast-to-coast and had most of the television media eating from his table. Even though Downs seemed to be an unstoppable force, he was still well aware of the Hamilton presence. Michael's name came up on a daily basis in the Downs' war room, and soon several cronies were assigned to follow Hamilton's Raiders. These were not "men of the cloth" by any stretch of the imagination, and were they allowed to have their way, the Hamilton bus tour would have been canceled due to unforeseen tragedy on the highway. Michael was messing with power, and it would be very easy to get burned.

The bus rolled out of the Ozarks on a charted path that would take them through Arkansas, Mississippi, Alabama, and eventually, Atlanta, Georgia. The bus was equipped with a flat-screen TV hooked to a satellite that was usually on, but seldom watched. Time spent on the bus was usually passed by telling stories. Dr. Nick was everyone's favorite, but Harry had actually surprised them with a few of his tales. Peter dished a little dirt on trustees and donors, while Henry reminisced about pastoring in small towns during the early years of his marriage to Grace. Michael and Jim shared stories from the campaign trail in Iowa and New Hampshire.

Michael also spent countless hours on the phone with the team in Iowa and Ben out west, not to mention Allie and the kids. Allie flew into Mississippi and spent a few days with the guys.

"Thanks, but no thanks," she said, and she left for the airport to fly back home. This was a guys' trip, and the bus was a bit cramped with a lady on board. Somewhere between Pascagoula, Mississippi, and Mobile, Alabama, Michael's phone rang, and the voice he heard was both welcomed and unexpected.

"Michael, it's Ed." He was frantic.

"Ed, where are you? Are you okay?"

"We're in Tennessee with some of Nell's family, but I think they've found us. I don't know what to do, Michael."

"Let me think, Ed. We thought you were dead." Michael's mind was reeling, and he could not make himself focus on a solution. It was Henry who finally came up with an idea.

"Ed, do you think you could get to Atlanta?"

Ed agreed to try and a timetable was established. Henry laid out his idea around the table as Jim throttled down for Atlanta. After several planned stops along the way, the Silver Eagle streaked into

Atlanta on July second. Part of Henry's plan counted on the reports they had been hearing for several days, that Downs would be in Atlanta for the Independence Day celebration. The plan was far from foolproof, but if it worked, it could restore Michael's reputation and provide safety for the Farmers with one simple act. Actually, with one incredibly difficult to coordinate, perfectly timed act that would involve several unwilling, hopefully unsuspecting partners.

Step one was to bait the trap. Michael scheduled several public appearances that would take him right across the Downs' path. Baiting the trap worked to perfection as their paths crossed at Centennial Olympic Park just across from the World Network News (WNN) Building. With cameras rolling, the senator caught sight of Michael.

"Ah, the good professor," he noted to the press and then called to Michael. "Where have you been, Professor? We haven't seen you in a while."

Michael, followed by his band of Raiders, walked over to the senator. Without answering Downs' question, Michael replied, "I hear things have been going well for you."

His vanity primed, Downs responded, "Why, yes they are, as a matter of fact, but you did not answer my question. Why did you disappear from the campaign? Don't you think that was a bit rude? Where did you go?"

"I went in search of answers."

"Answers to what?" Downs laughed out loud.

"Answers to the questions you have created. Questions like 'why doesn't my government care about its people?'"

"And have you found any answers?"

"Yes, sir, I have."

"Well, tell us, man. What are they?"

"Do you really want to know," Michael prodded, "or are you just pandering to the cameras?"

Hook...

"You, sir, are an arrogant little fly, and you had better beware the flyswatter."

Line...

"So you are really interested in my thoughts, thoughts I have gathered from those whom you would presume to serve?"

"Why, I most certainly am. What did you have in mind?"

"One-on-one, you and me, *Tom Allen Show* tonight."

"Tom Allen wants to talk to you?" Downs smirked.

"I'll bet he'd like to talk to *us,* or is that too much for you to arrange?"

"Tonight, primetime, seven p.m. sharp!" Downs snapped back.

And sinker...

The spat between Michael and Downs filled the airwaves for the rest of the afternoon and garnered its share of space on the evening network news. The plan was working beautifully, with one small exception: They had not heard from the Farmers since the original conversation. They had called the cell phone several times, but there was no answer. Michael did, however, receive a phone call from Sydney Porter with the arrangements for the talk show.

The Tom Allen Show aired live from the WNN Building.

Sydney gave Michael directions to the reception area and told him, "Be there at six p.m. sharp for preparations." Sydney had always been condescending to Michael, but where there was once the pretense of civility, there was now open hostility.

"Where are they, Michael? It's after five o'clock," Harry whined as the guys waited for the Farmers at the rendezvous in Centennial Olympic Park. Michael tried to reach them on the cell several more times, but there was no answer. Without the Farmers, Michael would be a sitting duck for Downs, but he remained the picture of calm as he sat on a bench watching the fountains in the park.

"It will be okay, Harry. Have a little faith." Henry kept a close eye on Michael.

By five forty-five, they still had not heard from the Farmers, but it was time to go up to the reception area. It was decided that Peter and Harry would remain behind to wait for Ed and Nell, while Michael, Henry, and Dr. Nick would go on ahead. They worked out a signal to let Michael know the Farmers had arrived: One ring, or buzz, as Michael had his phone on vibrate, would signal that the Farmers were in position.

"Any final thoughts?" Michael queried the group before they separated.

"I have seen many bad things in my life," Dr. Nick touched Michael's arm and spoke in his small, calm voice that filled the moment with humility as only Dr. Nick could. "I believe I will see something good here tonight."

Sometimes words don't have to be profound to be perfect. Michael took them to heart, and they helped him maintain his calm façade; a façade he would need to face-off against Downs. He was heading into the ring with a tiger, and the beast was hungry for his soul.

As they entered the WNN Building, it was obvious they were on Downs' turf. Everyone was cordial, but it felt like they were being led to the gallows more than the green room. Michael had anticipated receiving some basic instructions for the evening, but none were forthcoming. He also kept checking his phone to make sure it was still working, but despite seeing all the signs that it was on, he received no call.

Six…

Six fifteen…

Six thirty-two…

Six forty-seven…

"Five minutes, gentlemen," came a voice through the door.

Besides the fact that Michael knew Downs wanted a shot at his throat, he wondered if anyone would actually come to get them at seven. There was obviously a great deal of gamesmanship going on. Michael had led a charmed life before the cameras to this point, and he hoped his luck would hold out for at least one more night. Finally, at 6:57, the door opened, and a man who looked a lot like one of Downs' henchmen that had been dogging them over the last few weeks scowled at them.

"Follow me."

They did as they were told, and when they reached the studio door, the man of many words added, "Wait here." He went into the studio for a second and then returned. He motioned to Michael, "Just you."

As Michael entered the studio, Downs and Allen were waiting for him. Tom Allen stuck out his hand to shake Michael's and welcomed him to the show.

"Have a seat, Professor…Dr. Hamilton," he stumbled, leaving no doubt as to the bias of the evening.

"Thank you." Michael took his seat beside Downs. "Senator."

Michael felt the heat of the studio lights, but they were only part of the heat he was feeling: no phone call, no Farmers. This could be a very interesting evening. Before he knew it, they were live on the air.

"Good evening, America, and welcome to the *Tom Allen Show.* With us tonight are Senator Monroe Downs and Dr. Michael Hamilton. As a lead-in for tonight, I would like to play some video of the past several months."

With that he nodded to the control room and pointed to a monitor where those in the studio could watch the video that was airing. There were clips from the first town hall meeting in Hill City, the debate in Des Moines, and several other moments throughout the campaign—including clips of the Farmers.

Where are they? Michael wondered. *These guys are good,* Michael thought, as all of the clips had been edited to show Downs in a good light despite the flow of the actual events. The clips also included footage from the campaign trail after Michael had dropped out and concluded with the afternoon interaction in the park.

When the video was done, Tom Allen addressed Downs and Michael.

"Well, it would appear that you two have not become best buddies, but I suppose that is the nature of politics these days. Dr. Hamilton, let me speak to you first. You had a great showing in Iowa and New Hampshire, riding a Robin Hood-esque wave of 'take from the rich, give to the poor' economic plan, and then you seemed to drop off the face of the earth. Several weeks ago, you show up again on a tour-de-force bus trip, sweeping across the heartland with your band of merry men donning the cultish title of 'Hamilton's Raiders.' Tell me, sir, where will this mysterious road lead you next?"

Just as he opened his mouth to respond, his phone vibrated in its clip on his belt. He quickly reached for it and pushed the button to stop the vibration.

"Message from the men," Downs chided with a smirk.

"As a matter of fact." Michael hoped there were no beads of sweat showing as he gathered himself. "Interesting video, Tom. I'll bet your crew wins a lot of awards for editing. I'm not sure how to respond to the 'Robin Hood' or 'Hamilton's Raiders' titles. As to my knowledge, the only title or label we have given ourselves is Manna Network, through which we are distributing resources to those in need across the nation. Yes, I did disappear. Like so many in our nation, I thought I was finished. We started out on a mission, and we failed. But while the success we achieved was not final, we soon learned that our failure was not fatal. A wise man reminded me—"

"Please, Professor," Downs interrupted, "spare us the wisdom and the sermon. You said you had answers this afternoon. Let's hear them. But before you answer, let's talk about credibility. No one wants to hear the ravings of a mad economist, the sermon from a pastor whose pulpit is empty, a molester of children, for God's sake!"

"Senator, I do have answers for you tonight, but first I would like to ask you a question. Do you know where Ed and Nell Farmer are tonight?"

"At home?" Downs looked at Allen sarcastically.

"Well, I think you would know that is the one place they cannot be. They have not been there since you aired the story concerning their son. You and I both know the story of molestation is untrue, and tonight the Farmers are here to tell the nation the true story. Shall we invite them into the studio?" Michael looked at Tom Allen.

Allen and Downs both shifted in their seats, unsure of the next move.

"I don't think that's what we're here for tonight, but let's take a break and we'll sort it out when we come back." Tom Allen peered at the producer. As soon as the cameras were off, he and Downs stepped into the control room. Michael looked at his phone and realized he had a text message:

Downs' men took the Farmers. Police called. Need to hurry.

Michael stood up and left the studio. Henry and Nick were still waiting outside the door.

Henry filled Michael in as they made their way down the hall for the elevators. The Farmers had met Peter and Harry at the park, but when they entered the WNN Building, Downs' men identified and grabbed them. The public location was probably the only thing that saved Peter's and Harry's lives. Harry had managed to follow the men long enough to see them get into a "foreign" car, as he described it, with Georgia license plate number "TLZ 42 something." For their efforts, Peter had a broken rib and Harry had a black eye.

When the police arrived, one officer took Peter to a hospital for medical attention while Michael and the other three men were harshly escorted to the local precinct for questioning. They were each placed in separate rooms and held there for what seemed like hours. Actually, two hours passed before a Lieutenant Malone came into Michael's room.

"I have good news and bad news. First, you and your friends are free to go. Second, we have located the Farmers. Apparently, the men who abducted them crashed their car out on Highway 40. The Farmers are not in great shape, but they will make it. They've been taken to the same hospital as your friend. If you would like, I can have someone drive you over there."

"Thank you. That would be great." Michael stood, hoping to leave immediately.

They arrived at the hospital around ten forty-five and met Peter in the lobby.

"I saw the Farmers come in." Peter moved a little slowly. "It didn't look very good."

Security was tight in the hospital, and they were unable to get any information from the front desk, so they decided to go down to the cafeteria for some coffee while they discussed their next move. Things were getting more dangerous. Tonight had been a near miss, and Michael was apprehensive about continuing the trip. Sitting in the cafeteria drinking coffee, they watched the news on WNN. Michael expected to see himself massacred on the *Tom Allen Show,* but surprisingly there was no mention of him at all. An hour had passed when a nurse came to the table and told Michael that Ed Farmer was asking for him. She led them to the IC unit, where Michael was allowed to visit with Ed for a few minutes.

"I'm sorry for everything, Michael. We've made such a mess for you. Stupid, so stupid, how could we do this to you?"

"It's okay, Ed." Michael tried to keep Ed calm. "How is Nell doing?"

"She has a broken collar bone, and she banged her head pretty good. They think she has a concussion. Nothing life threatening, but they have her pretty doped up for the pain."

"And what about you?" Michael surveyed the numerous bandages and machines that covered Ed's body and filled his room.

"I don't know. I think I'm good."

A smile came to Michael's face over Ed's obvious denial. Ed seemed more concerned about Michael than his health. Truth be known, Ed had not always been Michael's friend. In fact, he had usually been a thorn in Michael's side back at Calvary, blaming him for the financial troubles of the church.

"I'm sorry, sir, but you'll need to let him rest now." A nurse stuck her head into the small room.

"I'll be right outside if you need anything, Ed. Is there anyone I should call?"

"We've already called his family," the nurse told Michael, and Ed nodded in agreement.

When Michael rejoined his friends, it was decided that he would stay in Atlanta with the Farmers until family arrived, and everyone else would go back to Iowa in the morning.

Michael spent the next day at the hospital. Nell was well enough to visit Ed's room, and the three of them spent several hours healing old wounds. Ed's leg had been crushed in the accident, and it would leave him with a limp and a large scar for the rest of his life. The scars that had marred his soul over the past eight years, however, were healed before Michael left.

Michael left the hospital the following day with plans to keep an appointment he had made weeks earlier. His cell phone was not receiving service inside the hospital, so he walked outside to call a cab. When he looked at his phone, he noticed a missed call and message waiting.

Maybe the message is from Allie, he thought, as she had not answered the phone last night or this morning. He always called her at nine o'clock every night, and sometimes at noon. Missing her voice last night reminded him of just how long he had been gone. The message, however, was from Jim telling him that he was in the parking lot with the bus. Michael thought Jim had taken the other men back to Iowa, so he was puzzled by the development.

The past two days at the hospital had been exhausting, so he was half in a daze as he walked out to the main parking lot in search of Jim. He was alert enough, however, for two men sitting in a white van just outside the main entrance of the hospital to catch his eye. Maybe he was just tired or overly paranoid after the events of the last few days, but it sure seemed like they were watching him. Just as he walked passed them, he caught sight of the bus in the parking lot, and that was enough to divert his attention.

Let's solve one mystery at a time, he thought.

When he got to the bus, the door was open. Climbing onboard, he looked at Jim.

"What are you doing her—"

"Surprise!" the entire Hamilton clan screamed from the middle of the bus and then mobbed him.

"Hey, what are you guys doing here?" Michael had a big smile on his face and kids hanging off each arm.

"Family vacation." Ian peeled Mark off Michael's arm.

"We missed you, Dad." Lana still hung over his shoulder.

"Larry worked it out for the guys to fly home and for us to fly here. Jim waited for us at the airport, and voilà," Allie cleared up the mystery.

Before Michael knew it, they were rolling down the road, immersed in conversation and sub sandwiches. They had spoken by phone almost every night, but it just wasn't the same. In typical Hamilton fashion, one sentence was barely complete when another one began. At times there were three stories going at a time. Jim admired the grand family in the mirror as he drove.

After several hours on the road, Jim headed off the highway and began a trek that took them somewhat over the river, through the woods, and well off the beaten path. As the conversation diverted to the road that was tossing them to and fro, the kids began to inquire about their destination.

"It's somewhat of a 'Robin Hood-esque' adventure." Michael smiled to himself as he recalled Tom Allen's comments from the WNN studio. Topping a large hill, they looked down on a large lake surrounded by forest on all sides. Through the trees, they could see what looked like a huge camp full of campers, tents, cars, and a few wooden shacks. The camp seemed to spread out through the woods as far as they could see. It was impossible to tell how many people were there.

"Look, Dad, it's a Manna truck." Mark pointed to a large truck on the road just ahead.

For months the kids had heard stories of the food and supplies that were being distributed across the country, but this would be a firsthand, up-close-and-personal look at the destination of those supplies. Michael had been communicating with a man living in the camp and was anxious to meet him because of the extraordinary stories he had heard.

The bus pulled up behind the Manna truck, and Michael got out and talked to the driver. A few minutes later he came back to the bus door and called for everyone to come with him. They were each given an armful of "stuff" from the truck to carry. Mark was mortified because he was given a case of toilet paper to tote.

"Gee, thanks," he said as he rolled his eyes at the man handing the supplies down from the truck.

He fell in with the rest of the long line of people who were helping to unload the supplies and followed them down a short path to a large metal building where they were met with other workers who told them where to stack their particular items. Mark was glad to see that he was not the only toilet paper toter in the group, as another girl about his age stood just ahead of him waiting to hand her case to the lady worker.

"Hi." She grinned at him through her braces. "Are you new here?"

"Well, I—"

"I can show you around. I know all the trails. Would you like to see some?" She grabbed him by the hand and gave a good pull.

Mark looked at Allie, who just smiled. "Have fun. Don't be gone too long."

"Thanks, Mom," Mark muttered sarcastically under his breath. "Toilet paper and now girls."

Ian and Michael dropped off their box of supplies and were now talking with one of the men who looked like he was in charge.

"Can you tell us where to find a man named Johnny Duncan?"

"Sure," the man chuckled. "In the office," he said, pointing inside the large metal building to a wooden ladder that led up to the office.

Allie and Lana were already talking with several ladies when Michael motioned toward the ladder and told them he and Ian were going up to the office.

They made their way over to the ladder and climbed up to the office. It was an open-air office on top of what amounted to a building within the large metal warehouse. The building below used to be office space, but had been converted into cold storage for food. There was a railing to keep people from falling off, but other than that there were no walls.

"Hello!" Michael called out to the people working in the office. "We're looking for Johnny Duncan?"

"That would be me," a pretty lady clad in a sleeveless flannel shirt and jeans said as she walked over to Ian and Michael.

That would be Jonnie, Michael said to himself. *That would explain the chuckle from the man down below.*

"Hi." Michael extended his hand to her. "I am Michael Hamilton, and this is my son Ian."

"Hi, Michael, Ian, we've been expecting you. I talked to Larry yesterday and he told us to watch for you. Did you have any trouble finding us?"

"No trouble," Ian was taken by the pretty lady, "just a bit bumpy."

"Are you hungry?"

"No, thank you." Michael peered at his son gazing at Jonnie. "We ate on the way. This is quite an operation you have here."

"Thank you. Would you like a tour?" She motioned toward the railing. "The food is separated by perishable and non-perishable and then stored accordingly. Anything that needs to be refrigerated is taken into cold storage downstairs. Clothes and other goods are stored in various areas around the warehouse. There is a store on the other side of this building where everything is sold."

Ian gave Michael a puzzled look. "I thought everything was given to the people. They have to buy it?"

"Earn it might be more accurate." Michael patted Ian's shoulder.

Jonnie picked up from there and explained that everyone in the camp worked to earn credits that they used to obtain food and supplies from the store.

"We tried giving everything away, but as the camp grew, we learned that things work better when people earn their keep. Too many idle hands led to lots of trouble. We learned a lot of lessons the hard way. Your dad gave us the idea for the system we use now."

"It was actually Larry's idea," Michael offered, trying to make sure credit went where it was due. He was incredibly proud of the students and amazed as he looked out over the warehouse. "You all are doing great work here."

"You are too kind and too humble. None of this would be working without Manna. Come on, let me show you around the camp."

They climbed down the ladder and went outside the metal building. Mark was still off with his new friend, and Allie and Lana were there talking with their new group of friends. They spent a few minutes exchanging "hellos" and "good to meet yous," and eventually Jonnie led the Hamiltons off to see more of the camp.

"This place is absolutely gorgeous." Allie looked at the lake and surrounding forest. "How many people live here?"

"It fluctuates from time to time, but we usually have around seven thousand."

"Wow! Where does everybody...How do you...sanitation, I mean?" Ian was amazed.

"This actually used to be a small town, so there was some existing infrastructure, but things were pretty tough before Manna showed up. Along with the food and supplies, your dad's group gave us ideas for distribution and work like we have already discussed, as well as ideas for governing ourselves. That sounds kind of 'cultish,' but honestly, with so many people coming in, we had to establish some rules and some form of governance. We still exist within the county government here, and the sheriff's office helps if we have any real issues, but the people here are good for the most part, and things are going smoothly."

As they crested the hill, they came upon what looked like an old town forgotten by time.

"This used to be an amusement park. It specialized in crafts and backwoods customs from the nineteenth century. Over the years, as the economy went downhill, it fell on hard times and eventually closed. I used to come out here when I was a little girl. I can still remember the smell of kettle corn and turkey legs. We've converted several of the buildings into housing, and about your sanitation question, Ian, there were several public restroom areas remaining from the park. They needed some work, but that gave us a start anyway. Manna is helping us construct more facilities that will make a big difference. It's no picnic living out here, but it has become home for many of us."

They spent several hours touring the town and the surrounding area. Mark and his new friend, Amy, eventually joined the group just in time for dinner. The campaign seemed a million miles away as they walked back up Main Street—if you could call the wide, dusty path a street. Michael was completely exhausted. He had spent the last two nights sitting up with the Farmers at the hospital, catching only an occasional wink in a chair or on a couch. He was beginning to drag, and Jonnie took notice.

"I have a surprise for you all." She led them down the street to a building with a sign that read "Saloon" above the door. "This will in no way repay you for all of your kindness, but we have been working hard over the last few weeks completing this project. We restored several of the upstairs rooms for you. They are not fancy, but I think you will find them to be comfortable. There are four rooms and two bathrooms. We have already stored your things there."

After showing them to their rooms and getting them settled, she invited them to a special meal that would be served in their honor. There would be fireworks and a dance to celebrate Independence Day.

"Oh yeah!" Mark remembered. "It's the Fourth of July!"

After resting for a while, the Hamiltons headed off for the celebration.

"How do we know where to go?" Lana drifted along behind the others.

"Follow your nose." Ian sniffed the smell of barbeque in the air.

"And the candles." Mark pointed to a path created using hundreds of luminaries. Following the candles, they wound their way down the path. They could hear music and laughter spilling through the trees, and they could see a glow from several large bonfires in a clearing just ahead. A large cheer began to rise as the crowd of several thousand saw the Hamiltons emerging from the path. Michael led the group to what seemed to be the center of the festivities and they found Jonnie waiting for them. A stage that held the band for the dance had been erected, and Jonnie motioned for the family to join her there. The cheers grew even louder as they made their way up the stairs.

So many thoughts swept through Michael's mind. *How in the world did we get here?*

*Be still and know...*came a gentle whisper in the breeze.

These people may have lost their houses, Michael thought, *but they have certainly not lost their homes.*

Jonnie invited him to join her at the microphone.

"Would you like to hear a few words from Dr. Hamilton?" she yelled as she winked at Michael, and the crowd roared again.

It was a few moments before things calmed enough for him to speak, and even then the lump in his throat demanded a few more moments of silence as he surveyed the crowd. Finally forcing the words, he said, "I am completely humbled and honored and overwhelmed at your hospitality and generosity. Thank you all so much. A few moments ago, I wondered how we ever got here, and a still, small voice reminded me of a few things. Life can move so fast, and we can begin to wonder, *Why are these things happening to us? Why are we losing everything, our homes, our way of life, and sometimes our families?* So many are suffering. It is so easy to be overwhelmed by the circumstances of life and so easy to feel insignificant and powerless to help. It can be easy to sit on the sidelines, not because we don't care, but more because we see ourselves as nobodies, just as many in power would have us see ourselves.

"I saw myself that way. I would not presume to preach to you, but there is a time and a place for everything, and tonight is a night to speak from the heart. That small voice reminded me that many great men of days gone by were not great because of some special talent, or strength, or anything in particular that distinguished them from their neighbor. They simply answered an obvious call that lay in their path.

"One man built an ark. He was six hundred years old when he started the process, and he labored at it for a hundred and twenty years. Good thing he was young when he started."

The crowd laughed.

"One man was a prince, but found no success from power or a throne. His destiny lay in the desert, in his blood, in his God. He heard that voice speaking from within a burning bush, and despite feeling like a nobody, he still listened.

"Across the ages men and women have listened to that voice. They decided that others were more important than self, and, taking their eyes off themselves, they found that their station in life was less important than their calling. They decided to forget self and press on, to listen and do whatever the task demanded. Build a boat, four hundred fifty cubits. It'll take a hundred twenty years. Sure! Demand the release of millions of slaves from the most powerful nation on earth. If successful, lead them across a desert with no food and water...Why not? Go on TV before a national audience, debate the most powerful politician in the nation, say we should forgive all the debt. Are you crazy? *Yes!*"

The crowd went crazy with applause.

"You are a shining star in a dark sky. You are a city on a hill whose light will shine for all to see. You are bread cast on the water by a crazy bunch of college students who look at you and see that bread returning...good measure, pressed down, and running over. Thank you so much."

And the roar went up louder than ever.

"Hamilton for President...Hamilton for President..." and it continued on and on. The night was filled with singing and dancing, fireworks, incredible food, and new friendships. It was deep into the night when they made their way back up the candle-lit path to their rooms.

Michael slept better than he had slept in years, not rising until after noon. The rest of the family had long since abandoned him for new friends and new adventures. Jonnie had only shown them part of the camp the day before. In other areas of the camp, they had rekindled several cottage industries from the old amusement park. In one area, they were canning all sorts of vegetables, jellies, and apple butters, while in another area they were making candy, baskets, glassware, and pottery. They had also resurrected an old lumber mill, which they were using to produce the materials for their building projects. Some campers were working in the cottage industries, while others tended to several fields of crops.

Michael found Allie up to her elbows in apple butter, while Lana was a few buildings away making fudge. Ian was out at the lumber mill, and Mark was running around with Amy back at the warehouse. Michael went up to the office, and Jonnie showed him some of the accounting for the camp.

From the second-floor office, Michael caught a glimpse of what looked like the two men he had seen outside the hospital. He asked Jonnie if she knew who they were, but she had not seen them. He told her about the white van and of his concerns regarding Downs and his strong-arm tactics. They decided to climb down and look for the two strangers, but as they walked out of the warehouse, they saw the white van driving away. Jonnie asked one of the men working outside the warehouse about them.

"They seem to be reporters," the worker gathered consensus from the others standing there. "They were here yesterday, too, with their cameras. They just left a few minutes ago. Didn't say who they were."

Michael realized that he had been out of touch for the past couple days. The camp did not have any televisions, and he had left his phone on the bus. He decided to get his phone and call Larry back in Iowa.

"Hey, Dr. Hamilton, I've been trying to reach you. You are all over the TV. Where are you? It looked like you were in the wilderness last night on the news."

Before Michael could answer, Larry spoke again, "Oh yeah, Senator Lawrence's office called looking for you. They want you to contact them when you get a chance."

Michael spent about twenty minutes on the phone with Larry, catching up on everything at Manna and all of the students spread around the country. Everything seemed to be going well. Larry had exciting reports from everyone. Michael got the contact information for the students so he could check in with them personally. He was puzzled about the men in the van, but they did not seem to be dangerous for the moment.

Later that afternoon, Michael's phone rang.

"Michael, this is Harold, Harold Lawrence. Did I catch you at a good time to talk?"

"Sure, Harold. What can I do for you?"

"Michael, have you been watching the news?"

"No, there are no TVs out here in this camp."

"Do you remember my promise at the last debate, my promise to find the answers?"

"I do, but I have lost track of the campaign. I'm sorry. Have you found your answers?"

"Yes, sir, I have. The answer is you. You and your team are doing unbelievable things, Michael. I don't know how you put it all together, but your name is everywhere."

"Harold, do you know anything about two reporters who have been following me?"

"Sorry, Michael. I tried to call you, but you have been hard to reach for the past few days. I do know the reporters. They are working for me. I saw you on the *Tom Allen Show* the other night. I sent some people to find out what happened on the show, and eventually the trail led to the Farmers. They told us their whole story, and we ran it on TV. Michael, people across the nation are screaming for Hamilton. You are their hope. You are the answer."

"Harold, I don't know what to say. I thought everything was over for the campaign."

"Well, Downs has most of the delegates from the primaries, but you won in New Hampshire. I have been talking to the Democratic Party leadership, and I have them convinced that they would be crazy to leave you out of the convention. It's the last week of July, three weeks from now. Do you think you can get there?"

"This seems crazy. Where is it?"

"New York City, the biggest stage in the world. I should warn you though. The city is on the verge of civil war. There are millions of homeless all over the city, and tensions are very high. Some parts of the city are under martial law. We thought about moving the Convention, but we're too close now. Tell me you will come. I will send a plane for you, anything you want."

"How about protection from Downs? I've seen what his muscle can do."

"I have that concern, too, but you are the only one with answers. Everyone else is lost, Michael. We can't wait another four years."

"I need a few days to think and run this past my family and the students. We are heading for Iowa tomorrow. I will call you back in three days with an answer."

"Thank you, Michael. I will be waiting for your call."

The Hamiltons spent the rest of the day making apple butter, fudge, pottery, and, most importantly, friends and memories. That evening there was another large celebration in their honor. After dinner, Michael said a few words to the crowd at Jonnie's request. Then he spent the rest of the evening standing just to the edge of the stage, shaking hands, and receiving countless well wishes and small gifts. By the time they loaded everything on the bus the next morning, it was packed. It was a tearful farewell, but they all promised to return. As they headed down the road leaving the camp, they noticed a new sign that stretched across the road.

Mark read it aloud for everyone, "*Welcome to Hamiltonia.*"

Stars in the Sky

They noticed the white van at several junctures on their way back to Iowa, and soon they were seeing pictures on the satellite news of themselves and the bus. Cheering crowds began to appear on overpasses and along the roadside. There were signs promoting "Hamilton for President" standing in farm fields, listed on hotel marquees, and filling rooftops that once said "Walnut Bowls for Sale."

The bus rolled into Hill City two days after leaving Hamiltonia. Michael felt like he had been gone for a century and traveled a million miles. After helping with the luggage and bidding Jim farewell, he went back out to the front porch and sat down. He peered up at the evening sky and let his mind wander back over the past year. He thought about the morning in the chapel with Henry before the first day of class, of Dr. Terry and the Department Chair controversy. He thought about Mark looking over his shoulder at the Jubilee notes and teaching those lessons to his class. The town hall meeting played through his mind, meeting Christine, hearing her story, and seeing her standing in the shadows while Downs spilled empty thoughts all over the airwaves...What if he had just remained invisible?

He thought about the Wallaces, especially Jim, how proud he would be of Ben. He wondered how Ben was doing, a question that was answered thirty seconds later when a car pulled up in front of the house and Ben stepped out. Without saying a word, they walked toward each other and embraced, squeezing until all the air in their lungs was gone.

"Where did you come from?" Michael finally loosened his grip.

Ben just shrugged. "It was time to come home."

Allie came out the front door and joined the welcome party. They sat on the porch telling stories well into the evening.

"It would seem you have a decision to make, sir." Ben looked at Michael with deep pride.

"What is your advice?" Michael turned the tables.

"I think you should take your own advice about calling and purpose. You believed in me, trusted me…cared, and didn't give up on me when I was lost. Call me Moses." He laughed a little. "I found my way out in the desert. I found my purpose, my faith. Doc, you are an awesome teacher. You're also a great leader. People follow you not because you are the loudest voice, maybe because you're not. You are calm when the whole world is falling apart. When darkness hides the light and all is lost, you are at your best."

Michael and Allie both gave him a hug as he prepared to leave.

Halfway down the sidewalk, Michael stopped him, "Hey, have you talked to Sarah lately?"

Ben glanced back over his shoulder and only smiled. "See you tomorrow, Doc."

Michael spent the next day—the third day since talking to Harold—calling all of the students. He filled them in on everything that had taken place while he was out on the road, and he listened to all of their stories. They were all excited about the news and the possibility of being back in the race. Allie invited Henry, Dr. Nick, Peter, and Harry over for dinner as a way to say thank-you for their companionship and hard work on the bus tour. They all advised Michael to at least go to New York. They talked about the dangers, both from the riots and from Downs, but decided that avoiding the issues would not solve anything. By seven thirty that evening, Michael picked up the phone and called Harold.

"I'll be there. Tell me where and when."

Harold was ecstatic. After several moments of jubilant celebration, he calmed down and talked about the details. He made arrangements in New York for the Hamilton family and the students. The convention was in two weeks, but Harold asked Michael to arrive one week early to allow for any travel delays and to give them time to talk about their strategy. That left one week to rest, rejuvenate, and prepare.

The next day, July ninth, was Sunday, and the Hamilton's went to church. Michael shook hands with Henry in the vestibule and chatted for a while before going into the sanctuary.

"It's been a while since you've been here," Allie reminded him. "We've had a few changes." She nodded toward the platform and the young man taking his seat just in front of the choir as they filed into the loft.

"Who is he?" Michael surveyed the young man in his late twenties.

"John Bane is his name, ask me again, I'll tell you the same," Allie replied with a spunky look.

"Not a Roe man?" Michael looked at him with an upturned eyebrow.

"No. All the Roe men have been busy saving the world," she remained in her festive mood. She was really glad to have Michael home, and it was nice to be sitting in church with the whole family. It seemed like such a simple thing, something she had taken for granted all of her married life. Allie slid her hand into Michael's and squeezed it as she smiled to herself.

Allie looked across the sanctuary and saw another lady who was happily seated with her son—it was Halley, seated with Ben, and who was that bright young face seated next to Ben? *Sarah Johnson.*

Allie said to herself, *You go, Sarah.*

After church, the two families met up outside, and Halley invited the Hamiltons over for lunch. The usual "are you sures?" were exchanged, but Halley insisted, so they all walked over to the Wallace house. While the ladies fixed fried chicken and all of the trimmings, the guys went into the family room and watched a little of the baseball game—Cards and Cubs—nothing better on a Sunday afternoon.

After lunch, Michael, Allie, Ben, and Sarah went for a walk. In no time they were strolling through the beautiful Roe Campus gardens. As they walked, Michael inquired about Hawk, and Ben shared the story about the PT boat, the palm branch, and Hawk's name. As the story wound down and questions began to arise regarding the seriousness of the relationship between the two new lovebirds, Sarah changed the subject.

"Dr. Hamilton, how did you meet my grandfather?" She looked at Michael, still blushing from the questions about Ben.

"Yeah, how did that happen?" Ben added, receiving a "you're not going to get out of this that easy" look from Michael.

While Michael pondered the question, Allie answered, "Henry Johnson went to seminary with Robert and Martha Hamilton."

"In Texas?" Sarah wondered if Allie was referring to Southwest Seminary.

"That's right," Allie replied. "After graduation, your grandfather went on to pastor several churches before coming to Roe College, while the Hamiltons moved to Thailand as missionaries. Young

Michael spent his summers there with his parents and the school year in the States with his maternal grandparents. Michael was an only child, the first grandchild of Lowell and Sharon Peters. His mother, Martha, was the eldest of six, being seventeen and fifteen years older than her two youngest brothers. Richard and Ron were like brothers to Michael, and they spoiled him rotten. Would you like to share some of your stories...dear?"

"Well, there were—" Michael started before being interrupted by his grinning wife.

"Well, there were many stories. Tomatoes lobbed into convertibles, jumping out of trees onto mattresses, stealing bathroom signs at the lake...Shall I continue?"

"I don't think we were exactly juvenile delinquents," Michael rebutted.

"No, I suppose not," Allie agreed with a tilt of her head as she reminisced proudly about her husband's life. "How about the motorcycle phase?"

"Hey, I just went along for the ride."

"Yeah, over the river and through the woods, up the levy and down the other side."

"It was motocross—"

"It was crazy, and they almost killed themselves."

"Allie." Michael cautioned with a smile.

"How many phone calls from the hospital?"

"Just one," he answered sheepishly.

"Just one," she repeated. "Just one call, but two hurt boys!"

"They lived," Michael defended the honor of his uncles as they both paused from their debate and laughed about the memories.

"They were my idols growing up," Michael turned a little more serious. "They could do anything, and I wanted to be just like them."

"What happened to them?" Ben sat down on one of the landscape walls.

Michael laughed. "They grew up, got married, had kids, and..." his words trailed off as he thought about them for a minute.

"And?" Ben urged Michael to finish his thought.

"And I would still give anything to be just like them."

"You are," Allie said as she and Sarah both wiped a tear from their eyes. Then they all laughed at themselves for being so sappy.

"Finish the story about your parents." Sarah's curiosity was peaked.

Michael looked at Allie for a minute before starting, but once again she interrupted.

"Michael spent some amazing summers with his parents, but there was a lot of guilt on both sides for the time they spent apart. They came home on furlough every few years, but it was hard to make up for lost time."

"They were home for graduations and our wedding," Michael continued. "We were pastoring our second church when they retired and came home for good, or so we thought. In the early winter of 2004, Dad got a call from the missionary board asking if he would go back to Thailand for one more visit. He was bored in his retirement, so he and Mom agreed to go back for a few months. They had been there for a few weeks when the tsunami hit. We don't know exactly what happened, but they had been visiting a remote village a day or so before, and we think they were washed away with the villagers."

They all sat in silence for a few moments, absorbing the story.

"I was born in Thailand," Michael continued as his eyes brightened, "and I remember the first time I came to the United States. I was four years old, and my parents were bringing me to the States to start school. All the arrangements had been made with Grandma and Grandpa. I was so excited to meet them and my other relatives, especially Richard and Ron. I had heard so many stories and I just couldn't wait.

"When we got to the airport, though, I was a little scared. It was my first flight, but that's not what scared me. I began to realize that I would not be coming back with Mom and Dad. As we walked across the tarmac to board the plane, Dad took my hand and stopped me. It was night and he pointed up to the sky.

"'Do you see those stars, son?' he asked as he bent down. I looked up and just nodded with a big lump in my throat. 'Those same stars shine on Grandma's house too. Did you know that?' Once again I nodded, but I could not imagine that it was true. Dad let me sit by the window on the plane, and I watched the stars while we flew for as long as I could keep my eyes open. I guess I was looking for the end of the sky, but it went on forever. It was so beautiful.

"When we got to Grandma and Grandpa's, I got so excited about meeting everyone, like any kid would, that I forgot about the lessons in the stars. On the last night before Mom and Dad flew back to Thailand, Dad took me out on the front porch and we looked at the stars again.

"'You're right,' I told him. We picked out our favorite one and decided that we would look at that star each night when we said our prayers. I remember it raining the first night after they left. Grandma let me sleep in by her bed because I was so upset about not seeing the star. There were many nights that Grandma's kindness and warm cocoa had to replace the star."

"It's still there, Doc," Ben whispered. "I look up there for my Dad too."

It was late afternoon before they walked back to the Wallace house, so Halley invited them to eat leftovers for dinner. They ate and talked until evening. Michael and Ben excused themselves from the table and went outside. They both lay down on the warm grass under a bright summer sky and just looked up.

The Suits

"He's crazy! You can't just forgive the debt." An angry Seth Randle threw the evening *Post* across the room. "Sydney, how long have we been working on campaigns? Have you ever seen anything like this?"

It was late in the evening of July second, and Seth Randle, the financial genius behind the Downs machine, was meeting with Sydney Porter.

"Hamilton is all over the news," he continued in disgust. "Even the press that hated him a few months ago are going weak in the knees. Forgive the debt," he mocked as drool slipped out of his mouth from his uncontrolled rage. "What's next? Give the land back to the Indians?" He marched over to the window and looked out across the Washington skyline.

Sydney was slumped in the chair behind his desk with a cigar burning in his hand. He had been in meetings all day long with the campaign team, but despite their efforts, no solution to the Hamilton dilemma had been found.

"We've been in tougher races, haven't we?" he asked without even raising his eyes toward Seth because he already knew the answer—*no.*

"How did we get all the way to this point, only to have some moron professor drop a few 'words of wisdom' and everything turn upside down?" Randle spewed in his unrelenting state of wrath. In his rage, he spun toward Sydney. "If you can't join 'em, beat 'em! I mean—"

"Wait, Seth," Sydney broke in. "Beat him…to a pulp. Eliminate him. Kill…"

They worked into the early hours of the morning hatching their plan to remove the fly from their ointment. Michael Hamilton needed to go, and they were about to ensure that he did. Their boss would expect nothing less; there was no room for failure.

Later that morning, Sydney summoned "the suits," as he referred to the army of men in dark suits that did all of Downs' dirty work. He spent a little over an hour with them before he sent them out of his office in the Hart Senate Building to visit one of Downs' fellow statesmen. The two men walked straight past the receptionist and made their way back to the senator's office door, entering without knocking.

"Senator Lawrence," one of them said, gaining his attention as the other closed the door.

Jubilee Express

It was early Monday morning, July tenth, when the Hamilton phone rang.

"Dad, it's for you." Lana brought the phone into Michael's office where he was already working.

"Michael, this is Derrick Jett. We are hearing word that you are going to the convention. Is that true?"

"Yes, it is."

"Good. The network has a proposition for you. They would like you to fly to California and take an old-fashioned train trip back to New York. We've made arrangements for a special train that will accommodate your team, and we will schedule all of the whistle-stops and events if you will consent to come."

Michael paused as he noticed Allie walk into the room. He covered the phone and told her what Derrick had proposed.

"Let's do it." She always amazed him with her spontaneity.

Michael's head spun. "This is crazy," he half whispered, half shouted back to her. "Okay, Derrick, we're in. What do you need us to do?"

They talked for a while but decided the students should be involved in the planning, so they set a meeting for later that evening when everyone could be present. The students were very excited, but there was much to do. Over the next three days they worked out the detailed schedule:

City	State	Time	Stop	Arrive	Depart	Event	T-Zone	Date
Los Angeles	CA			01:00 pm		Fly to CA - Marshallville Dinner	Pacific	Friday, July 14, 2028
Los Angeles	CA	4:00			4:00 am	Breakfast on Train		Saturday, July 15, 2028
San Bernardino	CA	1:44		5:44 am	5:44 am	Whistle-stop		
Victorville	CA	1:11	0:10	6:55 am	7:05 am			
Barstow	CA	0:46		7:51 am	7:51 am			
Kettleman	CA	3:10	0:10	11:01 am	11:11 am	Whistle-stop		
Williams Junction	AZ	2:44	0:10	02:55 pm	03:05 pm	Whistle-stop	Mountain	
Winslow	AZ	1:39	2:00	04:44 pm	06:44 pm	Dinner Stop		
Galup	NM	1:46		08:30 pm	08:30 pm			
Albuquerque	NM	3:31	0:10	12:01 am	12:11 am	Whistle-stop		Sunday, July 16, 2028
Lamy	NM	1:05		1:16 am	1:16 am	Sleep on Train		
Las Vegas	NM	1:45		3:01 am	3:01 am			
Raton	NM	1:47		4:48 am	4:48 am			
Trinidad	CO	0:59		5:47 am	5:47 am			
Lajunta	CO	1:42	0:10	7:29 am	7:39 am	Breakfast on Train		
Lamar	CO	0:52		8:31 am	8:31 am	Whistle-stop		
Garden City	KS	1:20		10:51 am	10:51 am		Central	
Dodge City	KS	0:44		11:35 am	11:35 am			
Hutchinson	KS	1:47	0:10	01:22 pm	01:32 pm	Whistle-stop		
Newton	KS	0:36		02:08 pm	02:08 pm	Lunch on Train		
Topeka	KS	2:19	0:10	04:27 pm	04:37 pm	Whistle-stop		
Lawrence	KS	0:29		05:06 pm	05:06 pm			
Kansas City	MO	1:37	5:00	06:43 pm	011:43 pm	Marshallville Dinner		
Independence	MO	0:19		12:02 am	12:02 am	Sleep on Train		Monday, July 17, 2028
Lee Summit	MO	0:17		12:19 am	12:19 am			
Warrensburg	MO	0:43		1:02 am	1:02 am			
Sedalia	MO	0:30		1:32 am	1:32 am			
Jefferson City	MO	1:14		2:46 am	2:46 am			
Hermann	MO	0:45		3:31 am	3:31 am			
Washington	MO	0:28		3:59 am	3:59 am			
Kirkwood	MO	0:45		4:44 am	4:44 am			
St. Louis	MO	0:42	4:00	5:26 Am	9:26 Am	Homeless Shelter - Breakfast		
Alton	IL	0:46		10:12 Am	10:12 Am			
Carlinville	IL	0:29		10:41 Am	10:41 Am			

Springfield	IL	0:42	0:10	11:23 Am	11:33 Am	Whistle-stop		
Lincoln	IL	0:28		12:01 Pm	12:01 Pm			
Blooming-ton/Normal	IL	0:30	0:10	12:31 Pm	12:41 Pm	Whistle-stop		
Pontiac	IL	0:27		01:08 Pm	01:08 Pm			
Dwight	IL	0:18		01:26 Pm	01:26 Pm			
Joliet	IL	0:35		02:01 Pm	02:01 Pm			
Chicago	IL	1:01	17:00	03:02 Pm	8:02 Am	Marshallville Dinner		Tuesday, July 18, 2028
Hammond/ Whiting	IN	0:27		8:29 Am	8:29 Am			
Cincinnati	OH	7:50	6:00	04:19 Pm	010:19 Pm	Marshallville Dinner		
Ashland	KY	3:00		2:19 Am	2:19 Am		Eastern	Wednesday, July 19, 2028
Charleston	WV	2:28		4:47 Am	4:47 Am			
Clifton Forge	VA	3:58	0:10	8:45 Am	8:55 Am	Whistle-stop		
Charlot-tesville	VA	2:28	0:10	11:23 Am	11:33 Am	Whistle-stop		
Washington	DC	2:50	18:00	02:23 Pm	8:23 Am	Marshallville Dinner		Thursday, July 20, 2028
Baltimore	MY	0:32	0:10	8:55 Am	9:05 Am	Whistle-stop		
Wilmington	DE	0:42	0:10	9:47 Am	9:57 Am	Whistle-stop		
Philadelphia	PA	0:17	6:00	10:14 Am	04:14 Pm	Marshallville Lunch		
Trenton	NJ	0:26		04:40 Pm	04:40 Pm			
New York City	NY	0:47		05:27 Pm	05:27 Pm	GRAND AR-RIVAL		

This schedule would not put them in New York a week early, as Harold requested, but Michael hoped the added publicity would more than make up for the delayed arrival. As he watched Larry say good-bye to Derrick and put away the wireless conference phone, he took a few minutes to survey the faces of the students. They were all present, even the ones who had been on assignment.

What was a band of bright-eyed college students is rounding into a well-oiled political machine, Michael thought, and then he almost laughed at himself. *It's just us folk.* He rolled his eyes. He was very proud of their efforts—especially those connected with Manna

Network. How many people had the students touched? He marveled at their enthusiasm after what had been an extremely grueling summer. Their energy knew no bounds. He hoped the trip from L.A. to New York would somehow reward them for their efforts.

Unfortunately, some would have to stay behind to man the network. Larry volunteered. Although it melted Michael's heart to hear his humble words, he knew it was for the best. Larry worked with the network staff to coordinate the Marshallville dinners that would take place at several points along the train route. It was an enormous undertaking, especially with such short notice. Fancy was not on the agenda, but moving mass quantities of food and supplies were. Larry and the Manna connections would work through some amazing obstacles, and their efforts would make everyone very proud.

The team accompanying Michael and his family would consist of Sarah, Shelly, Danielle, Ben, and, of course, Hamilton's Raiders—thirteen in all. They called themselves the "Colonists"—thirteen original colonies—on the Hamilton campaign trail. It would be a new revolution, and their odds of defeating Downs were about as good as those of the colonies defeating the British , but…

The plane carrying the faithful thirteen touched down in Los Angeles right on schedule, and a team from WNN shuttled them to the hotel. It was a little after three in the afternoon by the time everyone was checked in and settled. At three thirty, they all gathered in a large meeting room on the second floor of the hotel with Derrick Jett and staff from WNN to review their schedule for the upcoming week.

"I hope you are all rested, because this will be one busy week," Derrick opened the meeting. He had their schedule projected on a large screen. "There will be buses here at five o'clock to take us out to the camp tonight. It's a forty-five-minute ride, maybe more with traffic. We eat at seven o'clock, and there will be a dance to follow. The buses will depart the camp at nine o'clock for the hotel."

"That seems early." Michael wanted to spend as much time as possible with the people in the camp.

"It is, but the *Jubilee Express* pulls out of the station at four o'clock sharp in the morning." Derrick's response was met with a unified groan from the room. "Porters will be around to your rooms to collect your luggage before we leave for the camp tonight. Per instructions you received earlier this week, you should have a small overnight bag to keep with you tonight and each of the nights that we depart from the train for hotel stays. The buses will leave at three tomorrow morning for Union Station. Any questions?"

There were no questions, as they had all been given the schedule before they left Iowa. It would be an early start, but they were all excited.

"Okay, let's talk a little about the train," Derrick continued. "Our conductor will be Mr. Arthur O'Donnell, and he is here with us this afternoon to tell us about the train. When he finishes, Ms. Jones will give you your cabin assignments. Mr. O'Donnell, the floor is yours."

"Thank you, Mr. Jett. Our train is a very special lady. We'll call her *Jubilee Express,* but on her last voyage of this magnitude, she was called the 21st *Century Express,* and she carried President Bill Clinton. That was thirty-two years ago this summer. The train consists of thirteen cars, including three engines, a main dining car, an arcade/theater car, a media car for the press, and several cars with complete living quarters, which include onboard restrooms with showers. Several of the cars have overhead-viewing areas. Like I said, she's a special lady. I think you will all enjoy her company."

"Thank you, Mr. O'Donnell. Ms. Jones…"

"Good afternoon, everyone, and welcome to California. I have a packet for each of you that contains your cabin number and key. Our time is short this afternoon, but we will have daily briefings on the train as we travel. If there are no questions," she paused, and seeing no hands, she turned the meeting back over to Derrick.

Derrick dismissed the group but asked Michael to stay behind.

"We've not talked a lot about security, but it is a concern for this trip. You've become quite a celebrity."

"I think we'll be fine." Michael did not want anything to stand between him and the people he hoped to meet on the trip.

"Just the same, we have two secret servicemen that will accompany you anytime you leave the train."

Michael agreed, though he was not comfortable with the arrangement. He was just an ordinary guy, and he could not imagine needing protection from anyone except Downs.

Thoughts of his "I'm a nobody" talk with God the rainy morning after Jim Wallace's funeral ran through his mind.

It was four thirty by the time Michael got back up to his room. Allie was busy preparing their luggage for the porters.

"What do you expect at the camp tonight?" She was busy moving their clothes around.

"I don't know. There have been reports of riots all over the L.A. area, and I think this camp has had its share of violence. "

"Michael, I know you want to reach the people, but will we be safe?"

"I think the camps have been much safer since Manna supplies started arriving. These are not bad people. They are desperate people. They just need a little hope."

There was a knock at the door, and the porters were there to pick up the bags.

"Thanks, guys." Michael tipped them as they left. He looked out the door and saw porters loading luggage onto carts as far as he could see down the hall. He was beginning to realize just how many people would be traveling on the train, and once again the magnitude of the trip became clearer. Throughout the entire process—from debates to campaign trails and even on to the Manna Network—he had always just seen himself as one of the team, an ordinary guy who had simply been given an extraordinary opportunity.

Truth is, that's all that's really happening, he told himself, but special trains and secret servicemen tend to play tricks with your mind. Walking back into the room, he took one look at Allie and was thankful to have his family with him, which reminded him, "Hey, where are the kids?"

"Next door. They gave their bags to the porters as soon as we got back upstairs and then went off to explore. I told them to meet us in the lobby at four forty-five, ten minutes ago. Come on. We gotta go."

The buses pulled into the L.A. traffic and wound their way to the outskirts of the city.

What a mass of humanity, Michael thought as he surveyed the traffic stretching beyond the horizon. They drove for about twenty-five minutes beyond the city limits before they left the highway, another twenty minutes on back roads, and then, cresting a rise, they looked out over a city of nomads. It was a city of tents stretching out for a mile or so across the valley in front of them with tens of thousands of people moving about. Allie and Michael just looked at each other as they took in the sights all around the buses. The caravan of three buses made their way to the center of the camp, where preparations were underway for a great feast and celebration.

Many people had already gathered, but more were coming from all directions as word about the arrival of the buses spread.

They were greeted by a man named Bill Hedges as they got off the buses. He told them dinner would be ready in about an hour and led them over to a group of tables where they could sit. Derrick had his cameras rolling, interviewing people left and right. Michael took the opportunity to ask Bill about the camp.

"Our numbers vary, and it's by no means an exact count, but we have a little over forty thousand here. There are many other camps like this one in the greater L.A. area."

"What about sanitation?" Allie could only imagine the nightmare.

"It's not very good. There is a river just over the hill. It's not very private, but it is the best we have right now."

"How long have people been here?" Michael's heart was aching.

"I got here about eighteen months ago, but there were a lot of people here already. I don't know when the first ones came, but I know we'd all like to go home."

Bill shared stories about different people in the camp, and all were very similar. Most still had their jobs, but they had lost their homes when the housing market went down and interest rates went up. Many had lost the credit card battle. With no more equity and no other options, the day of reckoning finally arrived, and the results were spread out all over the valley in multicolored tents.

There was a huge area cleared for the dance, and a group of campers were setting up their instruments. Ian talked to them and learned that they were a group of recording studio musicians who were living in the camp. The camp was home to a huge range of people—studio musicians, actors, businessmen and women, teachers, lawyers, doctors...Debt had cut a wide path through L.A., and it knew no racial or economic barriers, as evidenced by the great diversity of the campers.

When the dinner bell rang, Bill invited Michael to the microphone to say a few words and to pray for the meal.

"Thank you all for having us this evening. These are tough times, and answers seem to be hard to find—"

"You have an answer!" came a shout from somewhere in the crowd.

"Yes, I do," Michael responded, "and I intend to shout it all the way across this nation over the next few days. It is my hope that this nation will listen to our answer, or come up with a better one. Please know that in the meantime, there are those who care about you. Manna Network is doing all it can with the support of the president and congress to provide food and supplies. We know that is not a long-term solution, but we will carry your words and hopes across the nation this week, and we will share them in New York. Speaking of food, I don't want to stand between you all and this meal, so let's bless it and eat." With that, he said a short prayer.

Their time was short, and it went fast. Michael and Allie managed one dance, but they mostly just made their way from table to table talking with the campers. By the time the buses pulled out of the camp, their stomachs and hearts were full.

After what seemed like five minutes of sleep, the phone next to the bed rang.

"Good morning, sir, this is your two o'clock wakeup call."

Allie was up like a flash as Michael sank back into his pillow. Moments later, he was attacked by an overzealous nine-year-old.

"Come on, Dad, get up." Mark climbed all over him.

"Watch it, pal." Michael flopped Mark over on the bed and tangled him up in a sea of sheets.

"Dad!"

The room was alive with activity. Allie was in the bathroom getting a shower, and Mark darted back through the door connecting the adjoining room. Michael sat on the edge of the bed gathering his wits. In another thirty minutes, they were all ready to go. Even the usually hard-to-wake Lana was standing at the door with bag in hand.

"Come on, let's go," she impatiently prodded the group to leave.

Michael laughed to himself at the thought of her impatience. Lana was usually the last one ready, but this morning—this early, early morning—even Lana was up and at 'em with the rest of the mass of people who were spilling into the hall and making their way to the elevators.

Good planning was already paying off. With so many people all trying to get down the elevators at the same time, the only thing helping the process go smoothly was the absence of their luggage. Each person had a small overnight bag in hand, but the major luggage was long gone—taken to the station and loaded on the train the night before.

It was still dark as they exited the hotel to the sound of three bus engines idling in the hotel circle. Michael caught sight of the students and ushered everyone onto the bus. The first seat after the stairwell was reserved, so the Hamiltons filled in behind it, followed by Henry, Peter, Harry, and Dr. Nick. As he peered out the bus window, Michael saw Ms. Jones directing traffic.

I need to remember her first name. He wondered if he even knew it. *Did they say her name yesterday, or did Derrick just call her Ms. Jones?*

Two men in suits stepped up into the stairwell, the first reaching his hand out to Michael.

"Good morning, sir. I am Agent Russell, and this is Agent Barnes. I believe Mr. Jett told you about us?"

"Yes, sir." Michael shook his strong hand. "Good morning, Agent Barnes." He took his hand next.

"We'll take good care of you, sir," Agent Barnes barked in his very official voice.

Michael wanted to click his heels and salute, but he just smiled and said, "Thank you."

"Mom, when do we eat?" Ian's stomach growled with emptiness.

"On the train." Allie looked at Ian peering over the seat. Soon Mark's head joined Ian's. Allie smiled at them both. "Are you excited?"

"Yeah!" came the obvious response from the younger of the two wide-eyed brothers.

"Me too." Allie eyed Lana getting settled into the seat across the aisle. Lana gave her a smile as she fixed her earbuds and fiddled with the buttons on her MP3 player.

Derrick Jett popped his head up into the stairwell of the bus and said, "Okay, folks, we're ready to roll. Is everyone here?" He looked at Michael.

"All here, Derrick."

He nodded and hustled off to check on the other bus. After a few moments he hopped off the second bus and darted back into the hotel. He was gone for only a few seconds when he reappeared through the revolving front doors followed by a rather haggard-looking lady hustling to keep up with him. Michael made eye contact with Derrick.

"Overslept." He rushed toward the bus shaking his head. "We're ready to roll now."

Three buses loaded with family, friends, students, and a sea of media rolled away from the hotel and headed for the freeway. The short five-mile trip to the station was quick since the highway was fairly deserted at the pre-dawn hour. The train station, however, was another matter. The brick walkways leading up to LAX Union Station were filled with hundreds of people hoping to get a glimpse of Michael Hamilton. A buzz went through the crowd as the buses arrived.

Shouts of "They're here!" went up all over the plaza. Others began to shout, "There he is!" and "I see him!" even before Michael got off the bus.

As the people began to surround the buses, the agents prepared to spring into action.

Michael reached up and put his hand on Agent Russell's shoulder and said, "Can we talk for a second? I know you want to keep me safe, and believe me, I'm all for that too, but I want to talk to these people. I know it may not be very safe, but I just need to do it."

The agents gave each other a look, and without responding, they stepped off the bus and began to move the people back.

Michael looked at Allie and said, "This is going to be interesting." He let everyone else get off the bus first and told Allie he would see her on the train. She nodded and took the kids with her. Ben stayed with Michael, and they climbed off the bus together. A huge shout went up from the crowd, and Michael waved at them, amazed at the pre-dawn numbers.

"It's only three thirty!" He shook his head at Ben. With the two agents in tow, Michael and Ben waded out into the people.

"Good morning. Thank you for coming," they said over and over as they made their way toward the station, a white stucco building with a red tile roof that stood about two hundred feet from the bus. They shook hands and talked to people for about twenty minutes before the agents moved them on into the station.

Michael could tell from their body language that the agents

were very uncomfortable with the number of people pulling at their charge.

"Thanks, guys," he said trying to ease the tension as they made their way into the ornate station.

"Wow." Ben surveyed the room. "The inside is much nicer than the outside."

Time was growing tight as the four men made their way through the station and out to the tracks.

"Wow, again." Ben caught sight of the train. She was beautiful—steel blue cars draped in bunting with flags flying. She seemed to stretch down the tracks forever.

"This way." Agent Barnes motioned them down the station platform. They had to hustle to keep up.

No sooner had they stepped up onto the train than Agent Russell spoke into his sleeve, "Twenty on board. Ready to roll."

Michael looked at his watch—four o'clock, straight up. A few seconds later, he heard the engines rev, and somewhere in his mind he could have sworn he heard a conductor say, "All aboard!" The train rolled out of the station as Michael stood on the back platform of the last car. He waved to the sea of well-wishers, and they cheered loudly.

Allie opened the door. "Come on guys, let's get some breakfast."

They wound their way through the train to the dining car where Derrick and Ms. Jones were waiting for them. Everyone else, including the kids, were already eating. After giving them a few minutes to get settled and order, Ms. Jones began to cover the schedule for the day.

"We should cruise through San Bernardino about five forty-five. Our first whistle-stop will be at 6:55 in Victorville and then 11:01 in Kettleman. You'll have about ten minutes to speak at each stop and then we'll be rolling again. We'll eat lunch on the train and then have another whistle-stop in Williams Junction, Arizona, at 2:55. We'll have a couple hours to get off the train and eat in Winslow before getting back onboard for the evening. We have scheduled time during the evening for an interview with Derrick."

Michael nodded at Derrick, as they had actually arranged several interview sessions during the planning stages last week.

"Do you have any questions for me?" Ms. Jones finished checking her agenda.

"Yes," Michael remembered his most important question for her. "Could you tell me your first name?"

"Amanda." She looked up from her list and seemed to relax. Her duties with the network were always so official, and she liked the regiment, but Michael, in his usual way, made her feel more… human, less robotic.

"Thanks, Ms…Amanda." Derrick followed Michael's lead, allowing a more relaxed look to fill his face as he, too, smiled at Michael.

"Do you always have this effect on people?"

"It's going to be a long trip. I just want you all to know that we trust you, and we thank you for all of your hard work. I'm sure there are a million details to fret, but I hope we can enjoy these next few days at the same time."

"Your breakfast, sir." The waitress delivered two plates heaping full of eggs, bacon, and French toast. She also brought juice, coffee, and water.

"Thank you, Consuelo," Michael read her name tag.

"'Don't care how much you know until they know how much you care,'" Derrick said as he looked at Michael with admiration. "Are you going to learn everyone's name on the train?"

Michael grinned reflexively and then tried not to lose his mouthful of French toast.

"I'm terrible with names," he dabbed his mouth with his napkin, "but I'll do my best."

"Where does this 'Mr. Nice Guy' thing come from?" Derrick was accustomed to being around media and celebrities, and "nice" was not usually in vogue—professional courtesy maybe, but seldom nice.

"They say our personalities are formed by the time we are two. I'm no expert, but if that is true, maybe I should thank the people of Thailand for my demeanor. I lived there until I was four. They are a kind and gentle people. Life is much different there, or at least it was when I lived there. I suppose I should also thank Grandma Peters. I was kind of shy when I came to live with her. People would say hi to me when I was out with her and I would do the usual, 'bury my head in the side of her leg' thing as a lot of shy kids do. Very gently, she began to teach me that there was a proper way to respond. She told me to just say hello. I didn't have to break into full conversation, but I did need to at least respond politely.

"Knowing someone's name is just the golden rule in action. We all like to be acknowledged, to hear our name, unless, of course, it is our first and middle name...*Ian Benjamin!* We make life so complicated sometimes. No speech or campaign slogan will fool people forever. If we say we care, then at some point we really do need to care. I think that starts with the basics, knowing their name."

"So how will you 'know the names' of the crowds you will see on this trip?"

Michael thought for a minute as he looked out the window at the California countryside flying by.

"People have many names...John, Bob, Mary, Sue...We will not learn them all, but they have other names. Some names give us insight into their heritage and ethnicity, identify them with their family. Too often in this high-tech information age, we replace names with labels, minority, white collar, blue collar, stay-at-home moms, absentee dads...Men like Senator Downs see them only as potential votes, as means to an end, his end, and he doesn't want to be bothered by the details of their lives. Sure there are homeless, but who cares unless it affects the economy on a macro level? Sure there are millions of children growing up in broken homes in a world that has lost its value of life, but how is that his fault? 'Don't blame me, just vote for me and let me be.' His billions insulate him from...from their names.

"We on this train will learn their names. We will see their pain, care about their pain, and do everything possible to alleviate their pain. We will see them as Smiths and Millers and Johnsons and Nguyens, Patels, and Martinezes. We will understand that the economy is broken long before the GNP is affected because it is made up of millions of names who wake up every morning and hope for a better day, a fighting chance to be successful, for someone to care about them. And no, they don't care how much we know, how brilliant we are, what legends we have become in our own minds. They just want to know that someone cares enough to at least acknowledge their pain, to look for real solutions...to at least shake their hand and, even if we won't remember it forever, ask their name."

Derrick looked away for a moment and then stuck his hand out and took Michael's.

"My name is Derrick Jett. I was a spoiled, rich black kid who got everything he ever wanted and never thought it was enough. I got a free education at the best schools and had my ticket punched all the way to the top at the network. I have worked hard, but where my work failed, my daddy's cash took over. I have a wake of broken hearts in my past, not the least of which is my momma's, and I've never cared about names unless they were written on executive doors that could get me somewhere." He let go of Michael's hand and sat back in his chair.

Michael gave him a kind, gentle look.

"Well, son, as Grandma Peters would have said, 'Pull your face away from society's leg and learn how to say hello.' She'll be looking you in the eye all the way to New York."

Their conversation was interrupted by the oohs and ahhs that began to spill through the dining car. They were rolling into the suburbs of San Bernardino, and there were people everywhere along the road.

"Let's say hello." Michael looked at Derrick.

"But there's no stop planned here." Amanda thumbed through the agenda.

"Make the call, Amanda." Derrick bolted for the camera with excitement in his eyes.

"Come on, Doc. We can make it to the back platform before we reach the station."

With that he whisked Michael away through the train for the platform on the back of the last car. They reached the back car with about a mile to spare. The air was rushing past as they stepped outside. The train whistle was blasting and the flags were flapping in the wind as they slowed to pull into the San Bernardino station. Michael waved and the people cheered.

Derrick was one big smile as he began to wave at the crowds.

"Hello!" he shouted at the top of his lungs. "What's your name?"

The train did not stop, but at least they made an effort to acknowledge the crowd. From the platform, they watched as several people jumped in their cars and took off for the next crossing or overpass—anywhere they could catch another glimpse of the train.

"What is it, Doc? I thought the train would be a good idea, but I never thought about seeing this many people."

"They're just looking for hope, Derrick."

An hour later they stopped in Victorville, where Michael had a chance to speak to the crowd for about ten minutes, as they had planned. They rolled on through Barstow before making their last California whistle-stop in Kettleman. They crossed into Arizona while they ate lunch on the train and stopped briefly in Williams Junction just before three o'clock mountain time. The crowds were unbelievable. Derrick and his crew were beaming some amazing pictures back to the studios via satellite. The crowds made for great news, and the news drew bigger crowds.

Larry called around four o'clock to give Michael a heads-up about the crowd that awaited them in Winslow, where they would be stopping for dinner. Larry had coordinated the dinner plans with Amanda for the short two-hour stop.

"Doc, it's amazing. We've been watching the pictures all day. Winslow is expecting over fifty thousand people!"

"Are we ready, Larry?" Michael asked, not so much questioning Larry as giving him a chance to realize they were indeed ready and to say thank-you for all his hard work and long hours. "I'm proud of you, son."

Sure enough, the roads were packed with people as they made their way into town. A full-blown dinner celebration awaited them as they got off the train. Michael spent the entire two hours shaking hands and talking with the people. Several of the students tried to get him to eat, but he was a man on a mission and there was no stopping him. Derrick and his camera crew followed him every step of the way. Reporters from newspapers and TV stations across the country were frantically writing and recording. The people were not shy about sharing their stories. They were hurting, many of them homeless, and they were tired of the politicians ignoring them.

"Manna is feeding my kids," one mom said as she held a baby in one arm and clutched a small child next to her side with the other.

Derrick Jett had been traveling in a suit when they left the hotel that morning, but little by little he had become more concerned with the people and less concerned with his looks. By now the tie and jacket were gone, his shirt was open, and he found himself kneeling down in the dust to ask the child standing at his mother's side a question. "What's your name, son?"

At first he just buried his face in his mother's dress, but she gently urged him to answer the question.

"Willy." He looked Derrick in the eye with a great big grin that revealed his missing two front teeth.

"Give me five, Willy." Derrick returned the smile. "You have a great day, okay?"

"Okay. Hey, am I gonna be on TV?"

"Yes, you are, Willy." Derrick looked up at his mom. "Tell your momma to watch the ten o'clock news when you get home."

Willy grinned and looked up at his mom.

The whistle on the train blew, signaling everyone to return. Michael took his place on the back platform and waved to the people as the train lurched toward the next town. He looked down at his shirt and noticed it was a mess. There were so many people pulling at him all day that at some point it had been torn. Allie was now standing next to him, surveying the damage.

"Anything you want to tell me?" She raised an eyebrow.

"She didn't mean anything." He hugged her tightly.

"Come on, partner, let's get you some supper."

Michael was exhausted and needed a moment away from everyone, so Allie went to get him some food and brought it back to the Hamilton car, where they could share a moment of peace. They went up to the observation area on top of the car and watched the desert roll by as the train raced east away from the setting sun.

Ian, Lana, and Mark were settled in front of arcade games with plans to watch a movie later in the theater car. Ben was busy introducing the newest member of the team that had joined them in Winslow.

"This is Hawk," he told them as he bent their ears with stories from the past winter and spring. The Arizona Fall League seemed a distant memory as Hawk watched his young protégé hold court.

Day one on the *Jubilee Express* had been amazing, but not all things were as they seemed. While Ben told his stories, the kids banged away at their games, and Michael and Allie watched the sunlight fade into starlight, darker deeds were also afoot in other areas of the train.

"Yes, sir. I understand, sir, but...No...No...*No!* I don't but... Good-bye, sir. Yes, I will." Derrick hung up the phone. He sat there in his dark room contemplating the call and forgot all about his interview appointment with Michael. Lucky for him, Michael was more wrapped up in Allie and the stars.

"I'm not sure we can trust him," an angry Sydney Porter hissed as he slammed the phone down. "We made that young man, and we can unmake him just as fast."

"Patience," came the calm, sullen voice from the shadows of Sydney's office in the Hart Senate building. "Those tracks are leading to one place...us."

"You're right." Sydney lifted his cigar to the hateful grin on his face.

Ben was the only one standing with Michael on the platform as they made the last whistle-stop of the day in Albuquerque. Despite the midnight hour, the station was still full of people. Michael spoke to them for a few minutes before the whistle sounded, and the engines of the *Jubilee Express* roared to life. A day that started at two in the morning came to a close at 12:11 a.m., as Albuquerque, just like California and Arizona had done before, faded into the distance.

Destiny Does Not Follow a Compass

> The LORD detests dishonest scales,
> but accurate weights find favor with him.
> When pride comes, then comes disgrace,
> but with humility comes wisdom.
> The integrity of the upright guides them,
> but the unfaithful are destroyed by their duplicity.
> Wealth is worthless in the day of wrath,
> but righteousness delivers from death.
>
> Proverbs 11:1–4 (TNIV)

Michael rose before the sun and went to the observation deck. It was Sunday, the day of rest. He knew it would be a busy day, but he would at least start out before the Lord. He spent about an hour reading and listening. When he had finished, he made his way down to get cleaned up for the day. He and Allie, along with the kids, went to the dining car for breakfast and the daily briefing with Amanda and Derrick. Arriving early, they were pleased to see that only the "old men," Henry, Peter, Harry, and Dr. Nick, were there. It was nice to spend some time with them and get their thoughts on the previous day.

"Good morning, Consuelo," Michael greeted her as she arrived at the table to take their orders.

"Good morning, sir. Did you rest well?"

"I sure did. What do you recommend?"

"The pancakes are good this morning."

"Sounds great. I'll take a stack with some coffee, thank you."

She took all of the orders and returned in a flash with their drinks. Consuelo was Hispanic and appeared to be in her early fifties with graying hair, beautiful eyes, and a gorgeous smile that she rarely shared, but she was beaming at the attention this morning.

Amanda came into the dining car just before seven o'clock to remind Michael that the first stop would be Lajunta, Colorado, in about thirty minutes. There were no other stops that morning, as Michael did not want to interrupt any churches. The next stops would be Hutchinson, Kansas, at 1:22 and Topeka at 4:27. Michael got a kick out of the exactness of the times, but Arthur O'Donnell ran a tight ship, or rather train, and old *Jubilee Express* was right on schedule. Most of the day would be spent on the train, as they were not scheduled to stop longer than ten minutes until they reached Kansas City, Missouri, at about six forty-five, where they would eat dinner.

Derrick Jett rushed into the dining room just in time to accompany Michael to the back platform for the Lajunta stop. He apologized profusely on the way back for his late arrival and for missing their interview the previous night. Michael was gracious, and they decided to make the interview up after lunch.

Although the Lajunta station, like so many of the stations they had passed through, was not nearly as fancy as Union Station in L.A., it was still surrounded by people gathered to get a glimpse of the passing train. Again Michael spoke for about ten minutes, thanking the people for coming out and giving them words of encouragement. Like the day before, the cameras were rolling, and soon pictures were beaming back and forth across the nation. *Jubilee Express* was the main topic on all the Sunday morning news shows and filled the front page on most, if not all of the major newspapers. They rolled past Lamar, Colorado, and then into Kansas, where they saw crowds of people along the tracks at Garden City and Dodge City. They made a whistle-stop in Hutchinson around one twenty and another in Topeka at four thirty.

Derrick and Michael spent most of the afternoon in front of cameras and microphones. Derrick interviewed Michael and his family, the students, and the other adults from Iowa, and he also spent some time with Hawk. Time passed quickly, and soon they were pushing through Lawrence, just a half hour from Union Station in Kansas City, Missouri, where another massive crowd and feast awaited them.

"Mr. Hamilton, sir, please take this," Consuelo pleaded as she offered him a plate with a sandwich and chips on it. "I know you won't eat when we stop, and it will be a long time before you are back on the train. Please eat."

"Thank you, Consuelo," he said and sat the plate down on the arm of his chair.

"No, sir." She raised his hand and the plate back off the chair. "Please eat it now before we get to Kansas City."

"Okay." He smiled, knowing she would not relent until he ate something.

"Thank you, Consuelo." Allie acknowledged that she, too, knew her husband would not eat once they reached the crowds.

Two familiar faces were waiting for them at the station: Dane and Christine.

"Hey, what are you two doing here?" Michael gave them both big hugs.

"We're second shift." Dane was happy to see him. "We're here to relieve part of the media crew for the second half of the journey."

"You look great, Michael." Christine gave him a hug and then Allie. It was hard to visit with the crowd cheering, so they all agreed to catch up later on the train. With his bodyguards in tow, Michael waded out into the sea of people crowded into the station, followed closely by Derrick and several cameras. They had about five hours to mingle before the whistle would sound.

There were several bands playing a variety of music at various points around the station. Dr. Nick made his way over to a section of people listening to a polka band. They were his kind of folk. They brought him a brat and a beverage and then bent his ear for the next few hours.

Henry took Ben and Sarah and found a group of folks sitting on blankets eating barbeque. They were mostly young families with small kids, many of whom were homeless living on the outskirts of the city in a camp they called "Mannaville" as a tribute to the support they received from Manna Network.

Peter and Harry took Shelly and Danielle over to a group that looked pretty scary at first. The group consisted of hundreds of bikers who they soon learned had left St. Louis early that morning on a ride to raise money for children. They represented many different bike clubs, including several from St. Louis churches. They planned to ride back in the morning to meet up with the train when it reached St. Louis.

Michael noticed a commotion in one area of the crowd and made his way to it.

"This food is not for you!" a man was yelling at a group of several hundred people who were crowding their way up to the food lines. They looked very poor, and the closer Michael came, the more he realized that they were homeless folk who had been drawn to the station for a meal. Although many of the people at the station had lost their homes and were living in the camps, they still had jobs and food. These were the truly poor and homeless.

"Wait," Michael interrupted the official, "there is plenty for everyone."

Too wrapped up in his own importance, the official paid no attention to Michael and continued to push the people away.

With a camera rolling right over his shoulder, Michael finally reached the official.

"What are you doing? There is plenty for everyone. Why won't you let them eat?"

Shocked by the camera, the official didn't know what to say, so he backed off and started to leave, but Michael beckoned him to stay.

"Wait, I know you're just trying to do your job, but let's see if we can't get these people some food, okay? What's your name?"

"Al," the man muttered in a gruff but easing tone.

The table in front of them was full of hamburgers, chips, cole slaw, beans, and cookies.

"Come on, Al, you give 'em burgers and I'll give 'em beans."

A little uneasy, Al made his way over to the pan of burgers, grabbed the tongs, and began to place burgers onto the plates of those coming through the line. Michael stood right next to him, dipping spoonful after spoonful of beans onto the plates.

"Thank you for coming, ma'am. Have a nice day. Good evening, sir. What's your name, little lady?" He scooped and talked for the next two hours. After a half hour of elbowing and prodding, he finally got Al to say hello to a little boy.

"Would you like a hamburger, son?"

"No, thank you. I don't eat meat."

"Well, then..." he started to yell at the boy, but then changed his tone, "would you like a bun with some cheese?"

"Yes, thank you." The boy grinned.

"Here you go. Why don't you take two?"

"There's hope for you yet, Al." Michael laughed.

Eventually, Michael turned his bean duty over to another man and began to move through the crowd. He never made it to the stage. He never delivered any sort of great oration. No one was wowed by any particular talent he possessed—other than his expert bean-dipping prowess—but no statesman or politician had ever touched them so profoundly.

He never did eat. Once in a while he caught a glimpse of a Hamilton kid carrying another package of hot dogs or buns from one food table to the next. He looked at one point and saw Ben flipping burgers, and later he found out that Allie, at least by her own estimation, had set a world record for lemonade distribution. At one point he even saw Agent Russell leave his guard duty to retrieve another plate of food for an elderly woman who had spilled hers.

"What if someone would have tried to shoot me while you were gone?" Michael teased.

"Sorry, sir."

Michael responded by filling a plate and handing it to him. "Go find someone else who needs a plate and give this to them. I'll take care of Barnes while you're gone."

At eleven thirty, the train whistle sounded, and Arthur O'Donnell began tapping his watch. "Thirteen minutes till we leave. We have a schedule to keep."

Another night of sleep on the train and early morning lay ahead for Michael. He was seated in the observation deck at sunrise when he caught the first glimpse of the St. Louis Arch.

Gateway to the West, he thought to himself and then chuckled at the irony of the fact they were heading east. He wondered if the motorcyclists had made it into town yet. Peter and Harry were full of biker stories, including one spunky biker named Peggy who was smitten with Harry.

They had passed through Independence, Lee Summit, Sedalia, Jefferson City, and the river town of Hermann before hitting the suburbs of St. Louis. There had been countless numbers along the route with torches and signs all cheering the train on her way. Michael and Allie had spent several hours watching from the observation deck before finally heading off to bed. They passed through the Kirkwood station at five in the morning and finally pulled into St. Louis Union Station just before five thirty. Even at the early hour, the station was full of people. The schedule in St. Louis was tight, but Michael waved at the people as he made his way from the train to the awaiting buses. They drove to a homeless shelter a few blocks away where they served breakfast.

The team split into three groups at the shelter. Group one made biscuits, group two made gravy, and group three served. Once again, using his wonderful scooping skills, Michael stood on the serving line dishing gravy onto steaming hot biscuits. Eventually, he talked too much so he was relieved of his serving duties so he could mingle with the men and women at the shelter. By nine o'clock, it was time to return to the train.

Michael had his game face on at the shelter, but as they stepped back onto the buses, his heart began to break.

Is there no end to the suffering? How many faces...How many names? The cheerleader would soon need some cheering himself. That's what good friends are for, and Michael's group of buddies were watching. Back on the train, they pulled him away for a few hours of cards and distracting conversation. Their tactics worked at least well enough to get him ready for the whistle-stops in Springfield and Bloomington/Normal as they made their way through the Land of Lincoln. In Springfield, a man tossed a book full of Lincoln quotes to Michael, and he had a good time reading for a while.

> *I have been driven many times to my knees by the overwhelming conviction that I had nowhere else to go.*
>
> *That some should be rich shows that others may become rich, and hence is just encouragement to industry and enterprise.*
>
> *Whatever you are, be a good one.*
>
> *The best thing about the future is that it comes only one day at a time.*
>
> *You have to do your own growing no matter how tall your grandfather was.*
>
> *I like to see a man proud of the place in which he lives. I like to see a man live so that his place will be proud of him.*
>
> *I don't know who my grandfather was; I am much more concerned to know who his grandson will be.*
>
> *America will never be destroyed from the outside. If we falter and lose our freedoms, it will be because we destroyed ourselves.*
>
> *Abraham Lincoln* (1809–1865)

Behind them lay the west and the prairies. Michael thought of the souls Henry had introduced him to in Valhalla. He thought about Martha's stone and the dollar bill. They were good memories; they reminded him that his trip was more about selflessness than self. Thinking of the pioneers, once again it seemed ironic to him that he was heading east in search of answers instead of west, but destiny does not follow the points on a compass.

Eventually, We Have to Pay the Bill

The Day of the LORD

You have abandoned your people, the house of Jacob. They are full of superstitions from the East; they practice divination like the Philistines and clasp hands with pagans. Their land is full of silver and gold; there is no end to their treasures. Their land is full of horses; there is no end to their chariots. Their land is full of idols; they bow down to the work of their hands, to what their fingers have made. So people will be brought low and everyone humbled.

Isaiah 2:6–9 (TNIV)

I will make mere youths their officials; children will govern them. People will oppress each other—one against another, neighbor against neighbor. The young will rise up against the old, the nobody against the honored. A man will seize one of his brothers in his father's house, and say, "You have a cloak, you be our leader; take charge of this heap of ruins!" But in that day he will cry out, "I have no remedy. I have no food or clothing in my house; do not make me the leader of the people."

Isaiah 3:4–7 (TNIV)

"Good afternoon. I'm Jennifer Linn with the WNN Midday Report. For the last several days we have been following the *Jubilee Express,* but this afternoon we will switch our focus to some incredible developments in New York.

"For over a year now there have been complications from the growing homeless problem all over the nation, but no area has been harder hit than the five Burroughs of New York City. These pictures are coming from our crew in Sky 5 hovering over Fresh Kills and La Tourette Parks in Staten Island. As you can see, there are thousands of people living in tents and cars scattered all over the area. This scene is being repeated in the major parks all over the city. We're going to be switching around, as we have several helicopters in the air. I believe this is a shot of the Gateway Recreational Area in Brooklyn. Here are some pictures from Central Park.

"The living arrangements have been deteriorating for a long time, but with the summer heat, tempers are also starting to flare. We have full-blown riots in several areas of the city, with many reports of youth gangs controlling whole city blocks. Some say the gang population has swollen due to the increasing numbers of homeless. Kids have abandoned their families for these gangs. Bill Simmons has been covering the story. Let's go to him now. Good afternoon, Bill. What can you tell us about the violence?"

"Jennifer, we are getting reports of several thousand youth holed up in the warehouses down on the riverfront along West Street. They have been raiding up into the Greenwich Village area at night and have caused quite a bit of damage. Here are some shots we took last night of a fire raging through one whole city block. It is still burning today, but firefighters believe they have most of it under control. Police are having a difficult time dealing with these gangs because their forces are spread so thin all over the city. They did manage to take a few gang members into custody, and here's the interesting thing; each of them went by the name of a U.S. president. Apparently, the farther back in history the president goes, the more power he controls. So, theoretically, George Washington would be the kingpin—"

"Bill, sorry to interrupt you, but we are receiving word of a large explosion out on the river. We take you live to Heath Johns over the Hudson. Heath, are you there?"

"Yes, Jennifer. Wow, what a mess this is going to be. The ship you see below was a Liberian merchant ship fully fueled and headed out to sea. The Coast Guard is very concerned that she may go down right here in the river. She has already lost a great deal of fuel, and as you can see, the flames on the water are creating an extraordinary sight."

"Heath, what caused the explosion?"

"Well, it's too soon to tell, but authorities are leaning toward the youth gangs that are in the area. They are wreaking havoc all over the city, so for now they are an easy target for the authorities."

"Thank you, Heath. We'll check back with you in a little bit. In other news, the economy continues to slide downward…"

A bright flash of lightning just outside the train window followed by a deafening clap of thunder brought a scream from Lana as the picture on the TV in the Hamilton car disappeared. The news was scary enough without the storm that was brewing outside.

It was two o'clock in the afternoon, and they had just passed through Joliet, Illinois, about one hour outside of Chicago. The news of the camps in New York had many parallels around the country. They had already seen several camps from the windows of the train as they rolled through Illinois. Danielle had spent most of the summer in Chicago, and she was with Michael and Derrick in the meeting room talking about the upcoming events in the Windy City.

"This weather could put a damper on things." Amanda watched the rain pound the train windows. "We are scheduled to have a huge block party tonight just off Michigan Avenue. I will make some calls to see if we can find an indoor facility, but we are expecting thousands of people."

"Danielle, I know you worked in several areas around the city this summer. Can you give us an overview of the state of the camps?" Derrick turned his attention from Amanda.

"They were pretty raw. I'm not surprised at the pictures we are seeing from New York, and I would say the conditions in Chicago could easily move to that point. People are desperate. The Manna supplies were easing the pressures on families to provide the basic necessities, but living conditions, not to mention sanitation, were deplorable. I think time is a big factor. People thought their situation was temporary, but some have been in the camps for eighteen to twenty-four months, and many of those I worked with this summer saw no end in sight."

"You said you could see things in Chicago escalating like those in New York. Are you referring to the kids?" Derrick made notes from her last answer.

"There's nothing to do. The kids are bored to death. Some have summer jobs, but so many are just hanging out."

"Danielle, tell Derrick about the ideas we talked about with the rest of the crew," Michael prodded her to share some of their thoughts on solutions.

"Manna is receiving and using federal funds to distribute food and supplies, and like I said, that is helping. But we think funds for a summer student work project would be good too, especially if those could involve housing projects. We also think the Education Department should take a global look at the school calendar. Why do kids still have twelve weeks off in the summer? So they can help harvest the crops? A year-round school calendar that consisted of smaller breaks would keep the kids in a more consistent routine and give them smaller blocks of time to find trouble."

Dane, who was also in the meeting, looked at Danielle and asked, "What about the kids who just don't see any point to school these days?"

Sarah took the question. "The Industrial Age is over. It's the Information Age now. Working hard is good, but not nearly as important as how smart you are, how much *information* you can process. We keep falling farther behind other nations in the area of higher education. That's not good in a global economy."

Now they were speaking Michael's language. For a long time he had been working with several national groups on projects to streamline the access to higher education process. He was dying to unload his thoughts on this question, but it was a good chance to let the students shine, so he deferred to them.

"Shelly, why don't you share some thoughts with us."

"This question is really a microcosm of the issue facing our nation today. We talk about debt and the economy, and to be sure these are big issues, but they stem from a larger issue, the issue of *change.* We don't want to change. Danielle spoke about the traditional school year and the sacred 'summer off.' We have this mental image of kids running free in the summer sun, and we don't want to change that heritage. The same aversion to change affects other areas of our society, and education is certainly one of the worst.

"For example, several years ago congress passed the 'No Child

Left Behind' legislation, good in theory and certainly well intended. No child should be left behind in our education system, but how do you define being 'left behind'? Does that mean not passing from one grade to the next, or does it mean that we guarantee that each student will be able to do the work of the next grade level, and if so, how do we measure that work? We have thousands of school districts, not to mention bazillions of individual schools, all using a different grading scale and different transcript. In the early 2000s, colleges across the nation stopped using GPA to evaluate students for college admission because they varied so much from school to school that it was impossible to gather a good measure of the student's capabilities—"

"I get your drift," Derrick interrupted, "but what is the solution?"

"Standardize the transcript nationwide," Sarah continued.

"I'm not sure I understand how that plays into the question of access to college," Derrick followed. "So they're standardized. I thought paying for college was the greatest barrier?"

"It is," Ben grabbed the floor. "Hold your transcript thought for a moment and we'll tie up the loose ends. Paying for college is one of the greatest barriers, especially for low-income families. And just for good measure, the fastest-growing portion of our population is the least educated. So many kids quit trying in school at an early age because they see no future in it. They know that in the end, they simply will not be able to afford it aside from taking on huge debt, and we see where that has gotten us these days. Congress needs to overhaul the federal student grant program, not just the amount of aid that is awarded, but the application process. So, here's the idea, overhaul the federal grant application process so that a tax return is basically the aid application, and standardize high school transcripts so they can be uniformly housed on a public clearinghouse site.

"A simplified aid process with real dollars available for those who qualify would help families understand that they really can afford a college education, and a standardized transcript would allow them to apply to multiple schools of their choosing with one streamlined application process."

Derrick's head was spinning. "I'm not sure that I follow, but it sounds like you've put a lot of thought into this topic."

"It's a question of hope," Michael said as he admired the students. "People stop trying because they lose hope, and they lose hope when they can't understand the process. One way to restore their hope is to give them a simplified process that everyone can understand and access. Like Shelly said, the issue is change. Do we really want to change the process, thereby giving true access to everyone, or do the educated elite want to hoard that golden nugget for themselves? Maybe we would rather hand out fishing poles than teach the world to fish. Maybe the economic elite would rather keep the not so fortunate buried in debt. That certainly leaves them with a larger slice of the pie, or so they may think. The truth is, the well is running dry. Credit can only take us so far. Eventually, we have to pay the bill."

A Man without a Home

It was a typical Midwest summer thunderstorm as the rain came down in buckets outside of Union Station in Chicago. Every inch of the station was packed with people waiting for the train to arrive. The local news stations were interviewing people for their evening broadcasts. Sherry Ferguson, one of the reporters on the scene, was interviewing several women in the back of the crowd who were disappointed with their inability to see over the mass of people in front of them.

"You said your name is Dannette?"

"Yes," responded the giggly middle-aged lady in her jeans and t-shirt that read "Hamilton Rocks."

"Why are you here today?"

"We are here to see the next president. He's so hot."

A man standing next to Dannette, obviously irritated with her answer, stepped up: "This is part of history. Candidates don't travel by train anymore. They fly everywhere, and they keep their distance from the people. Hamilton is a man of the people. He listens to us, and he's doing what he can to help."

"What do you think of Jubilee?"

"I don't know if it will work, but I think we have to try something. Millions of people are homeless! That's a recipe for disaster if you ask me."

The whistle blasted in the distance, and the crowd went crazy. Besides the throng inside the station, countless others were waiting outside in the pouring rain.

"Once you're wet, you're wet," a South Chicago man yelled from the crowd. "Let it pour!"

As soon as the last car pulled into the station, all of the Hamiltons stepped out on the back platform and waved to the crowd. The media blitz of the last few days had turned them into celebrities.

Allie and the kids were quickly whisked off to the TV studio of the *Larrine Show,* a national talk show that was hosted locally. They were driven by limousine to the studios through the downtown Chicago streets. The kids were in awe of the buildings. Allie was just nervous about being on TV.

On the show, they answered all kinds of questions about life as a Hamilton. Allie told a few stories about her mother and a little about Michael's missionary parents and his upbringing. Ian and Lana each had their share of adoring young fans in the audience, while Mark was more interested in the green room snacks.

"What has been the most amazing experience of the past year?" Larrine was really enjoying the family.

Lana and Mark each talked about surprising their dad in Atlanta and their visit to Hamiltonia. Ian talked about how proud he was of his dad and said, "He does really care."

"Allie, we'll give you the last word. What can you tell us about this amazing man?"

"My husband is a simple man who sees himself as just another face in the crowd. He does not see himself as particularly special, but he does feel a responsibility to respond to this extraordinary opportunity to make a difference.

"He has a big list of wise sayings in his desk at home. I'm not sure where he found them all, but once in a while I go in and read through them. I would like to share some of them with you today as together we face tough times.

"America is a melting pot…that is our heritage. We are red and yellow, black and white, rich and poor…We live in cities and on farms, we drop out of school, and we graduate with honors. We see the same glass as half full and half empty. For some the sky is blue and for some it is falling, for some it is full of clouds, while others have faith in the sunshine above the rain and they hold on to the hope that the storm will soon pass.

"To those who are rich I would say, 'No one is rich enough to be without a neighbor.'[b]

"'Many of us are self-made, but only those who are successful will admit it.'[c]

"'Much talent is wasted for a little courage.'[d]

"'Sometimes the best thing to get off your chest is your chin.'[e]

"'There are no rules for success that work unless you do.'[f]

"For my husband, who does not grasp after this power, I would say to our nation that real leaders do not always march at the head of the procession, and to those who do aspire to rise to the top, I would remind them that there is no room up there to sit down.

"'Yesterday is gone, tomorrow never comes, today is here. Let's get busy.'"[g]

A moment of silence passed as the host, along with a crowd filled with people living through tough times, contemplated the wise words of a kind woman. After that moment, Larrine hugged Allie and the crowd cheered.

Hamilton's Raiders were busy too. Harry met with a group of

ladies scheduled to have a tea on Navy Pier, but due to the rain, they moved it onboard one of the Lake Michigan tour boats. Henry met with the clergy while Peter met with several area school administrators. Dr. Nick and Hawk went to a local museum and met with a group of kids from a local daycare facility and then traveled to several retirement homes.

Michael and the students spent the day at City Hall in meetings with the mayor and several municipal leaders discussing the issues of governing the homeless in the camps. In a struggling economy, budgets are always tight, but they decided that being proactive was more cost effective than being reactive.

The rain continued all day, and while Amanda had no success finding an indoor venue large enough to host the entire block party, stores and vendors up and down Michigan Avenue were more than accommodating when the Manna Network trucks arrived with the supplies. Food courts were set up in buildings all over the Magnificent Mile, and despite the rain, the party went on. With umbrellas in tow, the Hamilton team made their way through the crowds, shaking hands and listening to countless stories from people who had come from all over the Midwest.

Despite the umbrellas, they were still soaked to the bone by the time they made it to the hotel, which was a welcome respite from the train.

Allie sank down into a tub of hot water and soothed her blistered feet. Michael took the world's longest shower, and then they both crashed into the extra soft pillow-top bed.

"Did you make the arrangements for Sunday?" Allie hoped Michael had not forgotten.

"For Sunday?" He feigned ignorance.

She smacked him on the arm. "Don't kid. This is important."

"Larry made all the arrangements before we left."

"He got the zoo?" Allie sat up on her arm and waited to pounce on any forgotten detail.

"Yep." Michael was admiring the comfy bed as he drifted toward sleep.

"In Philly?"

"Yeah." A touch of annoyance was starting to show in his tired voice.

"And the kids too?" Allie dropped off her elbow's perch onto Michael.

"Yes, he got it all. It's Larry, remember? Did you take care of your part?" He went nose to nose for a response.

"No." She flopped back onto her pillow feeling a bit guilty about her expectations of Michael. "I need a little mall time tomorrow."

He laughed at her and reveled in his victory. "No time tomorrow. Wednesday you'll get plenty of '*Mall*' time, but I don't think it's the kind you mean."

"I'll talk to Christine in the morning. Maybe she can help me." Allie gave Michael a playful shove.

Michael just smiled at her as he rolled over and closed his eyes. "I'm sure she will, you lucky dog."

They all met early for breakfast in the hotel restaurant before hustling back to the train for the 8:02 departure. It's amazing what a good night's sleep can do for a person. They were all re-energized for the downhill run of the trip. Bad weather continued to follow them as the train chugged east, but they passed the time with card games, movies, and books. They stopped around four thirty in Cincinnati to share dinner with a few thousand of their closest friends and then rolled east again.

The next day, Wednesday, the nineteenth of July, they completed whistle-stops in Clifton Forge and Charlottesville, Virginia, before turning their attention to the next stop: Washington, D.C. Receiving warm welcomes out west and across the Midwest had been one thing, but they wondered what kind of reception they would get from the east coast, especially D.C. and New York. Many of the media in the east were put off by what they called a "Folly Express," as they referred to the publicity-stunted train trip.

"It's just another one of Hamilton's crazy ideas, like Jubilee," they ranted.

Unfortunately, other more significant issues filled the news as well. Conditions around New York City were continuing to deteriorate, and the same things were happening in Los Angeles. People just could not live indefinitely in those conditions. A man without a home can be pretty desperate.

Someone Named Lincoln

"Hello. The meeting has been arranged. Randle just left, but Leveki and Bell are here...Yeah, I'm watching it. Makes me sick. They'll be done with that train soon enough and then we'll take care of business. I'll call you after the meeting."

"All right. Here are your tickets." Sydney Porter hung up the phone and turned his attention to the men in dark suits standing in front of him. "You're going to Canal Street. Here's the address. The guy's name is Lincoln, you know the plan. Any questions? What, Leveki?"

"Nothing, this just seems kind of over the top."

"Don't worry about it. Deliver the envelope and then call me. Okay?"

"Okay."

Five minutes later, Leveki and Bell walked out of the Hart Senate Building with tickets for New York in their hands and instructions to deliver an envelope to someone named Lincoln.

In God We Trust

"Fifty-eight, fifty-nine, two twenty-three on the nose," Arthur O'Donnell said to himself with a cocky grin as he snapped his pocketwatch shut, and cocky he should have been. The *Jubilee Express* had traveled over three thousand miles as she pulled into Washington, D.C., and he had managed to keep her exactly on schedule the entire time.

Despite the negative east coast press, any worries about the reception in D.C. were quickly blown away as the largest crowd so far awaited the train. Once again, the Hamiltons greeted the crowd from the platform. Michael was no longer the only Hamilton celebrity. The crowd wanted autographs from everyone in the family, especially Allie after her performance on TV the day before.

America had been watching every move the family made over the last four days. At first it was just a fascination with the train, but now they were really growing attached to the people. From public appearances to intimate moments on the train, Derrick's cameras were rolling the whole time; America had been watching the mother of all reality shows, and to be sure, many people stood to benefit. The network was receiving all-time high ratings, and Derrick Jett's star was shining ever brighter. He had taken a big chance when he pitched the idea to the network only weeks ago, but he was certainly delivering the goods. Michael's appeal as a public figure had grown to legendary proportions, and now his family's celebrity status was busting off the charts. Roe College also stood to benefit. *Loved professor makes good...*

More importantly, however, were the American people, especially those living the nightmare in the Marshallvilles, who stood to benefit if Jubilee really could be taken seriously. Derrick had tried to get a hearing before congress for Michael, but the time was too short and Senator Downs was too strong for it to happen.

The Hamilton team, with the exception of Michael, scattered to meet with their usual constituencies. He stayed with his family and made the rounds to several of the D.C. landmarks—obviously with Derrick, his cameras capturing every moment. Although it was not intended to be a parade, the Hamilton family carriage ride down Pennsylvania Avenue was accompanied by thousands of well-wishers who lined the street. They eventually wound their way over to the Washington Monument.

As they got out of the carriage and looked from the monument toward the Lincoln Memorial, the entire mall was filled with people. About halfway across the mall stood a huge stage setup for the benefit concert that would take place at eight o'clock that evening. Adam's Seed, a new band that had burst onto the scene in the past year, would be performing. Their songs had been climbing the charts all year, garnering them a Grammy Award for best new artist. The band's four members—Jon and Jeremy Adams, Luke Wells, and Matt Barr—had met each other two years ago in a Marshallville just outside Phoenix. Hawk had actually used some of his connections to help them get started.

Allie wanted to send the kids on to the hotel because of the huge crowd, but after much begging and pleading, she agreed to let them stay and work at one of the food stands with Ben and Sarah.

She and Michael made their way through the crowd, which was much different than those in the other cities. The crowd had come from all over the country. Many had started following the story a few days ago as the news broadcasts aired. Larry had posted the schedule on the Web site, and people got in their cars and drove to D.C. to be a part of what they hoped would be history.

The weather that had been a problem the last few days could not have been better. It was actually a little cool. All would have been perfect except there was not nearly enough food to feed the large crowd. No one would have anticipated numbers in the hundreds of thousands. There were several local bands playing on the stage throughout the evening, but at seven thirty Derrick Jett took the stage and introduced Michael. The crowd cheered for several minutes, and when Michael brought the entire team up on stage, they cheered louder and longer. Eventually, he took Allie's hand and walked to the microphone.

"Thank you all so much for coming. We are completely overwhelmed with your support tonight. I hope you got something to eat. We just did not anticipate so many of you. I would love to take credit for all of this, but I think we all know this is about much more than any one person. All of us have been affected by the issues facing our nation this evening. We have the best medical minds and facilities in the world, but most of us cannot afford health care. We have the best schools, but we cannot afford to go. We have magnificent stores filled with beautiful trinkets, but we cannot afford to shop. Some say our plight is our own problem, that we made this bed, and now we will have to sleep in it—"

"Boo!" the crowd yelled.

"Some say the Constitution guarantees the pursuit of happiness, but it does not promise to finance the chase. That may be true, and surely we should each look first in the mirror, but I would also say that there are those who do a good job of keeping the American dream just out of the reach of the American people—"

"Yeah!" the crowd responded.

"For decades we have been buying the American dream, a house, a car, an education for our kids. Seventy years ago we paid cash, fifty years ago we paid it off in fifteen years, and then twenty, and thirty. Eventually, we couldn't pay for it at all, so wealthy, wily, and wise men devised ways to expand credit into hybrid loans, interest only, negative amortization. They sent credit cards out by the billions, and with lust in our eyes we bought it all and now we find ourselves betwixt and between, a strange situation to be sure. We may have surmised that the borrower would eventually mortgage everything, but who would have imagined that the lender would also hit the limit? What does the lender do when no one has any remaining credit capacity?

"So where do we go from here? We've seen one major bank collapse, and it would not be surprising to see others follow. We see the millions of homeless—"

"We're with you all the way!" a single voice called from the crowd, followed by countless others. Allie squeezed Michael's hand as she saw him faltering with emotion. These were real people who had traveled countless miles to find hope. Michael wondered how he—how anybody—could possibly offer hope on the scale that stood before him.

He pulled a dollar bill out of his wallet and held it out to the crowd.

"Some say this is the problem, that money or wealth is the root of all evil. A few months ago a friend took me to a very hallowed place and introduced me to some special people, wise people beyond their years..." Pausing to remember his late-night walk to Valhalla and his encounter with Martha's headstone, he smiled to himself as a funny thought crossed his mind: *Actually, being dead made them all beyond their years.*

"While I was there visiting, I found one of these on the ground, and upon closer observation, I found a possible solution to our problem. Sometimes we find solutions where we least expect them. Sometimes we find them in an old, abandoned theme park like the folks in southern Tennessee—"

"We're here, Doc!" shouted a lady off to his left.

"Where are you? Who is that?" Michael shouted back as he tried to see through the blinding stage lights.

"It's Jonnie, Doc, and a bunch of us from Hamiltonia!"

"Bless your soul, woman! Like I said, some have found solutions in an old, broken down theme park that they have converted into a thriving community. Others, like our band tonight—"

A huge cheer went up as Adam's Seed had come out onstage a few moments earlier and were taking their places.

"Others have found solutions in the tent next door out in the camps. Don't give up hope!" And they cheered again.

"I found hope on the back of a dollar bill in this one little phrase, a phrase that has not been very popular for a long time. I'm sure it is not politically correct and probably not very politically smart, but I still found hope in it. If you have a dollar, take it out. Now give it to your neighbor. If your neighbor doesn't give you one, don't sweat it, but do look on with them because I want us all to read together. Are you ready?"

"Ready!" they shouted.

"Okay. Turn it over on the green side. It says 'one' in big letters in the middle. Got it?"

"Yes!" they all shouted again.

"You all sound really cool, by the way. Nothing like half a bazillion people all speaking with one voice. Hey, that could be profound...sorry.

"Okay, read the top with me...*The United States of America.* Now read the words with me that are written between 'USA' and 'one'..."

"In God We Trust," they all read in unison.

"Read that again."

"In God We Trust."

"Kind of an odd statement to find on money, don't you think? What dummy put that phrase there right on our money? I won't ask you to pass any more bills, but who's got a five-dollar bill? What does it say?"

"In God We Trust," thousands of voices responded.

"How about a ten?"

"In God We Trust."

"On a twenty?"

"In God We Trust."

"Wow, you guys are rich. Anybody rich enough to have a fifty?"

"I got one, Doc!"

"Was that Jonnie?"

"No, Doc, I'm poor!" an answer floated in from Jonnie's section of the crowd.

"Good enough. What does the fifty say?"

"In...In God We Trust!"

"I didn't know that," Allie said, looking at Michael; they both watched the crowd staring at their money and buzzing about the revelation.

"Sounds like a blatant violation of 'separation of church and state' to me, how about you? What were our forefathers thinking? Were they crazy? Didn't they read the documents they wrote?

They wrote them, didn't they? Or wait a minute. Where does it say 'separation of church and state'? The Declaration of Independence? No...The Constitution? No...Not even in the Bill of Rights? It's not in there, folks. It's just in a letter written by Thomas Jefferson to one of his friends, that's it!

"So, back to finding solutions in strange places...*In God We Trust* on our money, well, maybe just the small bills. After all, we wouldn't want to trust him with the big stuff, right? Maybe just the little stuff, stuff that religion can't mess up, maybe just with Junior's cold, or Aunt Martha's trick knee, maybe the weather. Oh, God, please don't let it rain tonight..."

Laughter drifted through the crowd.

"Well, let's see...No, there it is again, *In God We Trust,* on a five and ten. Well, maybe we can trust him with some of the middle stuff too. He is God after all. But the big stuff, we'd better take care of that ourselves. Stuff like the largest economy in the world. What does God know about that? He may have cattle on a thousand hills, but what is that compared to MasterCard? Like Senator Downs said, we should leave that stuff to the men in Washington, right?"

"Wrong!" they shouted.

"Wow, a twenty...*In God We Trust*...and on a fifty! *In God We Trust,* and I'll bet if we were rich enough to have a hundred or larger, they would say the same thing. Gang, I'm not trying to turn this into a prayer meeting. I know we are from many backgrounds and many faiths, but it is hard to deny our forefathers' intentions here. When it comes to money, they have spoken loud and clear, don't you think?"

"Yes!"

"What?"

"Yes!" the crowd roared back. He had them eating out of his hand.

Suddenly, memories of standing before a full sanctuary at Calvary ran through his mind, and then memories of that last Sunday. Allie was not holding his hand anymore, but he could still feel her support as he looked back out into the night sky and the mass of humanity in front of him. He looked at the stars and then at "the star," and he felt the encouragement of two fathers looking down.

"Proverbs 12:9 says, 'Better to be a 'nobody' and yet have a servant than to pretend to be a 'somebody' and have no food.' Did Senator Downs feed you tonight?"

"No!" they screamed.

"Proverbs 11:14, 'For lack of guidance a nation falls.' Proverbs 11:28, 'Whoever trusts in riches will fall, but the righteous will thrive like a green leaf.' So what does God say about debt? In Deuteronomy he says at the end of every seven years you must cancel all debts. He says every creditor must cancel all loans…forgiven…gone…no repayment…a fresh start.

"Some would say that these words are thousands of years old and meant for another time and another place. I tend to take God at his word no matter when he said it, but I am probably just crazy. So how does our world usually balance the scales between the classes, between the rich and the poor, the haves and the have-nots? Well, let's just say it's not usually peaceful. Remember the French Revolution? When enough people have nothing left to lose, they do desperate things. Look at the riots taking place around the country. So what is the state of our nation right now?

"Access to health care, *denied,* too expensive, health insurance not available for many, too costly for others, and too complicated for everyone." An energy began to surge through the crowd like the first strains of music when bow meets string and a symphony comes to life.

"Access to higher education, the greatest hope for the next generation living in the Information Age, *denied,* too expensive, too complicated. We'll just keep handing out fish instead of fishing poles. By the way, one of those wise sayings on the list Allie referred to yesterday says, 'An investment in education pays the best dividends.'[h]" More notes—more energy…building…The huge crowd began to surge.

"Access to the American dream of homeownership, *denied,* too expensive, no credit. Access to Christmas, *denied,* no credit. Access to *Life! Denied! Denied! Denied!* I don't know about you, but I'm tired of being on the outside looking in! Are we tired of being *denied?*" his voice cracked as he shouted into the night.

"Yes!" the huge crowd raged against their plight.

"Then let's trust in Washington to find the answers, yes?" he bellowed with his last ounce of energy.

"No!" they responded as one to their conductor; their symphony was at full crescendo.

"Then who do we *trust?*" he pumped his fist in the air, shouting with all the adrenaline left in his being.

With the climax of the final cymbal crash, the crowd roared as one: "*In God We Trust!*"

Right on Schedule

It was after midnight by the time they all got to the hotel. Michael and Allie had no sooner closed the door to their room when there was a knock. Michael answered, and to his delight, it was Christine with an armload of sandwiches and drinks.

"Oh, come in, come in!" He ushered her into the room.

"I didn't know if you all got to eat tonight, so I grabbed a couple subs on the way back."

"Thank you so much, Christine." Allie's mouth was watering. "We had a few chips, but we were running so low on food that we didn't want to take any."

They all sat down and devoured the sandwiches. While they were eating, Michael caught Christine and Allie exchanging sneaky looks.

"Whoa, those are the looks of two moms up to something." He finished the last part of his sandwich.

"Did you get it?" Allie was excited.

"I did," Christine squealed, pulling another little package out of her bag.

"Shhh!" Michael tried to control the two giddy creatures in front of him. "He's in the next room." Of course, they completely ignored him.

"Oh, he's going to be so excited." Allie examined the blue and silver box that held the V-Game 1000. "It's the newest one, right?"

"I think so." Christine crossed her fingers. "Josh has the 850, and the man at Game Corner said this was the newest."

Allie gave Christine a big hug. "Thank you so much."

The phone in the kids adjoining room rang at five thirty the next morning.

"Hello," came the sleepy voice of the now ten-year-old boy.

"Good morning, sweetie. Why don't you hop out of bed and come into Mom and Dad's room," Allie used her best early morning mom voice.

There was no response on the phone, but Allie could hear a commotion in the other room, and a few seconds later Ian showed up at the door with Mark on his back.

"Watch his head." Allie winced as Mark's head barely cleared the doorway.

"Good morning, birthday boy." Michael was standing by a table full of pancakes and sausage.

"I thought you were going to forget with everything going on." Mark was grinning from ear to ear.

"Happy birthday to you…You live in a zoo…" Ian sang to Mark.

"Hey!" Mark punched him in the arm.

The rest of them laughed, knowing what the day had in store. After a huge breakfast and a quick packing job, they all hustled down to the lobby to meet the buses. They knew better than to keep Arthur waiting no matter the excuse, and sure enough, he was watching for them as they arrived. The train pulled out of the station right on time as usual.

"8:23." Arthur all but kicked up his heels.

They had a thirty-minute ride to Baltimore, where they would make a whistle-stop, a forty-minute ride on to Wilmington for another whistle-stop, and then a seventeen-minute ride to Philadelphia, where a lot of fun awaited Mark and some very special kids from Sisters of Mercy Orphanage.

They pulled into Philly at 10:14 where, along with a large crowd, sixty kids from the orphanage awaited their arrival. They all loaded on school buses with the kids and sang their way over to the zoo. It was a media bonanza for Derrick and his crew. Kids and a zoo and a birthday...Who could ask for more? Larry had outdone himself with the arrangements, which included hot dogs for everyone and what Mark deemed as the "biggest birthday cake he'd ever seen." Mark made lots of new friends and promised to stay in touch. One little girl named Mandy gave him a great big hug as they were leaving and, in so doing, managed to get her cotton candy stuck in his hair. It was a very sweet moment.

Sometime during the festivities, a huge voice came over the loudspeakers at the zoo, making the following announcement: "Celebrating birthdays at the zoo today are: Katy White, Zach Burns, and Mark Hamilton. Happy Birthday and congratulations!"

For most families, celebrating their son's tenth birthday with sixty new friends while twenty-five hundred miles from home at the Philadelphia Zoo would probably be enough for one year. But for the Hamiltons, it would not even be the biggest event of the day. Climbing back on the train at four o'clock, Mark had just over an hour to get cleaned up before the *Jubilee Express* would make her final stop: Penn Station, New York City.

"We're ready for you here," Harold Lawrence informed a nervous Derrick Jett over the phone.

"All the arrangements are made?"

"Yes, Derrick. Three limos will pick the family and the team up at the station. There will be buses for the crew. They will take you to the hotel."

"The Crowne Plaza off Times Square?"

"That's right."

"How is the crowd?"

"There's a big crowd at the station and also at the hotel. There is a media city setup in the streets around the Garden preparing for the Convention. It's going to be magical."

"And Downs, how's he doing?"

"He knows the plan."

"Have you spoken to Sydney?"

"As little as possible, but yes, I spoke to him this morning when he got off the plane. He should be at the hotel by now. Why are you so nervous? You've done well."

"I've sold my soul."

"Well, join the team. Welcome to politics."

"Welcome to hell, you mean. Is this really going to work?"

"You just keep doing your thing. Keep the Hamiltons smiling and the cameras rolling. Everything is right on schedule."

An Answer before Tuesday Night

Penn Station was electrified. The crowd cheered the hope of the middle class as he rode into town on his steely blue stallion that had borne him from sea to shining sea. Like the desperate faces in D.C., many in the crowd had come from far and wide to place their last shred of hope in what they perceived to be the only honest man in politics. If he failed, their hopes would fail. Their last card was maxed, their equity tapped, and the bills looming. What had started as a dream in the eyes of a few college students was now Jubilee or bust for millions. The Hamiltons emerged onto the platform to thunderous applause that reverberated off the walls of the station. They were now on the sixth day of their "fifteen minutes of fame," and they had come to the center of fame's universe, where the pressure of a million critics could turn a lump of coal into a dazzling diamond or a shooting star into a cold, dark rock.

Henry stepped onto the platform and put his hand on Michael's shoulder.

"Is this crazy, Henry? I don't know whether to feel lucky or terrified. How long before my luck runs out and they realize it's just me?"

"Well, son, they say you can tell luck from ability by its duration. I think you passed luck somewhere back around Albuquerque. Now shut up and wave, you fool!"

They made their way from the train to Madison Square Garden, which was directly above the station. The main room was filled with workers making preparations for the convention that would start on Monday. They were turning the room into a sea of red, white, and blue. Michael looked across the wide expanse of the great hall, and memories of legendary sporting events ran through his head. He could almost hear the cheering fans...Champion of the *World*...How many had accepted the party nomination for president in this building? Jimmy Carter, Bill Clinton...It was a magical place.

Adding to the magic were three black limousines waiting outside to drive the Hamilton group to the Crowne Plaza Hotel in the heart of Manhattan. It was only a mile away, but everybody was wide-eyed as they made the trip. Amanda had given everyone a trip packet before they left Los Angeles, and Lana had her New York information out. She couldn't believe how close they were to so many fantastic sites:

- Radio City Music Hall - 0.2 MI
- Rockefeller Center - 0.3 MI
- 5th Avenue Shopping - 0.5 MI
- Broadway Theater District - 0 MI
- Empire State Building - 1 MI
- Statue of Liberty - 2 MI
- Central Park - 1MI
- Wall Street - 2 MI

- China Town - 1.5 MI
- Greenwich Village - 1.5 MI
- SoHo - 1.3 MI
- Times Square - 0 MI
- Garment District - 0.3 MI
- Metropolitan Museum of Art - 1.5 MI
- Diamond District - 0 MI

They were all still buzzing when the limos pulled up in front of the forty-six-story hotel.

"Wow!" Mark stood on the curb staring straight up into the sky at the top of the building.

Their rooms were incredible. This time Michael and Allie kept their suite because they would need the room for meetings throughout the week. With a little help from Larry on the phone, Ben was able to set up communication central in the suite, complete with computers and phones. The suite had separate living and dining rooms, as well as a master bedroom and bath. The kids had the next room, and the rest of the team had rooms just down the hall.

The students took the kids out for dinner and a walk around Times Square, but Michael and Allie stayed behind. They ordered room service, and Michael spent some time on the phone with Larry catching up on Manna business. Larry also gave him addresses for a few distribution centers in the New York City area. He especially recommended a visit to one of the sites in Brooklyn called The Gathering Place. It was located in a pretty tough area, but the folks who ran what was essentially a huge soup kitchen were doing some amazing work.

"Just ask for Keith," Larry told Michael.

When Michael finally hung up the phone, Allie was waiting for him with questions about their schedule. "So, what's on the agenda for tomorrow?"

"We have breakfast with Harold at seven o'clock, and then we are ringing the opening bell of the Stock Exchange at nine thirty. We are free then until one o'clock, when I have a meeting with the party leaders back here at the hotel. Larry has made arrangements for you to take the kids to a Broadway show tomorrow night."

"What are you doing tomorrow night?"

"The guys and I are going to a soup kitchen in Brooklyn. Apparently, it's not in a very safe location, but Larry thought we should go."

Allie called Lana on her cell to see what the kids were doing. They, along with the students, were in one of the hotel restaurants having ice cream.

"It's nine fifteen. I don't want you to leave the hotel again this evening."

"We won't, Mom. We're going back to Shelly's room to order a movie."

"Okay, but don't stay up too late. We have a big day tomorrow."

It was early to bed and early to rise for the Hamiltons. They met Harold in one of the hotel restaurants for breakfast.

"Welcome to Samplings Restaurant." The hostess showed them to the table where Harold was waiting.

"Thank you…Melanie," Michael read her name tag.

Harold, in his excitement, left the table and met them halfway. "Good morning," he said and gave Allie a hug and Michael a firm handshake.

How did we get to know this man so well? Allie thought as she politely returned Harold's embrace.

"Come, have a seat and tell me about your trip."

"Well, ninety percent of it was on the news," Michael shrugged, "but maybe we can fill in a few missing details."

"I've already ordered for us to save time. Enri makes a killer omelet."

Allie smiled politely, once again pondering Harold's assumptions, but Michael responded, "Sounds great. How long will the trip to Wall Street take?" He followed just to make conversation.

"It's only about three miles, but we'll want to allow plenty of time with the traffic around here."

They made small talk for a few more minutes before their food arrived. Despite Harold's warm invitation to come to New York, it was becoming obvious to Michael and Allie that they did not know Senator Lawrence very well. He was going to great lengths to make things seem cozy, but despite his efforts, the conversation remained strained.

"You have developed quite a following, my friend, and you too, for that matter, Mrs. Hamilton. I saw you in Chicago. Great job. Your kids are adorable."

"Thank you." Allie was not exactly flattered by the "adorable kids" comment. It somehow trivialized them, and she did not appreciate the sentiment.

What is this guy up to? She continued to wonder.

As they finished breakfast, Melanie brought a note to the table and gave it to Harold. "It seems your documentarian is waiting for us with the cars."

"Derrick?" Michael tried to swallow his last few bites quickly.

"Derrick." Harold stood and prepared to leave. "Please put this on my tab." He played the big shot with Melanie.

"I guess we're ready." Allie used a polite tone outwardly, but inwardly she was about done with Senator Harold Lawrence.

Derrick was waiting for them in the lobby, and Allie was glad to see his shining face.

Maybe things will be a little more normal, she thought, *that is, if riding in a limo across Manhattan to ring the opening bell for the Stock Exchange can be considered normal.*

Once at the Exchange, Harold led them to an office where they received some instructions, and then they were led to the balcony overlooking the trading floor. Michael rang the bell at exactly nine thirty, Eastern Standard Time. There seemed to be a certain irony to Michael ringing the opening bell. The main financial district had long since relocated to mid-Manhattan, but Wall Street and the Exchange still symbolized American business. Just as he had flashed back to historical moments in Madison Square Garden, he let his mind wander back in time as he watched the traders plying their craft below.

"At least it's not October." Michael scrolled through history as they made their way out of the exchange.

"Why is that?" Harold was looking at his Blackberry.

"October 24, 1929, Black Thursday. October 29, 1929, Black Tuesday and the Great Crash. October 19, 1987, Black Monday, twenty-three percent drop in the Dow, greatest one-day drop in history, and October 27, 1997, Mini Crash, over a five hundred-point drop in the Dow."

"Oh, I wouldn't worry about that stuff if I were you. We're much smarter now." Harold returned the Blackberry to his pocket.

"Oh, much smarter," Allie finally started to let her consternation show. "Twenty million homeless, we're much smarter. Major banks collapsing, much smarter."

"Bank," Lawrence countered in his now familiar friendly but demeaning tone.

"Bank?" Allie did not understanding his meaning.

"Only one bank has become insolvent," he reminded her. "Bank, not banks."

Just before they reached the door to the street, an explosion shook the building.

Despite the shock, Lawrence, in his still calm voice, demonstrated his knowledge of history. "You forgot to mention September 16, 1920."

"What was that date?" Allie cursed the fool in her mind.

"A bomb," Michael knew the story. "Thirty-three dead, four hundred wounded. The FBI investigated for twenty years, but they never solved the crime."

Smoke filled the street as they stepped out of the building. Harold quickly led them away to the cars, but later on the news they learned two men had been killed by the blast.

"Kids," Harold responded to the news. "They are going crazy around here."

"How do you know it was kids?" Michael had been hearing the reports, but he did not like assuming that kids were to blame.

"They have a stronghold somewhere in Brooklyn, and they've been exporting their violence over here. They're upset with the *establishment*...typical youth...rebels without a cause."

"Where have they come from?" Allie couldn't imagine all those kids just running loose.

"We think they're from the camps. Many of the parks in the city have growing homeless populations spilling into them. There have been reports of kids running away from the families in the camps and joining these gangs."

Michael's heart was torn as he thought of the turmoil families and their kids were facing these days, but he could not condone the violence.

"What's being done to solve the issue?"

"Nothing," Lawrence hissed, finally showing some emotion. "Stupid mayor doesn't want to hurt the kids. Well, they sure don't mind hurting us."

"Who is *us?*" Allie snapped.

"Us, the good citizens who pay their bills and don't lose their homes. Us, who don't spend every dime we have and then charge ourselves silly. Let's not glorify the homeless here. They mortgaged their futures and now the bill is due. They chose their path, and not very wisely."

"What happened to 'I pledge to search for answers'?" Michael was somewhat shocked at the change of heart he was witnessing.

By then they were back at the hotel. In the chaos of the moments outside the Exchange and the intensity of their conversation, they failed to notice the rain clouds, but the skies had opened up and it was pouring. Michael and Allie hopped out of the limo, but Harold did not follow. With the rain pelting down, Allie ran on into the hotel, while Michael poked his head back into the car.

"Are you coming?"

"No, I have to run some errands before our one o'clock meeting. I think you'll get some of your questions answered when you meet the National Committee."

Michael nodded and closed the door. It was raining too hard to continue the debate at the curb, not to mention the taxi blasting his horn behind them.

"I do not like that man." Allie was still seething. "Something isn't right here."

Michael tried to calm her, but she would have none of it.

"Why did he invite us, or maybe lure would be a better word? Michael, I think you should have a talk with Derrick or Dane. Something's just not right."

"Let me go to the meeting this afternoon. Harold said I would get my questions answered there."

"Ooh, Harold said," Allie mocked, not trusting anything that Lawrence had to say.

There was a message waiting on their room phone. The caller who left the message identified himself as Kerry and sounded like one of the students. "I will come to your room at twelve forty-five to escort you to the meeting."

Allie ordered sandwiches, and the whole family had lunch around the dining room table. The kids wanted to know about the upcoming meeting.

"Well, I don't know too much, but it will be with the Democratic National Committee." Michael filled his plate with chips.

"Who's that and what do they do?" Lana was trying to understand politics.

Michael did his best to explain. "It is a committee made up of a chairman, four or five vice-chairmen, a national finance chair, treasurer, and secretary. They are in charge of establishing the party platform and raising the money."

"So they are the ones that are going to help you with Jubilee?" Mark was so excited for his dad.

Michael made eye contact with Allie before answering. "We'll see." He tried to convince himself and his family that there was hope for Jubilee.

"But I thought that's why we came here."

"Politics are very complicated, Mark."

"What's so complicated? People need help. That's what the government does, and you have the best answer. That doesn't sound complicated to me."

"I hope you're right."

Sure enough, there was a knock on the door precisely at twelve forty-five, and it was Kerry, a polite young man in his early twenties. Michael knew his life history by the time they arrived at the fourth floor meeting rooms. He was a college student from the University of Arkansas, working as an intern for Senator Martin, who was from his hometown of Mountain Home. His mom was a single parent who had raised him and his sister by herself after his dad left. He was a senior political science major hoping to go on to law school and someday work on Capitol Hill.

A few of the committee members were standing in the hall just outside the meeting room.

"Dr. Hamilton, good afternoon. I am Edward Bosner, and this is Ted Arnett."

"Good afternoon." Michael shook their hands. Ed was a tough-nosed union man, and Ted was the mayor of Seattle. As they stood in the hall and talked, a few other committee members arrived: Treasurer William Bane, a self-made businessman from the West coast; Secretary Donna Luther; and National Finance Chair Daryl Lions.

At 12:55, William Bane suggested that they go in and find their seats. The meeting room was set up with a long rectangular table and sixteen chairs—nine for the committee members plus a few extra for guests like Michael. Ed offered Michael a seat next to his, and they sat down toward one end of the table. The National Committee Chairman was Landon Boggs, former Governor of Pennsylvania. He was seated on the other side of the table from Michael in the center. He was deep in conversation with Janet Dillon, one of the vice-chairs seated to his left, and Quentin Barrymore, another vice-chairman who was seated to his right. Barrymore was also the President of the Association of State Democratic Chairs. There were a few others seated around the table, but Michael did not recognize them.

Breaking from his conversation, Chairman Boggs greeted everyone, "Good afternoon, ladies and gentlemen. It is good to see you. We have been busy all year, and this is the big event leading to the election. We are very excited about our possibilities in November, not only for the Oval Office, but also for the two houses of congress." He took a few minutes to introduce the committee, and then he turned to their special guest.

"Let me say that we are very excited to have Dr. Michael Hamilton with us today." He gestured and Michael nodded in response. "He will be speaking for us on Tuesday night. Dr. Hamilton has become quite a presence in the past few months. I am sure most of you know that he is an accomplished pastor and professor, and more recently, the head of Manna Network. Let me give you some information that you may not know about the Network.

"From one hundred and twenty-five distributions sites spread across forty-seven states, Manna is providing food and supplies to an estimated thirty-two million people. Thanks to an innovative partnership with the pharmaceutical industry, they are also providing much-needed medical supplies to the Marshallvilles, where communicable diseases are spreading at epidemic rates. The Network's arsenal includes three hundred and fifty trucks, three hundred railcars, fifty dedicated planes, and countless volunteers logging thousands of man hours each week. This massive humanitarian effort started with a handful of students on a small college campus in Iowa. Welcome, Dr. Hamilton," Landon Boggs initiated a polite applause as he relinquished the floor to Michael.

"Thank you, Chairman Boggs. It has been a whirlwind these past few months. Fortunately, I have been surrounded by good people with a heart for their fellow citizens."

Janet Dillon spoke next. "Dr. Hamilton, can you tell us about Jubilee? Obviously your position on solving the nation's debt issue has made you very popular, but do you really think it is practical?"

"I have never thought of myself as a radical, but I do admit that the idea of Jubilee, the forgiving of debt on a national scale, is very radical...and practical? I think the time for practical solutions passed a long time ago...about twenty million homeless people ago, five million families ago. Sorry, I am probably preaching to the choir. I'm sure we are all looking for the same solutions. Debt is a tough issue. To answer your question, Ms. Dillon, yes, I do think Jubilee is practical."

"Doctor, what do you say to the lending institutions, many of which are already struggling?" Daryl Lions was notorious for watching the backs of the banks.

"Well, I guess I would ask a few questions first. Why are they struggling? Isn't it because people are not paying their bills? For years we have raised interest rates and charged fees. We have also penalized those who did actually pay off their bills every month, and we have encouraged people to carry balances on credit cards. We have encouraged overextended families to overextend themselves further with hybrid loans and fancy terms. Should people be wiser? Should they understand the world of finance and mortgages? Probably so, but the credit industry in general has been more than willing to prey upon an uneducated public and reap huge profits on the backs of the ignorant."

"Where is the precedence for such a move, Dr. Hamilton?" Treasurer William Bane began to press the questions with a little more edge.

"I think the tobacco settlement of the late nineties offers some precedence. The settlement exceeded $350 billion. If the tobacco industry was liable for deceiving the public, then there definitely seems to be precedence for liability on the part of the credit industry."

"But we are talking about $2-plus trillion dollars," fired Quentin Barrymore. "That's crazy."

"We're also talking about people." Michael tried to remain calm, but he could feel his blood pressure rising. "We are also talking about a national economy that is staggering under this debt, about a nation who leads the charge into debt as one of, if not the largest, debtor nation in the world."

Janet Dillon continued the assault. "Dr. Hamilton, what do we as a party communicate to our constituents in the credit industry when we fail to support them? When we severely, ultimately impact their receivables? How do they survive if we forgive the debt?"

"What do we communicate to people, to voters, if we do not support *them?*"

"We hear you, sir," Chairman Boggs replied, "but the credit industry pays our bills. We cannot ignore them."

"So we should ignore the people?"

"No, we should not," a voice came from behind Michael as Senator Downs stepped into the room. "May I suggest we look for some common ground with the professor and stop fighting with him? He and his Network pack a wallop of good will."

Michael was not sure how to process what he was hearing. *Isn't this the same man who has been opposing all of my ideas?*

"The senator is right." Boggs hushed the hounds following the master's lead.

Without saying another word, Downs left the room, but Lawrence subsequently appeared and took a seat next to Michael.

"Compromise, my good man. Don't lose the whole ball of wax over a few details," he whispered in his ear.

Barrymore spoke up as the meeting continued. "Dr. Hamilton, you have participated in the primary process this year as a candidate. I am sure you are aware that this convention is a mere formality when it comes to nominating our candidate for the election. Senator Downs has already garnered all of the votes he needs to win the nomination, so your presence here as a candidate will come to a dead end in a few days. You are, however, still very valuable to the party. While we cannot, or maybe I should say are not prepared to endorse your Jubilee plan at this time, we would like you to consider several party options."

Janet Dillon took up the pitch. "Dr. Hamilton, we would like you to consider a high-level party position in the new administration."

Michael was a little taken aback by the surprise proposal and did not respond immediately.

"Michael, that's a great deal." Lawrence patted his shoulder.

Michael was starting to get the same slimy feeling about Lawrence as Allie, and his body language reflected that newfound disdain as he pulled back from Lawrence.

"So where would that leave the Jubilee discussion?" Michael was beginning to get some answers to his questions, as Harold had promised.

"It would leave it on the table for a more appropriate time." Boggs' insincerity was way too transparent.

A time after the election when I "might" be given a "position," Michael thought to himself. *They can't alienate me, but they want me to go away. The position is a bribe for silence. Downs is running the game, and Lawrence is here to make sure I play along.*

Michael knew his answer, but he did not want to deliver it to a room of wolves.

"I would like some time." He stood to excuse himself from the meeting. Boggs thanked him and asked him to give the committee an answer before Tuesday night.

The Gathering Place

The Friday evening schedule was full. Allie and the kids were going to a Broadway show while the guys and students were headed to The Gathering Place over in Brooklyn. They all met at Samplings Restaurant for a five o'clock dinner. There was a lot to catch up on as everyone shared stories of their adventures in the city. The students had met several of the interns working at the convention and had actually managed to gain some limited assignments for the upcoming week.

"Be careful," Allie said, giving Michael a kiss as they all left the hotel for their evening events.

Michael, Henry, and Peter shared one of the cabs for the ride over to Brooklyn.

"You were quiet at dinner tonight," Henry probed Michael as they road along. "How did your meeting go today?"

"Not good. They want to bury Jubilee, but they need my cooperation to do it. Lawrence is in knee deep with Downs, and everything is just kind of spinning right now."

"Are you doubting yourself?"

Michael gave Henry a sarcastic look. "It's the presidential election process and it's just us folk here. Doubt myself? Of course not."

"What did they say?"

"We had a negative discussion about Jubilee. It was rapidly going south, and then Downs walked into the room. He put his thumb on them and they got all sweet again. They offered me a 'position' in the new administration."

"What about Jubilee?"

"We can talk about it at a more 'appropriate' time."

"And Lawrence?"

"He was a different person all day. Allie thinks he is a sleaze, and I am beginning to agree with her. Wow, where are we going? This neighborhood looks pretty rough."

They were weaving their way into the Old Navy Shipyard district where the buildings were dilapidated and scary looking. As they got closer, the streets buzzed with young people. Eventually, they pulled up in front of an old warehouse with the words "The Gathering Place" painted high above the door.

"Guess this is it." Peter was having some second thoughts about their visit.

Ben laughed at them all sticking close together as they exited from the cabs. "What's wrong with you guys? Just another day at the office." Ben had seen some pretty rough spots traveling with Hawk, so he was accustomed to the surroundings. Hawk smiled as they walked to the door where a large man was seated.

"Can I help you?" His body language communicated more "Can I hurt you?"

"We're looking for Keith." Ben walked right up to him.

"What's your name?"

Michael stepped to the front and gave his name. "We're with Manna Network. Larry sent us."

"Larry Finner?"

"Yes, sir."

"There's a name I know." The man's face creased with a broad smile and he pulled out a radio. "Ricky?"

"What."

"Group her from Manna for Keith."

"Tell them to step into the light."

The man motioned to the group and directed them under a camera that was hanging above the door.

"Okay, I'll send someone."

They waited for a few minutes until a mop-headed young man opened the door and motioned for them to follow. When he opened the door, an awesome aroma drifted out to the group.

"Man, that smells good." Shelly drew the atmosphere deep into her soul.

"You just ate," Danielle reminded her.

"Yeah, but that smells great!"

The door opened into a large converted warehouse. It was nothing fancy, but it was filled with tables where hundreds of people sat at tables eating sandwiches and soup from huge bowls. There was a stage with a band playing rock music at one end of the room, but their guide was leading them toward the other end. They came to a freight elevator and stopped.

"It's old, but it will get you there," he said as he opened the gate. "You pull down on the rope to go up, and you pull up to stop when you get to the top. You do the opposite to come back down." He closed the gate and stepped back from the elevator.

"Where are we going?" Harry did not like the elevator at all, and he was not alone.

"Up there." The kid pointed to some windows at the top of the warehouse.

Hawk grabbed the rope and gave it a pull. The elevator lurched into motion, giving everyone a start. "Rookies." Hawk laughed.

He stopped the elevator and opened the gate when they reached the top. They stepped out onto a walkway that was open to the large room below, leading them to a door where the kid had pointed. They knocked on the door, but no one answered. Finally, Michael opened the door and peeked inside. A man was coming toward him.

"Come on in. Sorry I didn't get the door. I was working in the back. Hey, everybody, I'm Keith. You must be Michael." He extended his hand. "I've seen your face all over the TV this week. I can't tell you how much we appreciate Manna. I don't know how we would make it without you."

"Thank you." Michael admired his firm handshake.

They stood around and talked until Keith urged them to go back downstairs for some dessert. "Cobbler ought to just about be ready, and I think the band should be starting in a bit."

"There was a band playing when we came in." Sarah wondered why he could not hear the music that was drifting up from below.

"Oh, that's not *the* band. Those are just kids. Wait till you here The Gathering Place band. They're smokin'!"

"Rock 'n' roll." Ben winked at Sarah.

They managed to traverse back down the elevator, and Keith maneuvered a few tables together at the foot of the stage. He was right…a band of kids. They looked to be mid-teens.

"Where do all the kids come from?" Peter wondered about the kids on the streets outside.

"All over." Keith motioned to a waitress. "We give them a hot meal and let them play their music. It keeps them off the streets."

"What about the violence we've been hearing about?" Danielle couldn't imagine the kids on stage committing such heinous acts. "Two people were killed today."

"It's New York City. There's always stuff going on here."

Michael pressed Keith a little more. "We've been hearing stories about kids leaving the camps to join up with gangs. Do you know anything about that?"

"There have always been gangs and kids joining them. I don't think that's really news."

"But what about the kids leaving the camps…running away from their families?"

"You guys sure do ask a lot of questions. Hey look, here comes the band. Let it rip, guys!"

With that, the band kicked into their signature song:

They're comin' from the corner, they're comin' from the street
Gonna have a good time tonight
Open up your heart and lay your troubles down
At The Gathering Place tonight
There's a hunger inside that's bustin' you wide
Gonna fill it all up tonight
Come in from the dark and fill your empty soul
At The Gathering Place tonight
There's a place on the corner where the weary find rest
At The Gathering Place tonight
Everyone is welcome when they come inside
At The Gathering Place tonight
Wine turns to water and stones turn to bread
The lonely are wanted and the hungry are fed
Everyone is here to worship in his sight
At The Gathering Place tonight
Tonight, tonight, a chance to make things right
Tonight, tonight, at The Gathering Place tonight
Tonight, tonight, won't you step into his light
Tonight, tonight , at The Gathering Place tonight…

Standin' there bare in the sight of the Lord
With our sin all hangin' out
Nothin' looks good in this neighborhood
Unless he covers it with his grace (hide your face)
So lay down your shackles and hang up your chains
Wipe off your tears and forget your pains
Come on down, come on down
To The Gathering Place tonight

It was hard to talk while the band was playing, but it felt good to sit back and relax. After a waitress brought strawberry cobbler to everyone, they ate and listened for a long time.

At about eight thirty, Michael's phone rang. "Michael, this is Dane. Can you talk?"

"Sure, Dane, hold on a minute. I can't hear you in here." He quickly made his way to the door and stepped outside, nodding to the large man at the door as he passed. "Okay, sorry about that. I couldn't hear over the music."

"Where are you?"

"We're in Brooklyn, somewhere around the Old Navy Shipyards at a rehabbed warehouse called The Gathering Place."

"Michael, what did you do in that meeting today?"

"Not much. I actually didn't stay very long. Why?"

"There's a lot of buzz going around through the ranks about you, and it's not good. I'm really worried for you. Do you know somebody named Lincoln?"

Michael was becoming aware of his surroundings. There were kids everywhere, and this was not a place for them to be hanging out. *What am I doing out here?* Michael thought.

"I'm sorry, Dane. What did you say?"

"Do you know somebody named Lincoln? I've heard that name

several times today linked with you, and it didn't sound very promising, mate."

"You mean like Abe Lincoln?" Michael was thinking of the presidential names the kids had been using, but Dane thought he was teasing.

"Shut up, man, this is serious! You know how to get under the skin of some pretty important people. I know, I've seen you do it. Who did you make mad this time?"

"I don't think the committee liked me very much. They made me an offer I can't refuse."

"So, are you going to refuse?"

"I'm sure that I am."

"Bad move, man. You need to be careful."

"I'll be careful," he promised before hanging up. "Where's Russell and Barnes when you need them?" he asked the breeze as he put his phone away. "Whoa." A little boy was standing just behind him as he turned around. "Where did you come from, little guy?"

The little boy did not speak. He just held a note out to Michael that read:

We are watching you
Meet here tomorrow night
Same time
Come alone

Lincoln

When Michael looked up from reading the note, the little boy was gone.

Well, I guess I'll meet Lincoln tomorrow night. He went back in and showed the note to Henry and Peter.

Henry looked worried. "You can't come back here by yourself."

"I'll just come and have some soup. If Mr. Lincoln is watching and introduces himself, I'll invite him to be my guest."

"It's not funny, Michael. These kids are dangerous. You saw that firsthand today on Wall Street."

"We have volunteers working in sites like this all over the country. I'll be okay. Besides, Henry, you should have seen the little boy who gave me this note. He was only six or seven. Somebody needs to do something for these kids, find out what they want, what they need."

"What happened to that doubting man in the cab? 'It's just us folk'...remember?"

"I remember." Michael shook his head, knowing that Henry was right.

"You remember, but you're still coming back tomorrow night."

Michael just looked at Henry and no more words were needed.

Pull Up to Go Down

Saturday passed quickly. Michael did some sightseeing with the family, but he was not very good company. He was thinking about the evening and his meeting with Lincoln. He was also feeling guilty about not sharing the news with Allie. He didn't want to worry her, but he was not in the habit of keeping things from her. She gave him funny looks all day, wondering why he was not himself. They had only talked briefly about the committee meeting, and now all of his thoughts were running together.

They decided to eat lunch in Central Park.

Nothing like a relaxing picnic, Michael thought, but it was far from relaxing. There were tents and homeless people all over the park. They had heard news stories about the parks in the city being overrun by the homeless, but seeing the mass of humanity eking out an existence was still overwhelming.

It's no wonder kids run away from this, Michael thought.

The sights put a damper on the day, and by mid-afternoon they decided to go back to the hotel and swim. While he sat by Allie at the pool watching the kids, he told her of his plans for the evening.

"Michael, you can't do that."

"Someone has to find out what's going on with these kids."

"But what if they are the ones blowing things up?"

"Then all the more reason to meet with them."

"Why you?"

"They've seen my face on TV. They've seen me with our kids and especially with the students. They see me as a teacher, as someone safe…I don't know."

"Do you have to go alone?"

"It's really not that far. I'll go, I'll listen, I'll come back to the hotel."

"What if they want you to do more than that?"

"Then hopefully there will be something I can do for them. Lord knows, somebody needs to do something for them. Little boys like the one I saw last night should not be running around on those streets…or any streets."

The kids were worn out from sightseeing, so they spent the evening in the room watching movies while the men kept Allie company playing cards. It gave her some comfort knowing that Henry knew where Michael was going. She gave Michael a kiss as he left.

"I'll call you when I'm on my way back."

He carried out his plan exactly as he had described to Henry. He arrived at The Gathering Place around eight o'clock. The streets were busy with kids, just as they had been the previous evening. He went inside and ordered some soup and, in his usual way, got to know his waitress. Her name was Katie, a twenty-five-year-old graduate student, but she looked more like eighteen and was a little fuzzy on her program of study.

Bad lie, Michael thought. *Never try to fool a professor with a story about school.* He chose a table away from the band, so, in the event that Lincoln did show up to talk, they might actually be able to hear each other.

He looked up to the walkway leading to Keith's office and saw him leaning on the rail just outside his door. They exchanged polite waves, but Keith did not come downstairs. A bowl of soup and a cobbler later, there was still no sign of Lincoln, and Michael was starting to get sleepy. It had been a long day, and now, with his belly full, his eyelids were getting heavy.

Man, I'm getting old, he told himself. *Don't answer that,* he responded.

At 8:38, his phone began to vibrate in its holder. "No Data Sent" read the caller id.

Hello, Mr. Lincoln, Michael thought before he answered the phone.

"Hello."

"This is Nixon, Mr. Hamilton. Are you ready to meet?"

The voice was young and serious. Michael wanted to laugh, but thought better of it given the situation.

"Yes, Mr. Nixon, I'm ready."

"Come out to the street. Turn left and walk to the streetlight at the end of the block. Wait there."

That made things a little more serious, as Michael could sense danger now. He did not like the arrangements, but he agreed and complied with the request. It was a warm summer night as he made his way to the end of the block. The streets that had been busy with kids earlier in the night were now strangely empty.

It's only eight forty-five, he thought, double-checking his watch to make sure the readout on his phone had been correct. As he neared the streetlight, two silhouettes stepped out from a nearby building and strode toward the light. They all arrived at the same time.

"Good evening, gentlemen." Michael was taken by their young faces. "Are you Nixon and Lincoln?"

With a look of disgust, one of them stepped forward. "I'm Nixon, he's Rice."

"Rice?" Michael questioned. "I don't remember a Rice."

"You wouldn't. He was only president for a day…long story."

"Sounds like a short story to me," Michael quipped, drawing their frowns. "I thought I was meeting with Lincoln."

"Not tonight."

"Am I meeting with you?"

"No. Please turn around. We need to blindfold you."

Michael did not like the sound of that request. "Sorry, guys, you're going to have to tell me what's going on or this meeting is over. I would like to help if I can, but—"

"We are taking you to Washington."

"Number one?"

"That's right."

"But I have to be blindfolded?"

"That's right. Now come on, he doesn't like to wait."

"Is it far?"

The final question did not receive a verbal response, but the nonverbal was effective enough. It was against his better judgment, but at this point everything was against his better judgment, so he allowed Rice to blindfold him. They turned him around a few times and then led him several hundred feet to a door, which they opened with a key. Once inside, Michael definitely thought he could smell soup, and he could hear the clanging of silverware. There was no band music, but everything else seemed like The Gathering Place. They walked a little way and then stopped. He heard the creaking elevator gate open and they stepped inside. This time they went down instead of up for what seemed like quite a distance. When they stepped off the elevator, the boys removed the blindfold. A long hallway stretched out in front of them, and, judging from the stone foundation walls, Michael surmised that they must be underneath the buildings above.

What a genius, he thought, laughing at himself. *We did go down in the elevator.*

He followed the boys through countless hallways, making turn after turn. After a while he was completely disoriented. At 9:09, his phone began to vibrate again.

"Mr. Hamilton?"

"Yes, is this Mr. Lincoln?" the voice sounded a little older.

"No, sir, this is Jefferson. Mr. Adams and I are waiting for you at the end of the hall."

"End of which hall?"

Click.

With that, the lights went out. Michael felt himself jostled about for a few seconds and then he was alone in the pitch black. After a few seconds passed, a light appeared several hundred feet in front of him, so he walked toward it. As he got closer to the light, its brightness made him squint. Walking through an archway and into a small room, there were two young men waiting for him.

"Jefferson and Adams?"

"Yes, sir, I'm Adams."

"What are we doing here, boys? Is there something you want from me, or can I go home?"

Jefferson looked at him with steely eyes and replied, "Mr. Hamilton, you can never go home. We've been watching you on the train. You have come too far and done too much to go home. Too many are looking to you for help. You can never go home."

With that, a heavy stone door slid open and a rush of loud music filled the room. They stepped into a huge theater-like room with a stage at one end. Thousands of kids filled the multi-story room to the rafters, and they were screaming over the deafening music. Jefferson and Adams led Michael into the room and let him listen to the band:

Lights and the fame of the cool fast lane
Out of control like a runaway train
Don't tell me what to think
I got enough on my mind
Don't tell me a thing
Just let me go blind
I'm in the in, I'm in the know
Freely it flows, freely it flows

Down to the River, never down to our knees
We lay down with dogs and wake up with fleas
Down to the River, never down to the word
We lust for the gutter and long for the night
Down to the River, Down to the River
Down to the River we go

Throw out your books, Throw out your gods
Throw out your children, Spare the rod
Trade in compassion for passions of Gold
Love like sand's gettin' harder to hold
The seeds are sown while the moon is red
A wild beast howls at the clouds of dread
The children of darkness are anxious to know
Where are their gods when they reap what they sow

Down to the River…

They led Michel back into the small room from which they had come, and now waiting for him was a young man dressed in a suit. The stone door closed behind them.

"Good evening, Dr. Hamilton, my name is Washington. Don't call me George, and I won't call you Doc."

"Who are you guys and what do you want?"

"We are the children of the scorned, the destitute, the homeless, as they have come to be called. Our families live encamped, but we have escaped to this haven where no one tells us what to do."

"Are you responsible for the violence in the city?"

"No, sir, you and your generation are responsible. You hear the clang of the coin, yet you are deaf to the widow, you watch the market and scorn the orphan, you steal from the poor and give to the rich. Early to bed, early to rise, may make a man healthy, wealthy, and wise, but in the end he only…dies?"

"Those are very disturbing words."

"Disturbing they may be, but unlike your generation, we will do more than just talk. We will care for our own, unlike your generation, who spits in the face of the man who is down while kissing the heel of the rich."

"What are you talking about?"

"You make the athlete rich and the teacher poor, you burn fossil fuel that kills our world because greed is greater than good, and you flirt with mass destruction like gods at play with dolls.

"'The Lord enters into judgment against the elders and leaders of the people; It is you who have ruined my vineyard; The plunder from the poor is in your houses. What do you mean by crushing my people and grinding the faces of the poor? Declares the Lord Almighty…'[i]

"'I will make boys their officials; mere children will govern them…The young will rise up against the old, the base against the honorable…'[j]

"'Woe to you who add house to house and join field to field till there is no space left and you live alone in the land…Surely the great houses will become desolate, the fine mansions left without occupants…'"[k]

"Don't twist the Bible. Those words don't condone your violence."

"'Do as I say, not as I do.' Is that it, Professor? Do you not twist the words of Moses for your purposes?"

"I do not twist anyone's words for any purpose. What is it you want from me?"

"I thought you would understand. You use the words from the good book to suit you. I thought you would understand us."

"Tell me your name, son. Let me help you…please. Why are you so angry?" Washington turned away from Michael.

"His mother was killed three years ago in one of the camps," Adams interjected.

"I am sorry, son. To all of you I would say I do believe that this next generation, your generation, can and will lead us back to where we should be, back to a place where people have more value than gold, a place where the air is more important than profit, and a place where we seek peace and beat our weapons into plowshares. I see hope everyday in the eyes of students who sit in my classes, and I believe in their goodness. I believe they trust in the good book from which you quote, and I think they believe in a God who gives us his wisdom and, more importantly, his grace. He is the God of forgiveness where obedience, not might, makes right."

"Leave us, Doc. I cannot think anymore."

"Take your little ones home, Washington. Take them back where they belong. Take yourself back there as well. End this violence."

The stone door opened, and this time there was only silence beyond it. The lights went out and the stone door closed. After a few seconds, the lights came back on and Michael was alone. He stepped out into the hallway and followed the lights. They led him down several halls, but eventually he came to an elevator.

Pull down to go up, he remembered. Exiting the elevator, he found his way out of the deserted building to the street—the empty street. He could see the streetlight in the distance and The Gathering Place a block beyond. He called a cab, and then he called Allie. It was very late.

My Good and Faithful Servant

Sunday was a gorgeous day. The whole team went to Trinity Church for services. The four-mile drive from the hotel to the church was unpleasant for Michael. Demons of young presidents haunted his thoughts along with pounding strains of "Down to the River." What had he witnessed last night? It seemed very surreal on this beautiful morning back above ground. Still, he knew there were mothers weeping for lost children, and despite his best efforts, he could not think of a solution.

Services at the church did not start until eleven fifteen, but Michael had requested an early arrival to give them time to look around the grounds—especially Trinity Church Yard, which held several interesting treasures. The church stood at the base of Broad and Wall Streets with its spires peering down at the heart of the American financial district—a stark reminder for all to monitor their priorities. Another ironic connection between the church and the issue of money was a man named Hamilton—Alexander Hamilton, the first Secretary of the U.S. Treasury. Killed in a duel with Aaron Burr in 1804, Hamilton was buried in the church cemetery.

"What's on your mind, my quiet friend?" Henry walked along with Michael through the beautiful church grounds.

"It's all a bit overwhelming. I know we've talked about this before, but those kids last night...We saw suffering as we traveled this summer, Henry, but can you imagine the suffering of the parents on top of everything else they're facing? Maybe this battle is too big for me, or anyone for that matter."

Henry led Michael through Trinity Church Yard to two bronze tablets commemorating the Battle of Washington Heights—some of the worst fighting of the Revolutionary War.

"Do you think Washington ever wondered, 'What am I doing here with this rag-tag bunch of misfits?' It was a question that likely drew the answer: 'I'm going to die here with these misfits.' Did you ever wonder what our history books would say if the color of Washington's coat had been red instead of blue? He would have made an awesome officer for the Redcoats. He was a gentleman's gentleman who could have earned great reward instead of great peril. What do you suppose history would look like if he had come to the Potomac and said, 'I'm not the one.'"

"But I'm not Washington."

"No, you are a nobody, just a simple college professor who couldn't possibly change your world. Let's walk." As they walked between the graves, Henry led them to the headstone of Clement Clarke Moore.

"Do you know who this man was, Michael?"

"''Twas the Night Before Christmas' Moore?"

"That's right, he wrote the poem 'A Visit from St. Nicholas,' a poem that gave us our contemporary concept of Santa and his reindeer. He wrote it for the amusement of his children and had to be coaxed into publishing it. It was first run anonymously. The poem was somewhat silly to the Colombia College Greek professor, who preferred to publish things like Hebrew dictionaries."

"I did know that he was a professor."

"Sometimes our world is shaped by warriors and sometimes by poets, sometimes by pilgrims and sometimes professors, sometimes by the old and wise." He puffed himself up and snapped at the breast of his coat, "And sometimes by the young."

"So, what am I, Henry?"

"You are a philosopher-poet. You dream with your heart, but think too much with your head. You believe anything is possible, but you think someone else will achieve it. You are always waiting to follow, but now it is time to lead. You don't have to win the day, just sow your seeds. Cross one more river, pen one more poem…I saw your 'Days of Rain.'

"Michael, you have treated me with the respect of an adoring son, and I have loved you like my own. If I am the 'old and wise' man, then that wisdom tells me it's time to pass the baton. We have already done so at the college with the passing of the department chair. Where you once looked to me for leadership, I now look to you. Where you once supported me, I now support you. You will not change your world with the sword like Washington, but you may change it with the pen like Jefferson or with your speech on Tuesday evening. Cross the river, Michael. Write the speech and deliver it with all your heart."

"Dad! Come on! We're going to be late," Mark shouted in the distance.

Henry put his hand on Michael's shoulder and they walked back to join the group.

Trinity Church was beautiful, its neo-gothic architecture topped with a gilded cross that once welcomed ships into New York Harbor. Long since dwarfed by skyscrapers, the church had a history of caring for the poor and misfortunate as it welcomed wave after wave of immigrants to a new land and new hope. Her magnificent bronze sculpted doors opened onto a street known for its commerce, but reminded all that greed must be tempered by good and that our faith must remain at the heart of even our greatest financial endeavors.

The rector welcomed everyone and read from Scripture before delivering his message.

> "Now faith is being sure of what we hope for and certain of what we do not see. This is what the ancients were commended for. By faith we understand that the universe was formed at God's command, so that what is seen was not made out of what was visible. By faith Abel brought God a better offering than Cain did. By faith he was commended as righteous, when God spoke well of his offering. And by faith Abel still speaks, even though he is dead. By faith Enoch was taken from this life, so that he did not experience death: 'He could not be found, because God had taken him away.'" For before he was taken, he was commended as one who pleased God. And without faith it is impossible to please God, because anyone who comes to him must believe that he exists and that he rewards those who earnestly seek him. By faith Noah, when warned about things not yet seen, in holy fear built an ark to save his family. By his faith he condemned the world and became heir of the righteousness that is in keeping with faith. By faith Abraham when called to go to a place he would later receive as his inheritance, obeyed and went, even though he did not know where he was going. By faith he made his home in the Promised Land like a stranger in a foreign country; he lived in tents, as did Isaac

> and Jacob, who were heirs with him of the same promise. For he was looking forward to the city with foundations, whose architect and builder is God. And by faith even Sarah, who was passed child bearing age, was enabled to bear children because she considered him faithful who had made the promise. And so from this one man, and he as good as dead, came descendants as numerous as the stars in the sky and as countless as the sand on the seashore. All these people were still living by faith when they died. They did not receive the things promised; they only saw them and welcomed them from a distance, admitting that they were foreigners and strangers on earth. People who say such things show that they are looking for a country of their own. If they had been thinking of the country they had left, they would have had opportunity to return. Instead, they were longing for a better country—a heavenly one. Therefore God is not ashamed to be called their God, for he had prepared a city for them.
>
> Hebrews 11:1–16 (TNIV)

"Faith," the rector removed his glasses, "being sure of what we hope for and certain of what we do not see. Faith - hoping that men have the capacity to love their neighbor, though we seldom see it. Faith that men of vision will rise up to lead this nation, for where there is no vision, the people perish. Faith to look forward with dreams of a bright future rather than turn into pillars of salt for looking back at golden ages past. Faith to join hands of different color, creed, and conviction and see one nation united under God, indivisible with liberty from anything that would enslave, and justice for all. Faith to live in hope of his promises, his grace, his calling until all faithful servants arrive in his promised city, his Promised Land and nation, his heavenly rest and hear his holy words: 'Well done, my good and faithful servant. Amen.'"

A Time to Love

Sunday was left open as a day of rest with the exception of an interview Michael had scheduled with Derrick. They decided to take advantage of a beautiful day and do the interview outside. For location, they chose Ellis Island, the famous "Island of Hope." Between the first immigrant, Anne Moore, an Irish girl who arrived at the island aboard the steamship *Nevada* on January 1, 1892, to the last, a Norwegian seaman named Arne Peterssen in 1954, over twelve million immigrants passed through the island into the U.S. Michael was fascinated with Anne Moore's story. She and her brothers, Anthony, age eleven, and Phillip, age seven boarded a steamship in Queenstown, Ireland, on December 20, 1891, along with one hundred and forty-eight other passengers. Legend has it that upon arrival on New Year's Day 1892, which just happened to be Anne's fifteenth birthday, her brothers shoved her ahead of a large man shouting, "Ladies first." As the first immigrant to arrive at Ellis, Anne was presented a ten-dollar gold coin.

Finding a good spot to set up for the interview was not difficult, as there were countless breathtaking views to use as a backdrop. Once settled, Derrick began to interview Michael.

"We have traveled literally thousands of miles together over the past week, and I have seen you do some amazing things, Michael.

What is the most important thing about yourself that you would like to share with the American people?"

It was still uncomfortable for Michael to talk about himself, especially in terms of being amazing. He pondered the question for a moment before answering.

"Derrick, the Psalms say, 'We are all fearfully and wonderfully made.' We are all unique with special God-given abilities and gifts. We tend to dwell on that uniqueness far too much these days. While our uniqueness is important, we seem to blow it out of proportion. We have turned that uniqueness into a 'me-centered' philosophy. Hundreds of years ago we thought the universe revolved around the earth, but now, being much more educated, we know that to be false. In our enlightened state, we now know that the universe revolves around the proverbial *me.* What do I want? What can I get? I'm a self-made man. I can do anything I put my mind to...

"What do I want people to know about *me?* Just that I am an ordinary man who, just like them, faces extraordinary circumstances, and I hope *we* will choose others over self. 'Do unto others as you would have them do unto you,' the Golden Rule. 'Love your neighbor as yourself,' part of the Great Commandment. We have twisted those words from the 'we' to the 'me.' Do unto others *before* they do unto you...unto thine own *self* be true.

"We need to learn to love each other. We've spent so much time insulating ourselves from each other that we don't know, much less love each other anymore. I don't want people to think I am something special, that I possess some special gift that allows me to do extraordinary things. If that were true, then the gift would pass with me and all would be lost. But the gift does not lie within one person. It lies within all people...not within the 'me,' but within the 'we.' It lies within our capacity to care about each other. If I could speak with the tongues of angels and do anything I put my mind to...If I was the most talented person in the world, but I did not love others, I would be nothing. If I gave everything I have to the poor, even my life, but I did not love others, it would all be for nothing. Three things last forever, faith, hope, and love, and the greatest of these is love."

"Michael, some would say that sounds like socialism, communism, Marxism...the 'we' over 'me' mentality. Where is capitalism?"

"All of the 'isms' you mentioned are 'manisms,' faith in man, not God. 'Then God said, Let us make man in our image, in our likeness, and let them rule over...all the earth...So God created man in his own image...' Genesis chapter 1. But man, in his wisdom, has decided that he does not need or want God, so he has re-created God in whatever image suits the moment. Who needs a meddling heavenly parent and a three-inch-thick book of rules?"

Derrick looked deep into Michael's eyes. *Who is this man? Isn't he just a small-time professor?* Michael was forcing him to look a little deeper at the American Dream. Derrick was so close to making his wildest dreams come true, but the cost seemed to be his soul as Michael peeled back the ugly layers of greed that tarnished the ideals upon which America had been founded.

"But isn't our nation built on capitalism? Isn't that what made us great?"

Us great, Derrick thought to himself as he asked the question. *I'm starting to sound like Hamilton.*

"'In God We Trust' made us great, pledging allegiance to 'one nation under God' made us great, 'we the people, holding these truths to be self-evident, that all men are created equal, that they are endowed by their Creator with certain unalienable Rights, that among these are Life, Liberty, and the pursuit of Happiness' made us great. Capitalism did not make us great, neither is there anything inherently evil about it. Capitalism offers each person the chance to profit from their hard work. Nothing wrong with that, but when the scales become dishonest, when we tolerate abject poverty in the face of absolute wealth, then I say we do not love and therefore become nothing."

"Do you want to be president?"

Again, Michael had to ponder the question.

"The easy answer is no. Senator Downs is right, I am not from Washington, and I don't understand all the ways of the politician, but leaders are not elected to represent Washington, they are elected to represent the people. The easy answer is that I probably will not even be on the ballot. Downs has earned the party nomination through the primary process. I am just here to speak."

"Again, I ask you, do you want to be president?"

"I want to be faithful. I want to be faithful to God and to his word that says, 'In the beginning God created the heavens and the earth,' words I can choose to believe or reject, faithful to a call to love my neighbor and treat him as I would have him treat me, faithful to care about those in pain and hardship, faithful to live a life before man and God as a truly good and faithful servant of both.

"A wise man offered me this advice during the early days of this process. I told him I was not worthy of this office. He didn't argue. Probably no one is worthy. He took me to a place and made me look into the eyes of those who have walked the path before us, who have paid the price for our freedom. Although I did not grasp after this office and after this power, and therefore did not want to run for it, he told me not to run from it. So is it time to run for office? God's word says:

> "There is a time for everything and a season for every activity under the heavens:

> A time to be born and a time to die, a time to plant and a time to uproot,
>
> A time to kill and a time to heal, a time to tear down and a time to build,
>
> A time to weep and a time to laugh, a time to mourn and a time to dance,
>
> A time to scatter stones and a time to gather them, a time to embrace and a time to refrain,
>
> A time to search and a time to give up, a time to keep and a time to throw away,
>
> A time to tear and a time to mend, a time to be silent and a time to speak,
>
> A time to love and a time to hate, a time for war and a time for peace.
>
> What do workers gain from their toil? I have seen the burden God has laid on the human race. He has made everything beautiful in its time. He has also set eternity in the human heart; yet no one can fathom what God has done from beginning to end. I know that there is nothing better for people than to be happy and to do good while they live. That each of them may eat and drink, and find satisfaction in all their toil—this is the gift of God. I know that everything God does will endure forever; nothing can be added to it and nothing taken from it...
>
> Ecclesiastes 3:1–14 (TNIV)

"So I will be faithful. Faithful to neither add nor take away from his work, and if that should include work for me at 1600 Pennsylvania

Avenue, then I will do that work with all my heart and trust in his guidance and his grace."

"Amen," Derrick concluded the interview.

8:30...Fingers Crossed

Observing Sunday as a day of rest meant that Monday was definitely a day of work. Although they had been laboring on the speech for several weeks now, putting it all together was proving to be difficult. Monday started with an early meeting over breakfast, during which everyone received their assignments. By now they were a well-oiled machine, so no time was wasted.

Shelly resumed her leadership role as they began to put the pieces of the puzzle together.

"It seems to me we need to clearly define the need for Jubilee, the urgency of the situation in the nation, possible alternatives, and some sense of historical perspective."

Sarah reminded everyone of Dr. Hamilton's mention of the French Revolution as an alternative solution to dire national situations. "Jubilee sounds much better than the riots we are seeing."

"So what do we have in common with the French Revolution?" Danielle probed the group.

Larry, who was dialed in for the meeting, wasted no time supplying some information.

"We have many things in common with the French. First, historically, their revolution and the late eighteenth century attitudes that drove them on were the same attitudes that drove us to revolt from the British. 'Liberté, egalité, fraternité, ou la mort!' 'Liberty, equality, fraternity, or death!'"

"Sounds good, Larry, but what about today?"

"Okay, Shelly, here's some info for you. The French resented the absolute rule of the king and the privilege of the rich and the clergy, who were supported by the national treasury at the time to the point of being rich themselves. They grew tired of watching Louis throw gigantic parties while the masses starved. The rich grew richer and the poor…Sound familiar? How about these facts, heavy national debt and taxation, wars, does that sound like France of the 1780s or America of today…Maybe both? On top of everything, the French grew tired of the bumbling Louis who, like our leaders of today, failed to deal with the issues.

"The people longed to choose their own destinies, both economically and religiously. Finally, in July of 1789, the have-nots, with nothing left to lose, banded together with some of the military and stormed the Bastille prison in Paris, and the revolution was on. By January of 1793, Louis XVI was guillotined, followed by Queen Marie Antoinette in October. The next year was known as the Reign of Terror. Between eighteen and forty thousand people were executed."

Regaining the floor, Shelly pushed forward, "Okay, so we know we don't want that to happen. What about this debt we're facing right now? How do we convince people that Jubilee is right?"

"I've been doing some research too, Larry," Sarah winked at everyone as she spoke into the conference phone on the table. "There is an incredible pattern in our nation. It happens every century. Century opens with war; with peace comes optimism and prosperity; with prosperity comes overconfidence and speculation, which leads to overextension, debt, and an eventual correction, usually a great depression."

"She's right," Ben added. "It started with the nineteenth century: First, war, the War of 1812. That was followed by a boom of the 1820s and early 30s. Even a growing national debt of ninety million that accumulated in the 20s was paid off by Andrew Jackson's administration. The boom that gave birth to our railroads, canals, and highway systems also ushered in grand speculation in land. Banks that once operated only on hard currency, coins, began to operate on soft money, paper. When the government withdrew their support of the soft funds, over half the banks in the nation failed, setting off a wave of economic corrections known as the Panic of 1837. The correction, or depression, was rivaled in scope only by the Great Depression of the 1930s and lasted until 1843."

"So, how did they fix it? Did they declare a Jubilee?" Danielle urged with excitement.

"Well, yes…sort of," Sarah replied, taking up the torch from Ben. "In 1843, the settlers of Willamette Valley in the Oregon Territory offered free land, three hundred twenty acres to married couples and one hundred sixty acres to single people. By 1848, the U.S. formally declared Oregon Country a U.S. territory, and in 1850 Congress passed the Land Donation Act, which replaced the less formal free land arrangement with a federal law. The Homestead Act, signed by Abraham Lincoln in 1862, extended the offer of free land from the Oregon Territory to the Midwest and eventually Alaska. That law stayed on the books until 1976, with the last homestead claim being completed in Alaska in 1986."

"And we all know the story of the twentieth century." Shelly paced as she let the new thoughts settle in her mind. "World War I…Roaring 20s…Stock market speculation…Crash of 1929, the Great Depression."

"Followed by the New Deal," Larry warbled through the speaker phone.

Danielle, beginning to think aloud, said, "So, war on terror, huge speculation in the housing market, crazy interest rates and hybrid loans, consumer debt spiraling out of control fueled by billions of credit card offers flooding the mail, buy now, pay later, use the equity in your house to reduce monthly payments by hundreds a month—"

"Twenty million homeless, riots, disease," Ben punctuated her sentence.

"A collapsing middle class, not to mention a collapsing family structure," Shelly added. "Where's a Bastille when you need one to storm?"

Morning gave way to noon, and breakfast to lunch. They talked; they wrote; they researched; they talked. Afternoon turned into early evening, and sandwiches gave way to pizza. They were making good progress, but the clock was racing on. By six o'clock, they were exhausted and decided to stop for the evening. The convention had been in session all day, and while they had taken short breaks to catch some of the proceedings, they were most interested in the evening events. Several prominent people were scheduled to speak, but the promise of an eventful evening disappointingly droned into the uninspired rhetoric of a party—and, indeed, a nation—lost in gridlock. There simply was no vision.

By nine o'clock, the students decided to go back to their own rooms where they could rest and prepare for the coming day. Michael and Allie took the kids down to Samplings for some ice cream before turning in early. After all the excitement of the past week building up to the convention, the day had been a letdown.

Michael rose early on Tuesday morning and met Henry downstairs for breakfast. They decided to go for a walk and found a small diner across the way. They sat down at the counter and ordered some eggs. Michael noticed a man staring at him, but when the eggs arrived, he turned his attention to eating and forgot about him. A few minutes later, however, the man came over and sat down on the stool next to him and began to ask about Hamiltonia.

"What's your name?" Michael tried not to spit eggs on him.

The man stammered a bit before answering, "Charlie." Charlie was somewhat haggard looking and didn't smell too good either, despite being dressed in what could best be described as business casual.

"Are you here on business?"

"I was," Charlie again stumbled over an answer to a simple question.

Michael was beginning to wonder why the man had come over. Other than a few questions about Tennessee, he did not seem overly talkative.

"Are you doing okay?"

"Not really," Charlie paused, hoping he could trust Michael with his story. "My friend was killed over on Wall Street a few days ago and...I'm just not doing very well with it."

"Oh man, I'm sorry to hear that." Michael assumed he was talking about the explosion he had witnessed. "Weren't there two killed? Did you know the other person too?"

"Yeah," Charlie started to answer, but then changed his answer to no. "I gotta go," he eased off the stool.

Michael caught his arm to stop him for a second and asked the waitress for a piece of paper and a pen. He wrote the eight hundred-number for Manna down and told Charlie to call if they could do anything. He also told Charlie about The Gathering Place.

"Ask for Keith and tell him Michael Hamilton sent you."

"Actually, you'd better tell them that Larry sent you," Henry snickered, knowing that Larry's name had more clout at the soup kitchen than Michael's.

Charlie took the piece of paper and thanked them. He shook their hands and walked out the door. It was a strange encounter, and it haunted Michael for a long time. As they walked back to the hotel, Michael remembered Dane's warning.

"I'm just glad his name wasn't Lincoln."

"Lincoln!" fumed Seth Randle. "Is he reliable?"

"Yes." Sydney was growing impatient with his irate partner. "Calm down. We've used him before. He's a pro. He knows what he's doing."

Although it was a bright, sunny day outside, seven people met in a dim room with shades pulled, and only a few indirect lights burning over the boardroom table. It was the daily meeting of the Democratic power-brokers led by the big man himself, Monroe Downs. He was calm, but the group knew how he could erupt without warning, and no one wanted to set him off.

"What's the status on Hamilton?" he directed his words to Landon Boggs, who immediately punted the question to Janet Dillon or Quentin Barrymore.

"He'll never do it," a voice not seated at the table replied. "I interviewed him yesterday, and I can tell you, he's never going to give up Jubilee."

"Who does he think he is?" Randle ranted.

Downs looked at Sydney, and no more words on the subject were spoken.

"What's on the agenda for today?" Downs moved on.

"Hello," Allie answered her cell phone. "What? Slow down, Henry, who took him?"

Henry was out of breath as he rushed back to the hotel. "The kids took him."

"Is he okay?"

"Yes, there was no struggle. He went willingly. He told me to call you, and he also said to call Dane."

Allie immediately tried to call Michael on his cell, but there was no answer, so she did as Michael requested and called Dane. It was about ten in the morning. At 10:20, Derrick knocked on the Hamiltons' door looking for Michael.

"He's not here," Allie told him as she recounted Henry's story.

"What did Dane say?"

"He asked about somebody named Lincoln, and then he said he wanted to find you. What's going on, Derrick?"

"I don't know, Allie. I need to talk to Dane," he excused himself from the room.

Everyone gathered in the Hamiltons' room. After an hour or so, Ben decided to take Peter and Hawk to The Gathering Place to see if they could get any information. Christine did her best to comfort Allie, but nothing seemed to help. Hours passed, and eventually the men returned from Brooklyn, but they had no new information. No one was really hungry, but they ordered dinner and went through the motions of eating. At seven o'clock, Dane called.

"Did you talk to Michael?" Allie was frantic.

"No, but I just got a call with instructions for you all to go to the convention tonight."

"Who called?"

"Jefferson, sounded like a kid. We're working on some stuff

here. I think you all should get ready and head to the Garden. I'll meet you there at eight thirty. I know this sounds crazy, but if everything goes as scheduled, Michael is supposed to speak at nine. I don't think any of the party people know he's missing, so let's just play it cool."

"Did you talk to Derrick?"

"He's with me."

"All right, we'll be there at eight thirty. What if...what if he doesn't show?"

"Let's just be there and keep our fingers crossed."

The Speech

The Hamilton group arrived at Madison Square Garden at 8:35. While the party folks that met them were puzzled by the absence of Michael, they escorted them to their reserved seating just to the left of the stage. A senator from Massachusetts was speaking, but he was distracted by the buzz of the crowd when the group was seated. He spoke for a few more minutes, but he had obviously lost the crowd. He concluded to polite applause.

Dane was stationed in his usual spot by the teleprompter at the foot of the stage. From the media booth, Derrick called him on the headset.

"Is he here?"

"I don't know. Roll the video and we'll play it by ear."

The lights dimmed and the spotlights combed the room.

First, the trumpets—"Bom, bom, ba," Dane sang into his headset as the first strains of "Fanfare for a Common Man" began to drift through the excitement in the air. Derrick's video essay from the past week, along with countless pictures supplied by the Hamilton team from the summer, began to fill the huge video screens. Each face, each scene told a painful story of a broken nation. As the opening measures of the song blossomed into full orchestrated surround sound, the room moved with emotion and beckoned a hero to come.

"Where is he?" Derrick thundered into the headset.

"Right on cue," Dane just shook his head. "Michael, you beggar, you, where do you get this flair for the dramatic?"

The doors farthest from the stage opened, and Michael walked in trailed by an unending line of kids. They followed him all the way to the stage and then split off to fill in the empty spaces on the floor. Other kids were filing in through all of the other arena entrances. There were thousands of them. Michael took the stage as if it were the corner of his desk and began to speak.

"The average American household[1] has thirteen payment cards, including credit cards, debit cards, and store cards. There are 1.3 billion payment cards in circulation in the United States. Americans make over one trillion dollars' worth of credit card purchases a year. Average household credit card debt increased 167% between 1990 and 2004. The average interest rate paid on credit cards is over fourteen percent.

"Total American consumer debt first reached one trillion dollars in 1994. Total American consumer debt reached $2.2 trillion in 2005 and has increased ever since. Americans carry, on average, eight thousand dollars in credit card debt from month to month. Making only the minimum monthly payments on that debt will take thirty years to pay off. On average, the typical credit card purchase is twelve to eighteen percent higher than a cash purchase. Over forty percent of U.S. families spend more than they earn. Over two million bankruptcies filed annually, almost one out of every one hundred households in the United States will file. Average homeowners stay in their home for 7.1 years. With an eight percent mortgage, they will sell their home still owing over ninety percent. Continuing this trend, they *will never* pay off a mortgage in their lifetime! Only two percent of homes in America are paid for!

"Over ninety percent of U.S. family disposable income is spent on paying debts, up from sixty-five percent in 1975. Ninety-six percent of all Americans will retire financially dependent on the government, family, or charity. Nearly half of all Americans, forty-six percent, have less than ten thousand dollars saved for their retirement.

"We see this stress on families played out in many ways:

"Family violence[m] accounts for over ten percent of all reported violence. One-fourth of all murders occur within the family, and of the nearly five hundred thousand people in state prisons for violent crimes, fifteen percent are there for a violent crime against a family member.

"Is it any wonder that our families[n] are breaking down? Surveys show that financial stress is the number one cause of divorce. Thirteen hundred new stepfamilies are forming every day. The average marriage in America lasts only seven years. Over fifty percent of U.S. families are remarried or recoupled. Is it any wonder we see the issues with our children?" He gestured to the thousands of kids standing around the arena. Pictures of broken families continued to scroll across the screens behind him.

"Fifty percent of the sixty million children under the age of thirteen are living with one biological parent and that parent's current partner. Two out of three marriages taking place under thirty years of age end in divorce. A breakdown at the family level is the most basic of all tragedies for any civilized nation. It impacts every area of life, and it is impacting our nation as a whole.

"In the area of education, we continue to fall behind other nations. Where a high school education once set us apart from other nations, we now see those nations pulling ahead of us with an ever-increasing percentage of their populations receiving higher education degrees while we have remained stagnant at about thirty percent for the last sixty years. While other nations make provisions for an ever-changing world, we hang our hopes on ivy-covered dreams for the wealthy, while the fastest growing portion of our population remains the least educated, resulting in decreasing per capita income, shrinking tax base, increased welfare, and, most importantly, shrinking hope. We are no longer living in the industrial age where hard work was king, but in the information age where knowledge reigns supreme. Educate or be left behind.

"From the young to the aging, our seniors work hard for a lifetime only to see the fruits of their labor expended on runaway health care costs and disappearing pension and benefit plans. Debt for seniors increased over ninety percent during the first decade of this century. Tens of millions of Americans who once used the equity in their homes as future security find themselves refinancing and utilizing that equity to pay down credit card debt.

"So where does this bad news end? According to the politicians of today, it does not even exist; everything is fine. They would lay the blame at the feet of the individual, and to be sure, each one of us should look first to the person in the mirror for a solution to these issues, but that same level of responsibility should fall to our national mirror. Our leaders of the past were certainly aware of the trappings of debt:

> *All the perplexities, confusion and distress in America arise not from defects in their Constitution or Confederation, nor from want of honor or virtue, so much as downright ignorance of the nature of coin, credit and circulation.*
>
> *John Adams*

> *If the American people ever allow private banks to control the*

issue of currency, first by inflation, then by deflation, the banks and corporations that will grow up around them will deprive the people of all property until their children wake up homeless on the continent their fathers conquered.

Thomas Jefferson

The money powers prey upon the nation in times of peace and conspire against it in times of adversity. It is more despotic than a monarchy, more insolent than autocracy, and more selfish than bureaucracy. It denounces as public enemies, all who question its methods or throw light upon its crimes. I have two great enemies, the Southern Army in front of me and the Bankers in the rear. Of the two, the one at my rear is my greatest foe. Corporations have been enthroned and an era of corruption in high places will follow, and the money powers of the country will endeavor to prolong its reign by working upon the prejudices of the people until the wealth is aggregated in the hands of a few, and the Republic is destroyed.

Abraham Lincoln

"So are we wiser tonight than those who formed this nation, who laid her foundation, and then put her back together again after civil war tore her apart? Is there wisdom in the apathy of our leaders? Can you look into the faces on the screens above me and the children who surround you and simply say 'be warm and fed'? Have we completely separated ourselves from *Common Sense,* even from its author Thomas Paine who said, 'A generous parent would have said, 'If there must be trouble, let it be in my day that my child may have peace.'

"For too many generations, we have passed these issues along… debt, health care costs, and a lagging education system. When will we resolve to answer these questions? When will we hold our leaders accountable, and in holding them accountable, when will we give them a fair chance to solve issues in the way they need to be solved, not for the short run, but for the long?

Michael surveyed the room as he caught his breath. Thousands of voices shouted in his head. Some represented the faces on the video screens above him, pleading for a solution, for some shred of hope. Others heckled his presence, screaming hatred for his beliefs, his ideals, his self-righteous mirror stuck in their twisted faces of greed.

"Some of you believe that Jubilee is crazy, and maybe it is, but at least it is a solution that offers hope to a broken nation. It shares responsibility among the classes, among the haves and the have-nots, among those who make the policies and those who lobby for those policies. Tear Jubilee apart if you will, but offer a *solution* in its place!" A man who once struggled to find words of farewell for a dying congregation now thundered with emotion, willing the stiff-necked nation to bend her knee and regain the God-given glory of her past.

"Our founding fathers pledged their lives, liberties, and fortunes to birth a new nation, and most of them paid an enormous personal price in doing so. It would have been much easier for them to be selfish. Many of them were well-to-do, but their principles drove them to choose freedom for all over selfish gain. In the early years of the nineteenth century, our third president, Thomas Jefferson, made the famous Louisiana Purchase, which doubled the size of the new nation. He commissioned Lewis and Clark to explore that vast new land. Eventually, the nation would offer free land to its citizens, and the rush west was on. The Oregon Trail was born, and thousands headed into the grand unknown to complete our Manifest Destiny.

"Do not be fooled looking back through your twenty-first century rose-colored glasses to think that these were anything other than incredibly brave and extraordinary people. There were no MapQuest sites or on-wagon satellite navigation systems. And do not be taken in by movies of the old west, these were not seasoned wagoneers. These were people from Jersey who purchased a wagon one day, loaded their family and all their possessions in it the next, linked up with a group of folks they most likely did not know, and headed into the wilderness with some 'guide' to whom they entrusted their lives. So again, just as the founding fathers, these patriarchs of the plains pledged their lives and fortunes to birth a whole new part of these United States, and once again, many of them, thousands of them, paid for those dreams with their lives.

"That is our heritage—men and women of incredible character and fortitude risked everything to make this nation what it is today. So who are we and what will we do with this heritage, this incredible gift, this responsibility? I urge you to look at the faces on these screens and give them an answer! Give them *hope!*

"Look at this picture on the screens, and I submit to you that we face the same three choices that our pioneer fathers faced…go back, stay where we are, or move ahead even as we face daunting, if not impossible obstacles. In this picture we see an unending train of wagons winding their way down a very steep embankment toward a wide rushing river. We see wagons crossing the river over a series of three islands and then winding their way toward incredibly high mountains on the horizon. The place is Three Island Crossing in Idaho.

"Again, I urge you to remove your rose-colored glasses and see the incredible drama before you. As I said before, these were not seasoned wagon masters. They were just people from the eastern seaboard. They bought a wagon a few weeks ago, and then they were doing their best to navigate rivers and steep grades. Folks, they were just hoping they wouldn't run over the wagon in front of them. They didn't have Wagon-101 class, and they certainly didn't have federally inspected brakes! In truth, they witnessed firsthand the brutality of the trail. They saw people washed away in swift rivers, attacked by wild animals, come crashing down a hillside. They pushed through bad weather and exhaustion only to arrive at this seemingly impassable river, and if they did manage to survive the current, they faced mountains twelve thousand feet high as a reward. Mountains may look beautiful today as we navigate highly engineered roads in our SUVs, but a Conestoga wagon was no picnic on a thirty percent grade.

"So, back to our choices. Those pioneers of our past could have chosen to go back. If they had, we would all still be huddled on the east coast, but something caused them to get in the wagon in the first place, something that made them willing to risk everything. Maybe it was the economic Panic of 1837 that left our nation in a depression, surpassed only by the Great Depression of the 1930s, or maybe it was the promise of free land and the hope that dreams of homeownership can bring. Whatever the cause, it must have been strong.

"They could have chosen to stop, stay where they were. No more crossing rivers and mountains, no more pushing on, no more dreaming…no more hoping…just giving up and stopping. But this was the wilderness, and they were not suited to survive there. They were not suited to *quit.* So they did the best they could with a rickety old wagon, bad brakes and all. They kept their eyes on the horizon, even when it was filled with mountains, and they pushed on.

"Were they all successful? No. Thousands were not. Did they make mistakes? Why don't we ask the Native Americans if mistakes were made? Did they go forward? Let's just say that California is the most populous state in the nation. Somebody got across those rivers and over those mountains."

A rumble went through the great hall.

"'Oh sure, Hamilton, that was two hundred and fifty years ago. What does that have to do with us today?' Everything is completely different? I emphatically say no to that way of thinking! I say we are still faced with the same choices of going back, staying where we are, or moving forward.

"Will we go back? Will we seek solutions to our issues with the same thinking that caused our issues? Will we become pillars of salt looking back to our 'glory days'? Will we stay where we are and ignore the issues altogether, telling ourselves that nothing is wrong? Will we ignore the millions of homeless? Will we only care if we are personally affected? Or will we face the fact that there are reasons to get in the wagon and go forward, maybe into places you can't Google or Mapquest before you get there? Will we cross the rushing rivers filled with the issues of health care and education? Will we cross the mountains of debt that stare at us from the horizon? Will we do more than turn a deaf ear to our neighbors in need that, somewhere beyond our broken religions, beyond our self-centered universe, we know in our hearts should be loved as ourselves?

"What say you? Will you be silent! Apathy is the opposite of love! What say you tonight?"

From somewhere out in the darkened arena, a single voice began to respond. It was Washington, "Jubilee! Forgive the debt! Love your neighbor as yourself..."

"Jubilee! Forgive the debt! Love your neighbor as yourself..."

Slow and steady the other kids standing all over the Garden began to join him.

"Jubilee! Forgive the debt! Love your neighbor as yourself...Jubilee! Forgive the debt! Love your neighbor as yourself..."

Within moments their voices were one, and they began to march in place until the arena shook under their feet.

"Jubilee! Forgive the debt! Love your neighbor as yourself…Jubilee! Forgive the debt! Love your neighbor as yourself…"

"What say you, people? Will you go back? Will you stay where you are? Or will you pledge your lives, your liberties, and your fortunes? Will you pledge your families? Will you pledge all that you are to make your life and your world all that it could be?" Michael boomed over the chorus of thousands of kids still speaking with one voice: Jubilee! Forgive the debt! Love your neighbor as yourself…Jubilee! Forgive the debt! Love your neighbor as yourself…"

Finally, they began to stand.

"What say you, Alabama? Where are you, New York? How about the Gateway to the West? Where are you, California, *are you still there?*"

"Yes!" they roared and joined the chorus. Soon the whole room erupted. The faces were rolling across the screens of countless "neighbors" in desperate need of the love that was rising in the room. The band blasted back into the mix with "Fanfare for a Common Man," and the roof rose to the heavens. Moments passed into minutes into timelessness as some continued to raise their voices, while others bowed their heads in shame.

"How could we let things sink so far?" one man wept with his neighbor.

Eventually, Michael spoke again. "I will close with this thought…

"You have one life

One childhood to enjoy

Once through primary and secondary school

One first everything

No second chance

No redo

You have many choices in the moment

Moments run into minutes, into hours, into days…

Years are filled with days determined by the choices of the moments

Memories are the results of those choices

Life is not designed to be fair

It is designed to be free

But freedom is not free, it costs everything we have and then some

My freedom extends to yours, and yours to mine, a billion times over

Today, I need more space, more room to swing my arms, to be free

Tomorrow, maybe you will need more space

Whose freedom is more important?

What is fair? Who will decide?

Are only the decision makers free?

You have one life

Act like it

You are free to act differently

You are free to pay the price

You have one life

Spend it well."

While he was speaking, a strange phenomenon was taking place around the city. Knowing that Michael Hamilton would be speaking that evening, many of the homeless had made their way to the streets surrounding Madison Square Garden. When he arrived with the kids and their faces began to show up on TV screens all over the city, parents of the runaways saw their children and began to make their way to the Garden. The streets outside were now filled with a multitude. From the teleprompter, Dane got a message to Michael at the podium of the events taking place outside. As he finished speaking, Allie joined him on the stage and the arena exploded with applause. With Allie on his arm, Michael left the stage and led the kids out of the building, hoping to reunite them with their families, a decision based more on adrenalin than common sense.

The crowd outside the Garden was held at bay by the National Guard, who had been called in to assist the police with the riots and the convention. The crowd had been pushed back about thirty yards from the doors, so Michael was able to lead the kids out of the building. As he walked toward the crowd, it occurred to him that he had no plan.

Seconds later, it would not matter. Two shots rang out. A man named Lincoln walked away from an open window across the street and disappeared into the crowd. Michael dropped to the ground…It was over.

Jubilee

Wasted Days

A day is wasted in the fray
As hours pass and minutes tread
On lazy moments in the midst
Of uninspired dreams and such
Where men of mischief lie in wait
For the uninformed and hurried late
Round and round the world does spin
On time's great path and at its end
The soul both spent and filled within
Will measure by immortal scale
The breadth of life's eternal sail
If not enough to move the ship
Will sink in silence and slowly slip
Away from light in ageless deep
And come to rest in timeless sleep

Or should this life be full of grace
Eternal blessings there bestowed
Be lifted up from earthly sod
To pass in peace
Eternal days...with God

Downs defeated Marshall in the general election of '28. Not only were all discussions of Jubilee silenced, but the federal funding of Manna Network ceased, and within a few months the Network was finished. Despite several efforts from the new president to reinforce the banking industry, several more major banks closed as more and more people failed to meet their monthly obligations.

For two years Downs reigned with an iron fist over a nation that shriveled in his shadow. On a dreadfully cold Sunday in February 2030, some mourned while millions rejoiced at the news of his death. In passing the news on to his congregation at the morning service, the rector at Trinity Church shared the following passage from Proverbs:

> Wealth is worthless in the day of wrath, but righteousness delivers from death. The righteousness of the blameless makes their path straight, but the wicked are brought down by their own wickedness. The righteousness of the upright delivers them, but the unfaithful are trapped by evil desires. Hopes placed in mortals die with them; all the promise of their power comes to nothing. The righteous are rescued from trouble, and it falls on the wicked instead. With their mouths the godless destroy their neighbors, but through knowledge the righteous escape. When the righteous prosper, the city rejoices; when the wicked perish, there are

> shouts of joy. Through the blessing of the upright a city is exalted, but by the mouth of the wicked it is destroyed...For lack of guidance a nation falls, but victory is won through many advisers.
>
> Proverbs 11

Downs was succeeded by his fellow degenerate, Harold Lawrence, and the nation languished in darkness for two more years. Where there is no vision, the people perish, and perish they did by the tens of thousands. The camps were besieged with disease from unthinkable sanitation issues. Only in the Civil War had Americans inflicted so much pain upon themselves.

By 2032, the nation was ready for change. They elected a new president—a Republican named Andrew Jamison. Party was not the driving force behind their choice for change. Both parties had failed the people, but Jamison allied himself with a voice from the past—a voice of hope, a voice with vision. Within weeks of his inauguration, as he prepared to meet with his cabinet for the first time, he called upon a group of men from Iowa to join him in Washington.

"As I convey these words to you now, I find myself standing on a white porch steeped in history with two men of whom I am most proud. To my left is a young man who married my granddaughter last year and now pastors a small church in rural Iowa. To my right...to my right is a man whom I have known all of his life. I saw him grow up as a child on two continents, watching the stars overhead to keep track of family spread across the globe. I watched him succeed with humility, fail with honor, and grow with grace over the years. I watched as, save for the tug of a little boy on his sleeve that allowed the marksman's bullets to miss his vital organs by millimeters and spare his life, he dropped to the ground four years ago. And then I watched him recover slowly, far from the public eye for his own safety. Today, I stand here to support him as he meets with the president, where he will once again present his plan of Jubilee. Is the nation ready for Jubilee? We shall see…We shall see…"

In a world that has gone blind there walks a madman
For he still believes that he can see
His mind tormented, still he is unbroken
By a siege of sages preaching blindness
In a world that has gone blind there walks a madman
For he still believes that he can see
Though demons rage against this rebel
Still he offers Jubilee

The Branch of the Lord

In that day the Branch of the LORD will be beautiful and glorious, and the fruit of the land will be the pride and glory of the survivors…

…Then the LORD will create over all of Mount Zion and over those who assemble there a cloud of smoke by day and a glow of flaming of fire by night; over everything the glory will be a canopy.

It will be a shelter and shade from the heat of the day, and a refuge and hiding place from the storm and RAIN.

Isaiah 4:2–6 (TNIV)

Endnotes

a Ralph Waldo Emerson http://www.quotedb.com/quotes/3641

b Danish Proverb http://www.theotherpages.org/quote-05d.html

c Anonymous http://www.motivatingquotes.com/success.htm

d Sydney Smith http://www.bored.com/findquotes/cate_740_Talent.html

e Anonymous http://www.quotesandsayings.com/finquoteframes.htm

f Anonymous http://www.quotesandsayings.com/finquoteframes.htm

g Anonymous http://www.quotesandsayings.com/finquoteframes.htm

h Benjamin Franklin http://quotations.about.com/cs/inspirationquotes/a/Wisdom10.htm

i Isaiah 3:14–15 (TNIV)

j Isaiah 3:4–5 (TNIV)

k Isaiah 5:8–9 (TNIV)

l http://www.newstepsolutions.com/debt-statistics.htm

m http://www.ojp.usdoj.gov/bjs/abstract/fvs.htm

n http://www.stepfamily.org/statistics.html